Inheritance

John F. Watson

First published by Emoter's Gap 2021

Copyright © 2021 by John F. Watson

This novel is entirely a work of fiction. The names, characters and incidents portrayed in it are the work of the author's imagination. Any resemblance to actual persons, living or dead, events or localities is entirely coincidental.

John F. Watson asserts the moral right to be identified as the author of this work.

First edition

ISBN: 978-1-80068-288-7

Cover art by Lyndsay Ford
Typesetting by Antony Wootten

This book was professionally typeset on Reedsy.
Find out more at reedsy.com

To my family.

It is what we learn after we think we know it all that counts.

'KIN' HUBBARD.

Chapter 1

ornament

The calm after the storm arrived abruptly, as if obeying orders from a higher authority. Minutes earlier the howling wind that cut through to the bone suddenly died to a whisper. The driving rain, ferocious upon the skin, immediately ceased. The destruction and damage caused by this freak storm would, possibly, only be witnessed at first light when river levels had receded. At present, the steep sided valley still reverberated with a low-throated rumble from the surging water that was carrying Henry Durville to almost certain death.

Stabbed and bundled into the water at the height of the storm and barely alive, Henry had entered a silent, ethereal world as a shaft of brilliant white light speared earthward from above, as Nirvana beckoned. On the verge of departure from a useless body, his soul reached towards the source of light where, surely, the pearly gates of peace awaited him.

But suddenly, he could no longer face the fierce brightness and was forced to turn away. As time stood still, the shaft of light slowly began to recede heavenward and the blackness of night closed in once again. The recent feeling of peace disappeared and Henry's battle for survival began.

The strong, twisting current tore the restrictive old sacking from his body, to wash away downstream. Henry, once almost a dead piece of flesh and bone, began to fight for oxygen, his chest solid as he tried to breathe. Finally, he thrashed to the surface, head thrusting clear of the water. His mouth opened in a scream for help but water-logged lungs only allowed a simpering gargled cry before being dragged under once more to swallow the filthy, brackish flood water. The blazing light that once offered peace had passed and was replaced by the cold, clutching hands of death.

Staying above the foaming water, his fingers grasped at thin air for a few seconds before clutching tightly to a branch torn down in the power of the storm. The red-hot blade of pain in his upper torso was excruciating and unrelenting, pushing him close to losing consciousness again and again. With mouth agape and gasping for breath, the force of the current had drained what little strength he had left and he teetered on the brink of death.

Clinging to the branch, a dull orange glow appeared in his vision from a low window and the flood water veered sharply and entered the old water race for the mill. The building loomed out of the darkness to his right, large and forbidding. A chance of safety if he had the strength to fight his way clear of the huge mill wheel. The rusted axle bearings squealed and growled in savage defiance after more than twenty years stationary. The wooden paddles slapped loudly against the rush of water ready to pull him beneath its deadly blades.

In a very last bid for survival, his bloodied fingers scrabbled for a handhold on the rough bankside and the jagged stone wall protecting the foundations came to his rescue. With a mighty effort, he heaved himself up onto a stone-flagged path below the flickering light from the grimy window. Hauling himself up onto his knees, he pressed his face close to the window pane, but the effort to hammer on the glass proved too much and he collapsed, once more, into a blessed world of unconsciousness.

Chapter 2

In its day, the old linen mill, built half a mile downstream from the small hamlet of Gallows Howe stood as a significant symbol of prosperity and power for its owner. It also provided, for a time, gainful employment for a lucky few that lived locally. Those days were long gone. Redundant and neglected for the past fifty years, with only a short respite grinding corn after the linen trade finished.

Although in a very poor state, the building had not relinquished everything from its past, as a certain grandeur remained in the surrounding grounds. Two imposing stone columns still guarded the entrance to the property and the long winding avenue of copper birch trees skirting the edge of the river led visitors in through a large courtyard. Sadly, this was where the splendour ended. The once cobbled driveway had deteriorated into a rough pot-holed dirt track. Most of the cobbles pulled up and re-used to build higher flood walls. The rusting wrought iron gates hung open either side on broken hinges, soon to be hidden from view in a neglected tangle of undergrowth. A couple of timber-built sheds, roofs sagging dangerously, doors hanging loose and ready to collapse, stood in a small garth close by, surrounded by a rough stone wall.

The property required urgent repairs, especially the exterior load bearing wall where the thudding powerful thrust of the mill wheel and heavy floods had caused damage. But immediate improvements were unlikely as the present occupant, Winifred Grey, was a disabled middle-age lady who lived here with her only daughter, Freda.

Luckily, Winifred possessed a remarkable knowledge of old herbal medicines and remedies and this provided their main income. Her unusual talent was well known throughout the dales and Winnie could often be seen by the early risers, roaming the moors, or foraging hedgerows and river banks for ingredients.

At this very minute though, Winifred was sitting by the small gable window overlooking the mill wheel, a lamp grasped tightly in her hand, keenly watching the rising water level. She screwed her eyes tighter for better vision, trying desperately to penetrate the blackness. But only her own sharp, troubled features stared back. The slightly hooked nose, which she hated, the pinched cheeks and thin lips and the quick, darting eyes. The deeply furrowed lines across her brow were accentuated more in the dull glow of lamplight.

Heavy floods always had this effect on Winnie, bringing alive memories of the day she slipped into the river and almost died under the paddles of the mill wheel. Only swift action from her late father saved her from drowning. She also remembered there was a time, while making her long recovery, she had dared to dream that someone was there for her. Not just to offer treatment and sympathy but because he loved her.

It was not to be. She would not only suffer the ordeal of an embarrassing pregnancy but also suffer the scars of the accident and a disabled limb for the rest of her life.

Winnie sighed at the memory. The affair, so short lived, she was not even sure it could be called an affair. It could so easily be a figment of her imagination if it was not for Freda, her daughter. Living proof that it happened and Winifred thanked the Lord every day for that. Not that Freda knew who her father was. No one knew for certain. Speculation and rumour circulated the village at the time but gossip soon finds other people.

Suddenly Winifred was brought back to reality. Squashed tight to the window, a horribly disfigured face pushed tight against the glass, replacing her own reflection, before collapsing out of her view. Eyes wide in horror,

Winnie instinctively jerked away from the window, the chair crashing to the floor and hands shooting to her face. The lamp glass shattered across the stone flagged floor as it fell from her grasp, plunging the room into semi-darkness. She screamed. A piercing, terrifying screech that echoed throughout the house.

Freda, sat reading in the sanctity of her bedroom, jumped up in panic on hearing the scream A sudden stab of fear clutched at her heart, instantly thinking her mother had fallen, or worse. Quickly dropping the book, she ran downstairs two at a time, lamp in hand, heart hammering madly and was relieved to see her mother still on her feet but in a state of shock. Setting her lamp on the table, Freda scuttled over and grabbed her before she fell and gently led her to a chair close to the fire.

"Mother, whatever's happened?" Freda asked, voice shaking. She knelt by the chair and held her mother's hand. "You'd think you'd seen a ghost. Is it the storm that's frightened you?"

Winnie's mouth resembled a fish pulled from the water, thin lips frozen in a round 'O.' No words formed and her face had taken on a deathly pallor. Striding to the cupboard alongside the fireplace, Freda reached for the whisky bottle and poured a fair old tot into a glass.

"Here, drink this!" It was an order. She held the glass in front of Winnie. "This'll steady your nerves and bring your voice back as well. Then you can tell me what happened."

Winnie took a large gulp. Like fire, it scorched the back of her throat, causing her to gasp and tears to course down her face and set her insides alight but it had the desired effect. The colour, rising from the neck upward until her thin cheeks glowed bright red and her voice, although just a croak, was audible. "There's someone outside, Freda." She stabbed a finger in the direction of the window. Freda brushed a lock of curly blond hair out of the way, as she cocked her head to one side and stared at the window in disbelief.

Freda was an attractive girl in her mid-twenties but her beauty was spoilt by a rather sullen, brusque manner, due mainly to her solitary lifestyle. For all that, Freda was not to be taken lightly and could read a weakness or a

5

blemish of one's character in one steady, studious gaze from her piercing sky-blue eyes.

Dressed in a pair of old working overalls that masked a solid body, she had a determined set to her chin, tending to give a more masculine look to her features than she would have liked. It also gave the appearance of one who knew her own mind and definitely not one to suffer fools. This she did not mind at all. It kept time wasters away.

"Outside? Now, in this weather?" she asked, incredulous. "There can't be. It's not fit to turn a dog out."

"There is I tell you. I saw a face, Freda. A hideous face at the window."

"That can't be right, mother. You sure you're not just seeing things?" Freda glanced at the whisky bottle. "You haven't been at the old firewater without my knowledge, have you?" Freda grinned and nodded towards the half empty bottle, believing her mother may just have had a tot too much and imagined it all.

"I certainly have not." Winnie was indignant. "I tell you there is someone out there." Her eyes once again strayed to the window. Freda, almost certain the drama was over, patted her mother's hand hoping to comfort her. Winnie would have none of it and refused to be quieted. Adamant she had seen a figure, she jumped up from the chair. "No, we must go check outside, Freda. See if anyone is still out there. They could be in trouble."

"If anyone's out there on a night like this, then they surely are in trouble. Or an idiot." But Winnie would not take no for an answer and Freda eventually gave way. "Oh, all right, don't worry yourself, mother, I'll go take a look. You stay here."

"No, I'll come with you. Better with two. Never know, there might be more than one out there. Anyway, I'm feeling better now you're with me."

Grabbing coats from the rack in the hall, Freda led the way carrying the lamp, venturing out onto the stone path leading to the river. The rain had ceased and just a whisper of a breeze kissed the few remaining leaves left on the trees overhanging the river. Treading carefully, the stones slippery with algae and the water almost at the same level, they turned towards the gable window and were confronted by the bedraggled figure of a man, face down and motionless on the stone flags.

"Oh my God, mother," Freda whispered, "you're right. Sorry I blamed the whisky. What the devil is he doing here on a night like this?" Freda did not pause for a second. "Come on, let's drag him inside. He might still be alive. I can lift him under the arms if you can take his feet?"

"Yes, I can do that, honey."

Even though slightly built, manhandling the sodden frame took every ounce of strength they could muster. Finally, after great effort, they hauled him over the threshold, through the hall and into the living room. Breathing heavily, Winnie rested but Freda rushed back, quickly checked outside, then slammed the door and locked it, fearing someone would walk in to discover this grisly secret thrust upon them.

By the time Freda arrived back in the room, Winnie had the man stretched out in front of the fire and was knelt clumsily at his side, her fingers on the cold white flesh of his neck. Nothing. She then tried his wrist in a desperate search for any sign of life. Finally shaking her head, she rose awkwardly and turned away, uncertainty clouding her features. Freda bent down, placed her face close to the man's mouth and waited a few seconds. Surely that was a breath she felt. She did the same again. Yes, it was. Only a whisper on her cheek, but a breath all the same.

"Mother, we need to work quickly. He's still alive. I'm sure of it." Freda was trying desperately to control the tension building inside her. "We must do something to help but you will have to tell me what to do."

"No." Winnie was adamant. "We must get a doctor, Freda. He's a goner. Look at him girl. There's nothing we can do to save him. There's not a drop of blood left in him by the colour of his face."

Freda avoided looking at the terrible facial disfigurements. Although inclined to agree with Winnie, she realized that if they were to have any chance of saving this unfortunate stranger Winnie would need every one of her special skills learnt over the years if they were to succeed.

Freda spoke crossly. "Mother, pull yourself together. Whatever's wrong with you? Remember, you pulled me through when all had given up hope, so it's best we do not waste any more time."

7

Rolling the sodden figure over, water immediately began to dribble from the slack, gaping mouth. Freda was just beginning to strip the man of his wet clothes, when Winnie's hands shot to her face again as she noticed a sliced cut in the fabric of his jacket and the chilling, dull red stain of blood, right in the middle of the man's back.

"Oh my God, Freda. It gets worse. Look!" With eyes wide, she pointed to the slit and the stain in the jacket. Winnie shivered, then stared directly at her daughter. "He's been stabbed, Freda." Winnie whispered. "Whoever's done it have thrown him in the river to make sure he's dead and that he would never be found, either. This is murder. We must get the police."

Freda turned the man back over, the lifeless eyes set in the disfigured, skeletal face, open and staring but seeing nothing. Freda's brain worked feverishly for answers.

"Well, someone stabbed him. He didn't do it himself, that's for sure. Talk about being stabbed in the back, eh," she said ruefully. "But let's think, mother. Do we really want police involved? You know our reputation among the locals. You and your healing powers, especially after nursing me back to life. All those stupid tales and gossip about witchcraft and such."

"Oh, that's years since Freda. All in the past."

"Don't be too sure, mother. Old habits die hard out here, stuck in the past. Anyway, it's too late tonight. I'll go for the police first thing in the morning, but for now, let's not waste a minute." Freda began to strip the upper clothing from the prone figure, searching every pocket as she did so for any sign of identity.

"Good God!" Freda exclaimed. "Look at this." She held a bulging wad of sodden money in her hand.

"I've never seen so much money. Definitely one o' the gentry. There must be well over five hundred pounds here." Freda spread it in front of the fire to dry and continued rummaging through the wallet for more information and with a cry of excitement, she held up a business card. "Henry Durville. 10, Darwin Court, York. Well, we now know the motive wasn't theft and we have a name and an address." Freda screwed her face up in concentration. "So, why would anyone go to the length of murder if it wasn't for money?

And how did he finish up in the river with a stab wound in his back?"

Freda paused but only for a second. "Right, let's have a few more logs on the fire before you start, mother."

"I'm not doing this, Freda. It's not right. We'll end up in trouble, it's a police matter and that's final." Winnie was determined. She folded her arms and sat down.

Freda jumped up and said, "Okay, I'll get the logs, 'cos we need to keep him warm. I'll bring some blankets from upstairs and I promise I'll go for the police first thing in the morning. I daren't drag 'em out at this time of night." Taking a couple of logs from the basket Freda placed them on the dwindling fire. The dry timber quickly took hold and crackled into life, the firelight sending eerie dancing shadows flitting silently around the room. The shelves, lined with row upon row of bottles and jars containing Winnie's medicinal compounds became a kaleidoscope of colours.

Recovering from her initial shock, Winnie realized she could not just sit and do nothing. She must try her best to save him.

"You're right, Freda. If we don't do anything he will certainly be dead by morning. We must try and keep him alive." Rising from her seat, she said, "Put the kettle on to boil because we'll need plenty of hot water. Then I need you to clean the wound. Use the spirit from the top shelf over there," nodding in the general direction. "It is labelled. I'll begin to mix the medicine. I'm sure I have everything I need."

Freda gave a wry smile. She noted Winnie's eyes scanning the lines of bottles, before reaching for her mortar and pestle on top of the old oak dresser, ready to crush a fresh compound. The necessary ingredients were all laid out on the table, as Winnie was about to start bottling just before checking on the river. She hoped they would do the job. Whether they would be in trouble if it failed, she dare not think about. But there was also a spark of excitement building inside her as she lapsed into her own small world. A world in which she found comfort. She loved working in this room exactly as her mother had. She inhaled deeply. The strong pungent smells and the aroma of the differing fungi, plants, berries and herbs caught satisfyingly at the back of her throat. All was as it should be and she settled to her task.

Fingers working feverishly, she placed the slippery elm leaves, puff balls, fungus and one elderflower into the mortar, before taking two comfrey leaves over to the fire in a small pan to boil in wax. Once done, she poured a teaspoon full of olive oil into the mix and began to grind to a fine pulp.

Winifred took great pride in her work. Often referred to as a quack, or even as Freda said, a witch by some, times were changing. Word had spread that these odd remedies worked, often after the doctor had informed them their illness was untreatable. It also proved a useful source of income. Although Freda brought a small amount into the household from her cleaning job at the infant school, the money earned from the medicine was their bread and butter.

Winnie glanced across at the prone form. "Is the wound clean, Freda?"

"It is. What now?"

"Good. Pop down to the cellar and bring me a handful of cobwebs off the old wheel mechanism. Also, the mouldy bread off the pantry floor."

Freda screwed her face up. Only ever seeing her mother treat minor ailments, Freda was astounded. "Surely you can't use stuff like that on him, mother?"

"Trust me, Freda. It will help seal the wound and stop infection. If we are to have any chance of saving him, we must do it now."

"Good grief, mother, I thought we were trying to cure him, not finish him off."

"Oh, you have a lot to learn. The mouldy bread will kill infection and the cobwebs will grip the open wound to prevent it ripping apart. Now, please go." Winnie continued pounding the mixing bowl.

Once Freda returned, both women knelt by the lifeless figure and with the flickering candlelight as their backdrop, they set to work.

"Hold the wound open, Freda, while I pour a couple of drops of this in." Freda turned her face away as her fingers prised the raw, jagged flesh apart. Just the thought of the mixture entering his useless body turned her stomach. Winnie tried to explain.

"This'll help with the internal healing, Freda. We don't know how deep the wound is, or what damage it's caused. The good thing is, he'll not suffer any pain while unconscious. When, and if, he does survive, we'll have the laudanum ready."

Freda grimaced as Winnie dripped the gluey substance into the gaping wound, then plugged it with the mouldy bread salve.

"Close it up now, Freda. You'll not hurt him." Freda's fingers eased the soft pliable flesh together. Winnie finished off by spreading a mass of the straggly grey cobwebs over the wound.

"Aah, mother, I'm sure you'll kill him with all that muck." Freda almost retched at this distinctly odd treatment of a dying man.

"I said before you have to trust me, Freda. I know what I am doing."

"I do, mother. Honestly I do." Freda paused, before adding, "Well, I thought I did, until now." Then her face lightened, a smile softening her features, "but I can see where the locals got the name, Winnie the Witch from."

The crackling of the log fire broke the silence in the room. Their eyes met for a moment. The nervous tension that had built since the man was brought in was beginning to pass.

Winnie groaned as she straightened her back and said, "We'll just put a light bandage over the wound. That's all we can do for the time being, Freda. If we drag a mattress downstairs, keep a fire going for warmth and comfort, I'll be as thorough as I can in treating the wound every day. It is all about patience now. Let's hope we've caught him in time." As Winnie hobbled back to her chair to ease stiff and aching limbs, she said, "Now, don't forget, we go for the police first thing in the morning and that should keep us clear of any trouble."

Chapter 3

After a restless night and with Winnie's words ringing in her ears, Freda roused early and rubbed the sleep from her eyes. Pulling the faded red curtains of her bedroom window aside, she stared out onto a dull low mist clinging close to the trees and the now subsiding river. Washing quickly, she rushed downstairs to check on the unfortunate Henry Durville. He was still alive, eyes staring blankly at the rough oak beamed floor above him. On checking his pulse, a sliver of excitement shot through her. It was stronger. Maybe her mother's strange treatment would work after all.

A few minutes later as she prepared breakfast, Winnie padded downstairs in her dressing gown and Freda told her the good news. Winnie was not at all surprised and after checking his dressings, they settled down to eat.

"I'll call on Sergeant Wright as I go to work, mother. He'll know what to do."

"That would be best, Freda. I'll look after this fella. Tell the sergeant I'll be in all day if he wants to call round."

Taking her hat and coat from the rack, Freda ran outside as the last of the wispy grey tendrils of mist were drawn up and away to disperse in the atmosphere. Water levels had dropped rapidly overnight and, thankfully, the mill wheel was silent and stationary once again. Freda strode out along the dirt track before tackling the steep incline that cut through the site of the old motte and bailey castle into the heart of the village.

Sergeant Wright lived alone in a small stone-built end of terrace house opposite the tin church at the base of the long straggling village. Although a two-storey dwelling, the long sloping pan tiled roof at the rear reached almost to ground level, the road rising sharply past the gable end with stone mounting steps alongside. Not that Sergeant Wright used them. He was no horseman.

A loud rap on the door soon had the curtains twitching and a sleepy-eyed, stubbly-chinned face peered out through the grimy window facing the street. A few minutes later, the portly figure of Sergeant Wright opened the door to his visitor, hurriedly hoisting a pair of brightly coloured braces over his shoulders as he did so.

"Morning Freda. You're an early bird today. Caught me on the hop a bit, I must say. What brings you out at this time of morning? Not trouble, I hope."

"I'm afraid it is, sergeant. Can I step inside? It is quite important." Freda glanced around to see if there were any prying eyes about, before stepping into the small passage.

"Come on through, Freda. I was about to have breakfast. Have you time for a cup of tea?"

"No thank you, sergeant. I'm on my way to work."

Seating himself at the small table, pen in hand, Bill Wright reached for a small notebook. "Righto, girl, I'm ready for business. Tell me all."

"This will come as a shock, sergeant, as it did to us. But mother and I dragged a man from the river last night, a victim of a stabbing we think. In the back. He's still alive but only just. Winnie treated him quickly and he's survived the night." Freda was nervously wringing her hands together, hoping the sergeant would take charge now. Earnestly, she carried on. "We didn't know what to do next and he's definitely too ill to move at present, so we need your advice."

Sergeant Bill Wright rubbed his chin, then ran a hand through his sparse thatch of grey hair before answering. "I see what you mean. Serious stuff, eh? Righto, young lady. Leave it with me. I shall call on your mother first thing. You get off to work and we'll have it sorted by the time you get back."

He rose from the chair, realizing the young woman was close to breaking down. "No need to worry now, Freda. You've done the right thing," and gave her a comforting pat on the arm.

"Thank you, sergeant." Relief flowed through her now she knew he would take charge. Freda was breathing hard by the time she reached the school, knowing she must have all the classrooms clean and tidy before Headmaster Haigh rang the bell and most of the smaller tasks as well before the children arrived. Working methodically through her chores, there was only the coke buckets left to refill in the cellar and carry up to the classroom for the stove. Freda hated this part of the job. No proper light, dark and smelly, she made as much noise as possible to frighten any lurking rats away.

Far too busy to think about any solutions the sergeant would come up with, the morning sped by. Freda returned home midday and dashed inside, keen to hear the outcome of Winnie's meeting with the sergeant.

Her mother stood carving bread to make sandwiches for dinner. Freda eyed the bread suspiciously. The way Winnie was struggling to carve a slice off, it appeared stale but it was all they had. It would have to do. Either that, or go hungry. She sighed and asked, "Okay, mother, what's the news. What had Sergeant Wright to say? Are the hospital coming to gather him up?"

"No, not right away. I told the sergeant everything, the address and his name. I also told him about the money. Bill said if we could look after him until a doctor checked his condition, he will be able to advise better on when to move him."

With sandwiches ready, they sat down to eat. "I'm glad you called him in, Freda. I definitely don't want any trouble at my age, honey."

Freda took her mother's hand. "It'll be okay now, mam," she reassured her. "We'll just keep him comfortable until someone else takes responsibility. Did he have any idea when?"

"No. Bill was going to try and get a message through as soon as possible. Oh, by the way," Winnie raised her eyebrows, stating, "Bill thought we might be able to claim some money from him, or the family for his care. That would help cover any extra costs, wouldn't it?"

Freda took a deep breath. "It would that as he might be here a while yet, especially if your treatment doesn't work."

They were interrupted by a knock on the door. Freda ran to answer it and was surprised to see a rather small and prim, well-dressed gentleman standing there.

"Good afternoon, Miss. I'm Doctor Rourke from further down the valley." He spoke quietly in a cultured accent. Not from round here, Freda realized. "I received an urgent message from Sergeant Wright asking if I could call as soon as possible. I believe you have a seriously ill man on your hands?"

"Yes, we have, doctor. Thank you for calling so promptly. Please come in." Freda ushered him into the hallway. "Pop through. Mother is in the kitchen."

"Thank you." Very neat and tidy, he reminded Freda of a tightly furled umbrella with legs as his short sharp steps clicked loudly on the bare stone flags of the passage.

He carried a smart black bag in one hand, a bowler hat in the other, now removed in the presence of ladies to reveal a shiny bald pate. A thin moustache and goatee beard confirmed Freda's assumption that he was a very efficient person. He entered the kitchen where Winnie stood wringing her hands together. Henry still laid out, prostrate, in front of the fire.

"Well, well, well, he murmured, bending down for a closer inspection of the disfiguration on the man's face. "Hmm," he said after a while, "now could you explain your treatment of this unfortunate man so far."

Freda tried to catch Winnie's eye mouthing, 'please don't tell him, for God's sake,' but was unsuccessful. Winnie explained every last detail, even the mouldy bread and cobwebs. Freda almost died with embarrassment while the doctor listened intently. Once Winnie finished speaking, he nodded sagely. "Odd, very odd treatment, Mrs Grey, if I dare say. Please do not think this impertinent but have you used these... er, this sort of treatment before on anyone?"

"Many times, doctor, and over many years."

"With success, I take it."

"Only a few failures doctor and only on minor ailments. Never on any serious illnesses."

The doctor stared at her with respect. "Your methods are very interesting, Mrs Grey, very interesting indeed. We must have a more in-depth conversation with you when we have more time to discuss the matter." He suddenly turned business-like. "Right, down to work." All efficiency, he gathered his bag close and knelt down by the side of Henry.

"If there is anything you want, doctor, just give us a shout, we'll be in the next room," Winnie said as they left the room.

"Thank you, ladies."

More than half an hour passed before Doctor Rourke emerged. "Well, as you realize, he is still seriously ill, but stable now. He has lost a lot of blood and will definitely need hospital treatment so I will arrange for his transport to Whitby. But it could be at least two or three days. Will you ladies be on hand later this week, most likely on a morning?"

"One of us will definitely be here, doctor, that's for sure."

"That is very good of you." He paused, then said. "Oh, by the way, I nearly forgot. I admire your medical skills, Mrs Grey. Unorthodox by medical practices of today but very effective." With that, he shook their hands and walked briskly out.

Freda and Winnie stared at each other in amazement. Freda spoke first. "Well, what a compliment, mother. I admit I nearly died when he asked how you treated him."

"I've told you many times, Freda. Do not doubt my ability. There are many things I can't do, but I can heal the sick." Then they embraced.

Chapter 4

⚬⚬⚬

The nights following Henry's attack were long and lonely for Ruth, with no one to confide in. God, how she missed Jim. If he was by her side, she would be stronger. Although desperately tired, sleep refused to ease her troubled mind. The very instant her eyes closed the terrifying image of Henry's slobbering face and the flash of the knife in the lamplight drove any chance of slumber away. But the real worry gnawing away inside her brain was the chilling thought, what if Henry was not really dead. Everything had happened so quickly. What if he did survive the stabbing and the flood. That night filled her with a nauseating guilt that refused to be locked away.

After one such restless night, at the first sign of daylight, Ruth realized it would be much better to be kept busy. Throwing the covers aside she decided to catch up on some household chores. Splashing water into the bowl, she dried and dressed quickly before taking a look outside. The rising sun was just beginning to break through a glowering sky, easing away the milky wisps of dawn. The weather had settled quickly after the recent freak storm. Soon to be forgotten by many, but not for her.

Glancing towards the head of the dale, Ruth saw the dull clouds shrouding the high moor and the sharp morning air decided her to light a fire in readiness for breakfast. Clearing the ashes into a bucket, she screwed up some old paper onto the open grate, placed the kindling on top and put a match to it.

The fire crackled steadily into life, spreading a welcome heat across the room. Although troubled by nightmares, Ruth did feel a warmth inside her, not just from the fire but from the sheer luck of meeting up with Jim again after such a dramatic and painful parting.

Also, Josh's voice had returned and he could communicate again. Jacob called it a blessing from above. Ruth smiled to herself, admiring Jacob's faith. It was always God's work to Jacob. Never circumstances.

Rising from the comfort of the fire, she wandered into the kitchen and washed the soot from her hands. Cocking her head to one side, she listened intently for a sign of movement upstairs. No familiar creak of floorboards or footsteps padding downstairs met her ears. In fact, no sign of life in the old building at all.

So, if the menfolk were not rushing up for an early morning, Ruth would make good her chance for a walk, hoping the fresh air and exercise would help clear her mind.

With a chance of rain, she slipped a cape over her shoulders and braved the fresh morning air. She was about to whistle but Nell had heard the click of the door and came bounding from her kennel ready to go with her.

Running hard down the rough moorland track, the sharp heather scratching and scrabbling at her bare legs, she never once paused. But fleet of foot as Ruth was, she was no match for Nell. Every once in a while, the dog halted, turned its head as if to say, come on, Ruth, keep up.

Gasping for breath on reaching the point where the two rivers segued into one, Ruth couldn't believe the devastation caused. The narrow footpath close to the river, which she often walked, was left strewn with broken branches and debris. Even some of the stout stone walls that had stood for centuries were reduced to heaps of rubble, unable to halt the force of water.

Ruth's gaze followed the snaking line of trees overhanging the stream, the green leaves of summer, torn away by the storm. The branches, devoid of such colourful dressing, reached skywards like gnarled, arthritic limbs, to claw at the dull, pregnant belly of a rain laden sky. The sun, not to be beaten in this battle of nature, occasionally broke through to offer its welcome warmth. And the once silver ribbon of water, still murky brown, continued on its never-ending journey to the sea.

Once past the old mill, Ruth branched right and up through the main street where the General Stores, Methodist Chapel and Primary School were all peacefully quiet at this time of morning, before striding out for home.

Arriving back brighter and refreshed from the walk, Ruth found Josh preparing the table for breakfast. He greeted her with a broad smile on his face. "Morning, Ruth. You were out and about early this morning. You and Nell had a good walk?"

"We have. We followed the footpath by the river. It's almost back to normal now but I was amazed at the height it had reached." A shiver ran through her at the memory and Josh realized the terrifying events of that night were still vivid.

Josh spoke quietly, sympathetically. "Ruth, you know that if you want to talk, I'm a good listener?"

Ruth had settled into a chair and picked up a book. She studied Josh her expression serious. "Do I make it that obvious, Josh?"

"I can read you better than you are reading that book clasped in your hand," he said.

She smiled up at him. "Well, you're right, Josh. There is something, but maybe only time will provide the answer."

"Okay then, let's hear it then we'll know for sure, won't we?"

Although only the two of them in the room, her voice lowered to a whisper. "You remember when you actually stabbed him?"

"Yes." Josh spoke quietly, hoping to ease the words gently from her.

"Then we quickly bundled him up on the horse and took him to the river?"

"Yes, and watched as he was taken by the flood."

"Well." She paused. "What… what if he was still alive, Josh?" Ruth's eyes were wide with fear and her voice trembled slightly. "I was too frightened to check, Josh. It all happened so quick." She paused again, then added, "Did you?"

Josh gave her a smile and wandered over to her chair. He placed an arm on her shoulder, apparently unperturbed by his action on the night. Or if he was, he hid it well. So unlike his God-fearing father, Ruth thought.

"So that's what making you miserable is it, little sis." A favourite term he used, usually answered by an angry glare as she liked to be called by her proper name. But not this time. Josh decided to tread carefully.

"Now listen to me, Ruth Brennan," his voice serious as he settled back on his haunches close to her. "What happened, has happened. Nothing will ever change that. As I see it, the evil swine got what he deserved and can rot in Hell for all I care. We know now that other young girls will not go through the horror that you and others have endured. In answer to your question, no, I didn't check if he was dead but if the knife didn't kill him, the river will have claimed him. And, imagine, if I hadn't arrived back when I did and you could have grasped a knife, what would you have done? Exactly the same, I bet. Am I right?"

Ruth nodded in agreement. She would certainly have stabbed him in a bid to save herself.

"Yes," she said. "I would have done anything to keep him off me. Oh, I know it makes sense, Josh, but it is not right to take a life."

"True, but it was not right what he was intending to do, Ruth. Now, just say, by some miracle he did survive. He's not going to strut around bragging about his evil intent with young girls, is he? It will be kept quiet. Should he do so, he knows damned well that gaol would be the only place for him and for that sort of a crime, they would most likely throw away the key."

He rose and walked across the room, ready for his breakfast but then carried on. "Also, the shock of that night unlocked part of my brain that had left me unable to communicate with anyone since my mother's death all those years ago." Even Josh appeared to be reliving that personal nightmare. "Yes, I could hear but I was never part of anything. An outsider for years. So, on that night, Ruth, although a death occurred, three very important things happened. You were saved from a frightening experience, the world is rid of a despicable man, and my voice returned."

A smile broke out on Josh's face. "That is my sermon over, dear girl. A slightly differing version to what my father's would be, I admit, but to me still makes perfect sense. Now, wipe away that worried expression. It really does not suit you and let me see that bright-eyed young girl thrive again. What do you say?"

Ruth couldn't help a smile breaking through. "Thank you, Josh. I don't know what I would do without you," She threw her arms around him, "I am a worrier but I do feel better after talking it through."

He was very much like an elder brother to her. She did not always agree with some of his views but, in Josh's world, there was never a dull cloud, always one with a silver lining.

Chapter 5

⚜

Henry's eyes flickered open. The room he occupied was quite small and lit by one single light. A strong antiseptic smell stung his nostrils and throat. Although feeling weak, he was suffering no real pain and his mind quickly grasped that he was now in a different environment. Crisp, white sheets covered him and the pillow felt soft to the touch under his head. No glowing embers from an open fire here, glinting light on a few meagre furnishings and medicine bottles. Could it be his mind playing tricks, or was it the drugs? Or maybe just a dream. He could not be sure.

He tried moving his arms. They responded sluggishly. There was also movement in his legs as he worked them up and down the bed. He could also hear activity in the adjoining room. But a feeling of panic seized him when he was unable to remember who he was, or where he was from. What was he doing in this strange place? Nothing made sense. A scream formed in his throat but no sound left his lips. Frustrated, he forced himself to lie calmly and tried to think.

Eventually the door swung open and a young nurse entered, interrupting his thoughts. She wore a starched white cap perched on top of curly auburn hair, which framed a kind, sympathetic face. She moved close to check his dressings and the warmth of her body set his fevered mind racing. Once finished she checked his pulse and frowned. It was slightly faster than expected. She would mention this to matron, hoping it was a sign of him gaining strength.

Working quietly and efficiently in just the soft light, she put her arms around him and eased him further up the bed. A rush of desire coursed through his wasted body at such intimate contact. Once happy with his position, she slowly spooned the liquid into his mouth. Henry swallowed greedily.

The nurse gasped in astonishment at such a positive response. "Steady now. Try not to take too much at once, young man. You are a miracle. Back from the dead, eh?" She paused, giving him time between each spoonful. "Be careful, please, just take a small amount each meal time until your strength returns."

Henry's health had made good progress thanks to the care and dedication of the staff. The nurse was pleased, but concerned about brain damage? If so, how serious would it be? After all, he had been unconscious for a long time. The nurse wiped his mouth and left the room. She found matron sat at her desk and related the good news.

"It looks promising for Henry Durville, matron. He's awake and swallowed his first fluids since being admitted. His pulse was a little high, though."

"Well done, Jane. You've done a fine job with him. His pulse rate could vary for a while yet. He's gaining strength every day and well on his way to recovery. As you rightly say, brain damage could be a problem but we'll not know for a few weeks yet. Doctor Rourke will be pleased with the outcome. I shall put this in my report."

Jane, in this her first year of nursing, beamed with delight at this unexpected praise, instead of the usual steely response from this bossy woman.

"Thank you, matron."

"I must admit, the state of him when he came in, I thought he was too far gone to actually pull through. We'll assess him each day but I would be surprised if he ever remembers anything at all."

Henry continued to gain strength and although his mouth made signs of movement, twisting and gaping open when trying to talk, the effort taxed him far too much and he would flop back on the bed in exasperation. No sound had yet escaped his lips but as matron said, "It is early days. Recovery cannot be rushed."

Chapter 6

Back in the city of York, John Durville made a coffee for breakfast, then slipped the early morning mail from the letter box and sat down at his desk. Nothing of interest until he came to the last one. The letter, from Whitby Police Headquarters, almost made him choke as it contained information on Henry. John had almost given up hope of making contact with his son again but, apparently, he was seriously ill in Whitby hospital. It gave no other details.

With breakfast forgotten, John instantly began to arrange a couple of days away and, if possible, try to find out exactly what had happened. Quickly packing a few essentials into the back of the car in case of an overnight stay, he then placed a hurried phone call through to the orphanage with an explanation, followed by a call to the hospital.

Donning his familiar black cape and hat from the hallstand, he was soon on the road, heading towards the coast. What fantastic news, but it also brought many unanswered questions with it. Where the devil had Henry disappeared to for all this time? And what had brought him to the hospital? Trouble or accident? Seriously ill, the letter said. John stared hard at the road ahead and concentrated on driving to stop his imagination running wild.

The weather was kind, a bright clear day. Under normal circumstances John would have enjoyed the drive but the uncertainty troubled him.

Eventually, stiff and tired he arrived at the hospital, a dour looking building that had once been the workhouse. He took the opportunity to stretch his legs and wandered across the recently opened swing bridge and gazed out beyond the sheltering harbour walls to the far horizon. The sound of puttering engines from the fishing boats were almost drowned out by the swirling mass of screeching seagulls eagerly following in their wake towards the fishing fields of the North Sea.

Feeling refreshed by the saline taste of sea air on his lips, John brought his thoughts back to the task in hand and entered the building. A door to his left was marked ENQUIRIES. He was about to knock when a formidable lady in a dark blue uniform opened the door, a simple nameplate pinned above her left breast indicated her status in this hospital, MATRON.

John gave his name and asked what information she had on Henry.

Matron told him everything she knew, explaining how he was saved by the two women from the mill at Castle Moor.

"Would it be possible to see him, matron?"

"Of course, Mr Durville." Turning quickly, she called for Nurse Rose. "Would you be kind enough to show Mr Durville to ward six, nurse."

"Thank you, matron," John replied. Although the interior appeared dull and dismal and in need of decoration, John admired matron's efficiency and authority.

"Follow me, sir," the nurse said quietly over her shoulder. "He may be sleeping at present but he is making good progress." John assumed Nurse Rose to be in her late teens, petite, with short brown hair and delicate features. Entering quietly, Henry lay dozing but roused quickly.

"Right, I shall leave you two alone for five minutes, then I'll be back to administer his medication. Just give me a call if you need me."

Thank you, nurse." John drew a chair up to the side of the bed, gently taking hold of Henry's hand laid out by his side. Cold. Cold as marble. Henry pulled his hand away, obviously disliking such an intimate gesture. Not a hint of recognition from him but the furtive black eyes were alive, darting around the room.

"Hello, Henry. My goodness, I am heartily pleased to find you still alive but how the devil did you arrive here?" A moment's silence with not a flicker of response. John tried again. "So, can you remember anything at all, Henry?" Still nothing forthcoming. John could see Henry was not too ill to respond, it was more like stubbornness. He patiently probed for the next five minutes until a light rap on the door interrupted them and Nurse Rose entered.

"Sorry, Mr Durville, time for Henry's medicine." Bending close to Henry, Nurse Rose checked bandages, monitored his breathing and pulse before administering the pills.

"Well, you are making a remarkable recovery, Henry. Improving every day." While the nurse fussed over making him comfortable, she was oblivious to the steely sinister gaze of Henry, his eyes following her every movement. But John didn't miss it. A cold shiver ran through him. Good God, even in this state, he could still be a menace to unsuspecting women. Finally finished, the nurse breezed out of the ward again. "Thank you, both."

Once the door closed, several more attempts at conversation brought no answers, John eventually asked, "Do you know who I am, Henry?"

Henry steadily shook his head before letting it drop to one side and looked the other way, showing total disinterest.

"I am your father, Henry. Can you remember anything of what happened?" But John already knew there was no chance of an answer. Eventually, Henry's eyes closed. John was not sure if he had actually drifted off to sleep, or whether he feigned it. Shaking his head, John left the ward and returned to the front desk where matron told him everything she knew. Before leaving, John asked if there was a room where they could talk in private.

"Of course, Mr Durville. Come through to my office." Opening a door behind her desk, John followed her. "Now, how can I help?"

"How much of Henry's background do you really know, matron?"

"Nothing. Nothing at all, apart from he is a very lucky man."

John thought matron had a right to know the facts. "This is very difficult for me, matron, and I am ashamed to tell you this about my own flesh and blood but I feel that you should know for the safety of yourself and your staff. Although never convicted, Henry is a sexual predator, well noted by all who know him, especially in the York area, for attacking and assaulting defenceless young women."

Matron stared hard at John before answering. "Thank you, Mr Durville. Do the police know this?"

"No." John bowed his head. "You are the only one I have given this information to. The worrying part is, even lying on that hospital bed, a seemingly helpless figure, I believe he is stronger than you, or I, think. When Nurse Rose came in with the medicine, I noted his behaviour. I believe, if possible, you should never have a nurse attend him alone. Just to be on the safe side."

"I understand, Mr Durville. We will try to do as you ask, but the difficulty will be when we are really busy."

John nodded in agreement. He could do no more. Thanking them all, John waved goodbye. He was baffled and still no wiser as to how, or why, Henry made the trip to these outlying villages without telling anyone. More importantly, who had stabbed him and for what purpose? It was not for gain as matron said he still had a large amount of money on him.

To try and find some answers, John decided to visit Winifred Grey, Henry's saviour, who may be able to shed light onto this mysterious stabbing of his son. While in the vicinity, he would also grasp the opportunity of catching up with Jacob and Ruth.

John hit the steep climb out of Whitby and once again the freedom and beauty of the open road helped banish any black thoughts for a while. The road soon branched onto the rough, winding tracks which led him over the brown, rolling moors and valleys he loved.

Dropping the car into a low gear, John hit the long slow ridge of high ground that took him through the village of Castle Moor. On his last visit to this area, the village was quiet. Not today. The weekly market was in full swing. Ahead of him the narrow high street was packed with stalls, horse and carts selling all manner of goods and home-made products. Rather than drive through the crowded, bustling street, he quickly took the sharp right turn that descended toward the river. The entrance to the old mill was easily recognisable and he drew the car to a halt, hoping that he would finally meet

Winifred Grey.

He was in luck. Winnie answered his knock and appeared quite taken aback by this well-dressed stranger stood before her on the doorstep.

"Good afternoon." John doffed his hat and made a slight bow. "Winifred Grey, I take it."

"Indeed, it is." Winnie looked bemused. Cautious, in fact.

John noted her nervousness and tried to put her at ease. "There is nothing to be alarmed about Mrs Grey. Let me explain. I am Judge John Durville from York and I have reason to believe you and your daughter, Freda, rescued a man from the river after a violent storm."

Winnie thought it best to remain silent for a while longer and let the man continue. She was not about to say anything that might incriminate her. John continued. "Well, the man you rescued was my son and I have come to give you my heartfelt thanks for your bravery and kindness in saving his life. I have just…"

At this moment, Winnie found her voice. Relieved, she said, "Ah, please excuse my manners, sir. I was quite taken aback by such an unexpected, er, visit, should I say. Come in. Please come in." Winnie ushered John into the hallway and limped through to the kitchen. "I was just having a cup of tea. Will you join me?"

"Thank you, I would be glad to and you might be able to tell me what you know about my son's unfortunate accident."

"Right. Well, sit yourself down there," she pointed to the chair, "and I'll pour you a cup of tea." Winnie settled in the chair opposite and began. "Oh, it was no accident, Mr Durville." Winnie, quite dramatically emphasised this information with a vigorous shake of the head. "He was stabbed. Clear and definite. In the back as well, I might add. No, no, definitely no accident."

"The hospital also told me it was your care and knowledge of medicine, albeit not gained from modern doctoring that saved his life. You are indeed a very clever and knowledgeable woman, Mrs Grey. The profession could well learn from your good self."

Winnie beamed at this praise, the thin lips almost curling into a smile. "Well, we did what we could, me and Freda, my daughter, that is. Some

29

people laugh about these old methods, Mr Durville, but they work you know." And she wagged a finger at him.

John smiled. "They surely do and Henry for one is living proof. Now, as you might know, Henry has no memory of what happened. I don't suppose you will be able to shed any light on it?"

"Not at all, Mr Durville. The only thing is it must have happened close by or Henry would have been a goner, that's for sure."

John, deep in thought, nodded in agreement. "Possibly upstream toward Gallows Howe, you think?"

Well, yes, must o' been, because there is only one other farm between us."

"Interesting, Mrs Grey. Very interesting."

Finishing his cup of tea, John said, "Well thank you for all your help and also the tea, Mrs Grey. I will always be in your debt." Taking in Winnie's living quarters, John brought out his wallet and handed Winnie a ten-pound note.

"This will help for the expense in taking care of my son so well, Mrs Grey."

"Well, thank you kindly, sir. It is very much appreciated. As you may realize, times are hard at present." She paused, adding, "but we manage."

"I understand but this is for your kindness and for any extra cost you may have incurred in keeping my son alive. Thank you once again, Mrs Grey." Shaking Winnie's hand he left for Gallows Howe to call upon Jacob who might know more.

John decided to tackle the high street in Castle Moor now it was later in the day and drove up through the village. It was beginning to return to normality. The hustle and bustle of market day had come to a close, horse and carts were loaded with unsold wares but, all in all, it had been a successful trading day. Many were heading home but some were making their way to the local hostelry.

After witnessing the busy trading street of the village earlier, Gallows Howe appeared almost deserted. Surprisingly quiet. John remembered the optimism shown by Jacob and others for the future when warmly greeted on his last visit here. But as the mining industry began to suffer and the labour force continuing to dwindle it was beginning to take its toll.

John realized the hamlet had deteriorated in a very short space of time, only the hiring of horses still operating successfully. John smiled as he noticed a beckoning light flickering dimly from the interior of the church. Although the light was welcoming, the building itself was showing signs of neglect. As John walked the well-worn stone path, he noted the newly quarried stone, stacked in readiness for Jacob's dream of a new church of worship had disappeared. But the grisly silhouette of the gallows stood, stark and sombre against the darkening sky, still firing its grim message across these moors. But, for how much longer, John wondered.

Entering the church, John stood quietly at the rear of the building until Jacob lifted his head and turned to greet his visitor. Jacob could not contain his astonishment. "Goodness me, what a surprise to see you, John. But a most welcome surprise."

He strode forward and grasped the big man's hand. "What brings you to this neck of the woods, John?" He studied John's face, already sensing a problem. "Is it a social visit or, as I suspect, could it be trouble?" It was more a statement than a question.

"It is good to see you Jacob and I truly wish it could be sociable but I'm afraid it does mean trouble. You see, my son Henry was stabbed the night of the big flood and was either thrown or fell in the river." John related Winnie's story and Jacob, standing silently in the dim candlelight began to recall the events of the night.

"Come, John." He put his arm around John's shoulders and ushered him out of the church. "We can talk more freely in the comfort of home over a drink."

Once settled around the table, John opened his heart to Jacob on Henry's problem. All the sordid details as he remembered them.

"I believe he is uncontrollable." John remarked. "Prison, or hospital the only possible outcome."

Jacob listened intently until John finished. "This is sad, sad news, John. Have you any ideas at all? If money wasn't the motive, it can only be a fight or a quarrel of some kind and if it hadn't been for Winnie, it would be a murder inquiry."

31

"Yes, the doctor freely admits the lady worked a miracle. There is no telling if Henry will recover completely. On opinions from the medical staff, it appears very unlikely but if he continues to respond to treatment, he could well return closer to York where I can be on hand more often. A few more weeks we shall know better."

"That would be good, John. In the meantime, if I hear any fresh information, I will be in touch with you."

As an afterthought, Jacob added. "By the way, John, you may not have heard, but Josh's voice has returned."

"Well, that really is good news, Jacob. I am pleased for you all. It will mean so much to him, especially at this time in his life."

After more pleasantries, John noted the time and rose from his chair

"Thank you, Jacob. Now, I must take my leave. I have a long drive back. I've certainly enjoyed our meeting, although not in the best of circumstances. Let us hope for better news in the future." Promising to keep in touch, John climbed into his vehicle and drove off into the darkness, the rear lights soon just a glimmer in the distance.

Jacob returned inside, lingering at the table, an icy sliver of fear beginning to fester at the back of his mind. Why, he was not sure, but on hearing Ruth's revelations of her experiences with Henry and now his own father revealing the man's lustful past, Jacob understood they were dealing with a troubled and violent man.

Chapter 7

⟨decorative flourish⟩

With lack of money always a constant problem, Winnie appreciated John's generous offer. Both her and Freda were quite prudent and looked after the pennies. They were not on true poverty street but it was never far from their door. On occasions, when they could afford, they dressed in their Sunday best to enjoy what they called one of life's little luxuries. Winnie would prepare a beautiful roast dinner, with home-grown vegetables, plus a few special trimmings from her herbs, making it as good as a royal feast.

Apart from the freak storm, the summer had been hot and dry and Winnie's medicines were not in big demand so Freda's small pay packet came in very useful. It was the winter months that were popular for Winnie's cures and this always helped see them through.

Talking idly in the flickering candlelight following one of their special meals, Freda, deep in thought, remarked, "Mother, one of us should really try and visit Henry Durville. We can't expect Doctor Rourke to always keep us up to date. If we miss one of our treats, it could pay for a trip to Whitby?

A smug expression appeared on Winnie's face.

"Well, as it happens, Freda, Doctor Rourke has offered to take one of us in his car, if we can spare the time."

Freda stared at her mother. "Mother, are you telling the truth, or is this one of your so-called jokes?"

"No, I wouldn't joke about such things as this, Freda," she said, disgusted that her daughter would even think such a thing. "No, that's exactly what he said."

"Wow, I can't believe it, mother. This is something special, isn't it? Are you going to take him up on the offer, or could I go?"

"Well, I'm certainly not going to be travelling that far but if you would like to go, I think we should accept. After all, you've never been to Whitby, have you?"

Freda studied her mother. Was this a new Winnie, about to let her daughter out for a whole day. With a man. Wonders will never cease, she thought.

"You know fine well I haven't. I've hardly ever been allowed out of your sight." Amazed, she went on. "Do you realize, I've never ventured over the moor top to see what's on the other side of the hill in case I happened to meet up with some unsavoury character, or in case I got lost, mother." Freda's head was spinning. This was so unexpected. "I can't believe this is happening. Did he say when? Have we any idea at all when he will call, cos I could be at work." Freda was bubbling with excitement at the prospect of the trip.

"Don't worry about that. I've told him your work hours, honey."

"Aw, mam, I love you to bits. You don't realize how much this means to me." She went over and flung her arms around Winnie, hugging her close. "What's brought this change of attitude in you all of a sudden?"

Winnie sat in a quietly contented mood after their meal, but proved she was still in charge by saying firmly, "It's not a change of attitude, Freda. I've been doing a lot of thinking these last few weeks after recent events." She leant forward in her chair to make the point. "What I am trying to say is you need to experience life and get out and travel a bit, especially when the offer is made by a man of Doctor Rourke's standing."

Freda was shocked. "Well, I never thought I'd see the day when you would begin doffing your cap to the upper classes, mother," she said with a smirk. "Just because he's a doctor, it's okay for me to be seen out with him, is that it?"

"It's not that at all, Freda," Winnie said, quite indignant. "I just think you'll be safe with him and he'll look after you, that's all."

Freda let it rest at that. She was not about to jeopardize her chance of a day out and risk Winnie changing her mind. Freda did not have long to wait. The very next day, Doctor Rourke arrived at the front door of the old mill in a shiny new Model T Ford, one of the first in the country. In truth, Doctor Rourke felt quite important and could hardly wait to show off his new purchase.

Excitedly, Freda quickly changed into her better clothes, pulled a comb through her hair, packed a drink and a couple of sandwiches into a carrier bag and jumped in alongside the doctor as Winnie watched proudly from the door.

"Bye, mother," Freda shouted.

"Goodbye, Mrs Grey. Don't worry, I will look after her," he shouted, while expertly reversing the car around in front of the house.

"This is very good of you, Doctor Rourke. I never thought I would be lucky enough to visit Whitby and in a new car as well. Would you believe I have never ever visited Whitby and I'm twenty-four years old? Nearly twenty-five in fact."

"Well then," he said, a prim grin parting the thin lips. "It's time you did. We'll make this a nice little day trip. I have a few calls to make in Whitby, so while you visit Henry, I will call on my patients and then pick you up. Then, if we have time, we can have fish and chips together for dinner. What do you think to that?"

"Oh, no, I'm sorry doctor. I couldn't do that. I didn't bring enough money." She giggled to cover her embarrassment. "To be honest, I wouldn't have had enough money to buy lunch even if I'd raided my piggy bank savings. But, don't worry, I packed sandwiches so I won't starve."

"No, Freda, I insist. This is my treat. You and your mother saved a life. Quite remarkable. This is a day that restores my faith in human nature."

"Well, seeing as you put it like that, I shall be glad to accept, Doctor Rourke." Freda felt quite light headed and as they chugged steeply away from the moorland villages out onto the open highway, the scenery changed dramatically to what she was used to. The stunning view before the sudden drop toward the historic town of Whitby, which she had only heard about, took Freda's breath away. The ancient abbey perched high on the cliff edge was a marvellous sight as the sun highlighted the azure blue of the sea and the rolling white breakers as they smashed against the rocks. Inside the harbour wall, the water was mirror calm, dazzling, not a ripple, providing a safe homecoming for the fishing boats. Freda had learnt a little history on the fishing and whaling industry at school, but to witness this true vision of the coast opening up before her meant so much more.

Absorbed in this unexpected journey, her excited chatter ceased. Doctor Rourke stole a quick glance at this naïve, young girl out of the corner of his eye. But Freda wasn't a young girl. Naïve maybe but in her mid-twenties and never having left the shelter of a small moorland village. He shook his head in bewilderment.

Parking in front of the main hospital entrance, the doctor ushered Freda inside to the reception desk and made sure Henry Durville was still in the same ward.

"Now, all you need to do Freda, is pop along to ward six and a nurse will take you in. If he is awake, just have a few words with him. If he appears to tire, that will be your signal to let him rest." He smiled gently. "Right, young lady, I will leave now and pick you up at midday and then we'll go for a spot of lunch."

"Thank you, doctor."

Doctor Rourke asked a passing nurse if she would show Freda to the ward.

"I certainly will, doctor. Follow me, Freda."

Waving a hurried goodbye, Freda ran after the fast-disappearing figure along the sterile smelling corridor, the nurse ushering her toward Henry's ward.

"Thank you, nurse."

Although experienced with the nursing methods and medicines that Winnie administered, this was a totally new concept of health care. I bet there are no cobwebs or mouldy bread used in this building, she thought, supressing a grin. Freda entered nervously, not knowing what to expect. Only one iron bed in the ward and the slight body of Henry, covered by a fresh white sheet. He lay motionless, eyes closed. Walking quietly to his bedside, Freda leaned over the bed and listened to his breathing which appeared quite normal. Suddenly, Henry sat bolt upright in bed and Freda stumbled backwards, heart pounding madly in her chest at the shock of such sudden movement. His eyes, terrifying black pearls, searched hers and seemed to reach her very soul, before he realized where he was. Slowly, he settled back on the pillow and began to speak in a breaking, hesitant voice but his gaze remained wild. Frighteningly so. "Who... are... you?" It was a harsh croaking noise.

Freda, recovering from the shock, made her voice calm, replied. "I'm Freda from the mill at Castle Moor. Mother and I pulled you out of the river."

"I... don't.... remember... anything." His voice brittle, breaking up, like a young child under stress.

"Don't try to speak too much. I just called to see if you were improving, and you are. All you need to do now is give yourself time and regain your strength."

A nurse breezed in. "Hi, I'm Rose," and pointed to her name tag. "And you are?"

"Freda, Freda Grey. Doctor Rourke brought me in to see how Henry was progressing."

"Well, Freda, you are the first person, apart from his father, to hear him talk since his accident. It could be we need you to call again if that's the case. Are you related?" Rose enquired.

"No, not at all. It was my mother and I who found him."

"Ah," Rose's face lit up with this news. "So, you're the heroine then. I heard about this from Doctor Rourke. You've made quite an impact on him I believe, the way he was singing your praises. An amazing recovery made possible by you and your mother's expertise in old types of medicine he tells me."

Freda felt slightly embarrassed by this disclosure, but could see the nurse was not making fun. "Well, yes, she has unusual remedies," then earnestly, "but they do work. I know many people, myself included who she has saved from serious ailments.

"I'm sure she has, Freda. We could do with someone like your mother to help out around here."

Freda grinned, shaking her head. "1'm not sure that would be a very good policy, nurse. You haven't met her." They both laughed as Henry's contemptuous stare followed the two young women's movements.

Chapter 8

Word quickly spread around the villages that Josh Thrall's voice had suddenly returned. Some regarded it as a gift bestowed by the Lord above, others more sceptical, were prepared to accept factual medical opinion. Whichever way, it was greeted as good news by everyone.

Only Jacob remained in subdued mood. Not because he wasn't delighted for his son but a troubling thought niggled at the back of his mind. A thought that Ruth and Josh shared a secret of some kind and he was unable to hazard a guess at what it could be. An uneasy feeling that something of great importance happened to one, or the pair of them, on the night of the flood. The sudden return of Josh's voice. The unnatural calmness from both that very same night. It was beginning to make sense. But how to confront them? Would it be better together? Or separately? He knew only too well the harbouring of a lie takes its toll over the years. The longer it continues the harder it becomes to face the truth.

The situation resolved itself the very next day, when Jacob answered the door to Toby who was in a state of excitement.

"Reverend Thrall, I just thought you should know you being the preacher man, like." Toby drew in a deep breath. "Sergeant Wright'll be coming round later asking questions about an attempted murder. I can't believe it. Out here of all places. "Nowt exciting ever happens round here, does it? He's already been to our house."

Jacob felt the kick in his stomach, his worst fears already coming to fruition.

"Well, it will certainly be exciting for some, Toby, but it could well bring heartache for others. Thank you for letting me know." Jacob somehow forced a smile on the boy, before Toby turned and headed for the stable.

Josh heard from his friend, Pete Eccles, that Sergeant Wright was making enquiries about a stabbing and Josh decided there and then to admit his guilt. Feigning indifference at Henry's death, mainly for Ruth's benefit, he now felt a sense of relief on hearing of his survival. The enormous burden of guilt instantly lifted from his shoulders once he'd made the decision to confess. He didn't have to think it over.

If he went voluntary, Jacob and Ruth would not suffer the humiliation of the police calling at home. Josh headed straight to the police house and made a statement, explaining everything. From the attack on Ruth in York to the night of the storm.

Reliving the terrible moment took a lot out of Josh. "I do want you to realize, sergeant, that none of this was Ruth's fault. I stabbed and disposed of what I thought was a dead body."

"Good God, Josh, you must have gone through hell." Sergeant Wright shook his head in disbelief, before adding, "although I sympathise, I have to abide by the law and this is attempted murder and a long prison sentence awaits if charges are pressed."

Josh's shoulders dropped. "I understand, sergeant." He looked up at the officer's stern face. If Sergeant Wright was expecting a show of emotion from the boy it was not forthcoming, as Josh added defiantly, "I have no regrets, sergeant. I would do exactly the same thing again to save anyone from an ordeal such as that. He is no better than an animal."

Admiring the young man's attitude and courage, Bill Wright's face softened. "I understand how you feel, Josh, but for God's sake when in court do not make any statements like that in front of the judge."

Josh gave a wry smile. "Thank you, sergeant. I'll remember that."

"Now, you realize I will have to take a statement from Ruth."

"I understand, sergeant." A worried look crossed his features. "Don't be too hard on her, will you?"

"No, I will be at my diplomatic best, Josh. You can depend on that."

"Thank you," Josh replied.

Stoically accepting the consequences, Josh followed Bill Wright to the rear of the house, where many years ago, a quickly adapted room became a small cell with just the addition of a steel barred door. Furniture was a bed, chair and washstand. No window. More suited to cage an animal Josh thought, flinching visibly as the door clattered shut on him. On his life and his freedom. Caged, like some kind of monster. For how long he did not know. That would all depend on the court hearing. Alone in the cell, he thought of the worry and shame he'd brought upon his family, this act of violence finally hitting home.

Once Sergeant Wright left, Josh flopped on the small bed and in the quiet loneliness of this lock-up, body-wracking sobs shook his strong frame. For how long, he knew not. Eventually, with all tears shed, he slept.

Jacob, although aghast at the news, accepted it calmly having realized much earlier there could be only one possible outcome. Gathering a few personal belongings together for Josh, he called at the police house and asked the sergeant if it was possible to see Josh.

Bill Wright nodded, hoping he could ease the burden that weighed heavily upon Jacob's shoulders. Unlocking the cell door, Bill knew he was breaking every rule in the book but decided it worth the risk. "I'll leave you two to have a talk. If you want me, I shall be in the front room.

After a moment of silence, Jacob was the first to speak.

"Strange as it may seem, Josh, I knew something had happened that night but I believe I was so relieved your voice had returned it blinded my vision to any kind of reality. I was not thinking clearly."

"I did what I did. I will serve my sentence, whatever it happens to be. I will carry no guilt. It is out in the open. Only the shame I have brought on your good self, and Ruth, will keep me awake at night."

"That we shall overcome. Many of us carry secrets. Some are shared, some are hidden. I admire your courage. I wish I were as strong." He hugged his son close and there were tears in his eyes as he asked the sergeant to come do his duty and lock the door. Jacob heard the metallic clang of the door as it slammed shut behind him, visibly shuddering at the sound. Heavy of heart he walked out into the cold night air, knowing the next time he would see his son would be in court. He now had to face Ruth when he arrived home and also his parishioners on Sunday.

Chapter 9

A lthough the hospital was a buzz of activity, Henry's room remained quiet. He lay motionless upon the bed in the dimly lit ward, his breathing steady, anticipation building as the nurse would soon enter to check on him. He knew the routine off by heart. She would lean in close, as she always did, and he would inhale the soft sweet smell of her body. His heart began to thud hard in his chest just thinking of what was about to take place, the excitement already building in his mind.

A few more minutes and the tension heightened along with a passion he could not control. The door opened and Nurse Rose flitted quietly to his bedside to check his pulse, unsuspecting. A gasp of shock escaped her lips but that was all as Henry's claw-like fingers dug tightly into the soft flesh of her neck. The bony fingers gripped tighter until her mouth fell open and her flailing body gave up struggling, sagged and went limp. Then with an almighty effort, he heaved her onto the bed.

Matron sat writing at her desk, but the recent information from John Durville left her uneasy. Knowing the nurses were busy she decided to heed his warning and check on Henry.

She entered the room quietly in case he was sleeping. For a second, she froze rigid at the scene in front of her. A nurse lay helpless on the bed, a pillow over her face. Henry, half naked, sprawled on top of her. Obsessed by his insatiable desire and lust, he was oblivious to everything else.

Matron was across the small room in a split second, hurling the full force of her body, and she was no lightweight, against the slight stick insect figure of Henry. He crashed off the side of the bed, his head slamming hard against the tiled floor. Leaving him there, she shouted for help before concentrating on Nurse Rose. The pillow had fallen from her face and the girl's cheeks were drained of colour but there was still a pulse. By God's grace, she thought, I might be in time. She is still alive. The commotion and shouting had brought more help and as she began to administer chest pumps to Rose's motionless body, a male caretaker and two more nurses were busy trying to revive the still unconscious Henry.

Gasping for breath and sweating with the effort, she pulled a whistle from her pocket and blew hard to raise more help in case Henry recovered. The piercing whistle soon brought two more staff running and they began to help with the stricken Henry.

"Please, someone dress that monstrosity of a man." She spat the words out. "Quickly! The mere sight of him makes me sick." Nurse Rose began to revive, matron advising her to keep still. A few minutes later and trembling with fright, Rose asked what had happened. Matron had no need to tell her. Rose understood. Horrified, through stifled sobs, she stammered, "has he... ? Did he...? She stopped. "Please tell me no, matron. Please tell me no..."

Matron hugged her now, comforting, like a mother would a small child.

"No, no, no, Rose. We were just in time, thank God." She breathed a sigh of relief as she was pretty sure she had barged in at the right time. A moment or two longer, Rose could have been dead. The words of John Durville had come to pass. There was no telling what this evil, twisted man was capable of.

Matron handed the distraught Rose over to the two nurses while she escorted the male staff to a secure room where Henry could be kept for the night. First thing in the morning, the Psychiatric wing could be notified and, hopefully, Henry Durville would be off her hands. Prison was no place for him. He needed a different kind of treatment and matron had a feeling he would be placed in a mental institution for a very long time, if not for life. That is if he ever roused from his present unconscious state.

Her worries were now for the safety and well-being of Nurse Rose and also herself. She realized there was a possibility she could be struck off for serious misconduct. The man could still die from his injuries, especially in his state. What the medical profession would make of it was anyone's guess. An attack by the matron on a patient under her care would carry a very serious outcome. But what else could she have done?

Two police officers had arrived and were waiting patiently to interview Rose when sufficiently recovered. Matron asked if it could wait until morning as the poor girl was still in shock and had been sedated to help her sleep.

"Of course, matron. I understand. Would it be possible for us to take a statement from you?" the older of the pair asked. "Do you feel up to it?"

"Of course, officer." She definitely did not feel up to it but the sooner it was done the better. The shock would come later. She gave an exact account and also added if Henry's father had not been so brutally honest it could so easily have ended on a much more serious note.

With Nurse Rose sedated and the ward tidy again, the hospital returned to its usual quiet efficiency. Once the police had left, in the sanctity of her office, matron contemplated how else she could have handled the situation. In her mind there was no other way. Rising from her chair, she reached for her hat and coat, and for once, was glad to hand over responsibility to Miss Ransome who would take charge for the night. As for herself, she would return straight home and enjoy a little tot of whisky, for medicinal purposes, to relax her before retiring to bed.

Chapter 10

News, especially bad news, spreads quickly and the attempted murder charge hanging over Josh Thrall, a well-respected young man in the locality, was talked about with great sadness. Many offers of support flooded in from close friends and acquaintances and Jacob and Ruth took heart from this.

Ruth, although upset, asked if she could go see Josh but Jacob advised her to wait, as he would be transported to Police Headquarters at Spring Hill, Whitby, first thing in the morning. The police would be in touch with John Durville, Henry's father and it was just a case of waiting on a date for the trial.

All Ruth wanted to do now was ride over to Roston and be with Jim, tell him the bad news. Have him wrap his arms around her, assure her everything would turn out all right. Instead, she walked slowly out to the stable in an effort to try and gain some normality. A bright moonlight night, usually enough to lift her spirits, did little for her on this occasion. The horses brought a smile to her lips though, greeting her with a toss of their heads as soon as the door opened.

"Oh, horses," she said. "If only us humans could live an uncomplicated, simple life such as yours." She put her arm around Pal, taking in his animal smell and the soft pleasing warmth of the taut skin and powerful body. He nudged her hand. Laughing, Ruth said, "You're only pleased to see me, cos' you expect a sweet, you greedy animals." She produced his favourite titbit, then walked up to the others to treat all equally, as if they were her children.

"You certainly make me feel better when I'm down, not only out riding, even when I just come in for a talk." Pal suddenly jerked his head up high as the stable door opened and who should walk in but Jim.

"So, this is where you spend your nights, is it? I was sure you were living it up in Castle Moor. When I heard your voice, I thought someone was in here with you, but I'm glad it's just the horses." He grinned and the whole place suddenly seemed brighter. Striding across to her, he took her in his arms and kissed her long and hard. Reluctantly, he released her. Ruth caught her breath, her face aglow with this sudden, unexpected meeting.

"Oh, Jim, how did you know I wanted to see you so much. Have you heard the news? Josh is in prison."

"Yep, I'd heard. Such news travels fast. One o' the miners walking into Roston told me. Thought I should know. I knew you would be upset, so I came straight here."

"I feel so guilty, Jim. He did it to save me, you know, from being raped. Or worse. That man is evil." Her voice broke. Taking her in his arms, he kissed her again, gently this time, then pulled away, wiping dry her falling tears.

"You know, Ruth. You don't have to worry about Josh, he'll be fine. He's a strong character and, although the law will state he was in the wrong, public opinion will be in his favour as many people will speak up for him. If the jury have any sense, they'll see what he did was on the spur of the moment and his sentence will be light." Jim hoped he was saying the right things. "And as for feeling guilty, just dismiss that, Ruth. The man is sick and should be locked up or put in a lunatic asylum before it happens again. Because it will do."

They settled on the rough wooden bench that Toby used when cleaning saddles and bridles, and sat in the warmth of the stable just hugging each other, Jim tenderly stroking her hair, before pushing her gently over into the pile of hay at the side. Laughing, he dropped down beside her. "How come you are not struggling with me, Ruth?"

Her eyes locked onto his, her gaze steady, serious. "Because I want you, Jim

Styles," she whispered. "Want you to make love to me more than anything in this whole wide world and I'm not sure how much longer I can fight such a fire that burns inside me. It never releases me. Do you understand, Jim? Am I making any sense at all?"

His voice was quiet and caring. "I think you're making perfect sense, Ruth Brennan." His lips found hers again. Tender, inviting. His hands began searching, becoming more adventurous, more daring. Fingers, clumsy in their haste, fumbled with the buttons on her blouse, eventually creeping gently inside. They both gasped as his fingers suddenly found and touched the warm flesh of her firm, rounded breast. His hands felt rough and calloused against the smoothness of such delicate skin, the fire in his belly almost unquenchable. Ruth lay still among the hay, eyes closed, breathing heavily. No denials as in the past. Jim had no idea what he was doing but he was sure he would be a quick learner.

At that very minute, voices sounded outside as if approaching the stable. Ruth was oblivious to it. He put a finger to her lips and she opened her eyes.

"Shhh, there's someone about, Ruth." He ran to the door, squinting through a crack in the timber. He spotted a lantern in the distance, swinging loosely in someone's hand as a couple of people headed their way. It could only be friends of Jacob's at this time of night. The two figures wandered slowly past the stable, Jim watched until the house door slammed shut behind the pair. He breathed a sigh of relief.

Ruth was beside him. The moment was over. For now. Jim helped brush the hay from her clothes and hair. "Better have you looking respectable when you are staying under the same roof as the vicar. Don't want people to think you jump in the hay with anybody just passing by." He laughed at the shock on her face.

"Jim, you know I wouldn't do that with anybody else." Then, the colour still high in her cheeks, she added, "But it could be different with you." She smiled and they sat down once more on the seat to talk. They were happy that the special moment still awaited them, knowing there would be more moments and opportunities such as this in the future. At present they could not share the ultimate pleasure that they both yearned for.

Chapter 11

J osh Thrall was a strong-willed character but waiting for the date of the trial stretched his nerves to breaking point, the time passing painfully slow. He paced his cell constantly, only four strides by three, in a bid to keep his body active and also to retain a degree of sanity. The dull grey painted walls, ugly and defaced with names and crude caricatures gouged out of the flaking paintwork revealed its cruel and sordid history. The crumbling brickwork and damp only added to the wretchedness of his situation.

A barred, grimy window, high in the wall opposite the steel door let in a small amount of light. A rusty steel bed and a pillow stuffed with straw, were his only comforts. A week had passed and Josh had requested no visitors in a bid to avoid more emotional stress. This was his problem and he would see it through alone, although he knew he would rely heavily on his lawyer, Mr Ingram.

He was expecting a visit from him and a tap on the door announced his arrival. The guard opened up and spoke directly to Mr Ingram. "Just knock on the door when you are finished, sir."

"Thank you, guard," Mr Ingram had a kind face, more appropriate to a religious faith than acting for criminals, Josh thought. Lean in stature, mid-fifties and smartly dressed, the wispy hair falling over his ears gave him a Dickensian type appearance, especially once the rimless glasses were placed on the end of his long nose.

"Right, Josh, down to work. We have good news. Since our last meeting, Judge John Durville has contacted me. He does not want to press charges. So much so that he is willing to speak on your behalf. If proceedings go according to plan, which he fervently hopes they will, it may help Henry to be referred for treatment."

They both sat on the edge of the bed, Mr Ingram with briefcase on knee and Josh leaning forward, listening intently to every word.

"This is now the mainstay of our defence and it is our only hope of saving you from a prison sentence, Josh. I am much more optimistic now Henry's father is on board." He paused, scribbled notes on a pad. "A judge of his standing will carry more weight. I think your only option is to plead guilty, tell exactly what happened. As you were unable to shout for help, you panicked and picked up the nearest thing at hand to save the victim from a vicious and violent attack. That is how I see it. Are you agreeable?"

"I'm entirely in your hands and will take your advice."

Mr Ingram rose from the bed and tapped the door, shook Josh's hand again, adding, "Try not to worry Josh. I think we do stand a very good chance of an acquittal." These words of encouragement lifted Josh's spirits.

Once alone, Josh began pacing the floor with monotonous regularity. Apart from a quick walk around the small yard with other prisoners, this constituted part of his daily exercise. Boredom proved the biggest threat to his sanity and he had devised a game of making words from the hundreds of names scrawled into the walls. But after this final talk with Mr Ingram, he was ready to face the court.

Come the day of the trial, the dark, sombre courtroom prickled with expectation and packed with people and reporters curious about this young would-be killer from the countryside. Everyone hushed and turned their attention to Josh Thrall, as looking neither right nor left, he was led handcuffed into the chair alongside his solicitor, Mr Richard Ingram.

The court usher rose to his feet. "The court rise for Judge Strickland." A shuffling of feet as everyone stood. Judge Strickland, in red robe and white judicial wig, made his entrance and sat down at the head of the room, adjusting his gown as he did so.

"Be seated."

The rustle of clothing sounded loud in the silence of this revered oak lined law room. Josh raised his head, studied Judge Strickland and then let his gaze wander over to the jury of seven men and two women. There sat the nine people who would decide his fate. A solid knot of fear lodged tight in the base of his gut, as heavy as lead. A terrible feeling of nausea swept over him and beads of sweat popped out on his brow. For God's sake, he must not faint now. He swallowed, forcing himself to concentrate, knowing he must be strong for the sake of his family. He knew Ruth and his father were sitting directly behind him and had also spotted the unmistakable figure of John Durville.

The court usher broke the brittle silence.

"Mr Joshua Thrall, of Gallows Howe, you are accused of attempted murder and disposal of the body of Henry Durville of York. How do you plead?"

Richard Ingram rose to his feet. "Mr Thrall pleads guilty to the charge, your honour but will also plead mitigating circumstances which will become clear as the case unfolds." Reporters began scribbling on their pads.

The court usher ordered. "The prosecution will call their first witness, your honour."

Mr Bowes rose quickly to his feet. "We have no witnesses, your honour. The only other witness to this act will be called by the defence. We only have the full confession of the accused, Joshua Thrall, as to what happened on the night of the attempted murder as taken by Constable William Wright of Castle Moor."

The judge looked up from his papers and peered over the top of his spectacles at Mr Bowes, bafflement written all over his face. "No witnesses. If I may say so, Mr Bowes, this is an odd way to proceed with a prosecution."

"Your honour, there were no other witnesses of the attack, so we have no one to call, but we will be cross examining when the defence put their case."

"Very well, Mr Bowes. That is all for the time being."

The judge whispered across to the usher. He instantly leapt to his feet.

"Will the defence call their first witness."

Mr Ingram rose and walked to the front of the courtroom. "Call Ruth Brennan to the stand." Ruth trying hard not to show her nervousness, walked to the stand and a Bible was placed in her right hand. "Please read from the card, Miss Brennan."

Ruth spoke with a confidence she did not feel. "I swear to tell the truth, the whole truth and nothing but the truth, so help me, God."

A kindly man, Mr Ingram did his best to put Ruth at ease. "There is no need to be nervous, Miss Brennan. You are not on trial here. All the jury want to hear is exactly what happened on the night the attempted murder took place. In your own time and in your own words."

Ruth stared out at the assembled crowd, and there, right at the back was the dark tousled head of Jim, smiling at her. The uncertainty vanished. She could face anyone now.

Ruth had no trouble relating the attack. It would be with her until the day she died. Once again, she relived the horror of what happened but, this time, in front of a packed courtroom. When finished she was emotionally drained, hung out to dry, but with her heartfelt explanation every person in that room experienced her fear, lived every moment with her. Gripping the support rail, she sank to the chair. Thinking it was all over, Ruth was just about to rise and leave the witness box when Mr Ingram spoke again.

"Thank you, Ruth. Your witness." He gave a curt nod to Mr Bowes.

Mr Bowes, a thin man with an aggressive set to his gaunt features, took his time, shuffling papers before eventually rising to address the witness. His manner was no less aggressive than his appearance and in a sharp clear voice that grated, he asked, "How old are you, Miss Brennan?

"Seventeen, sir."

"I believe you were raised in an orphanage at York. Is that right?"

"No, it is not. My parents lived in Lady Peckitts Yard, York and that is where I was born." The abruptness in Mr Bowes voice put her on edge. She well remembered her first appearance in court. With a feeling of anxiety, she realized there could be some tough questions ahead. She was proved right.

"Until what age, Miss Brennan?"

"Nine years old, sir."

"Then what happened?"

"My mother died and my next-door neighbour could not afford to keep me and I was taken to the orphanage."

"Why didn't your father take care of you?" Straight to the point. He studied the jury, then stared hard at Ruth.

Ruth was not about to buckle. She had faced meaner characters than this one in her short life.

"Because he went to prison for murder." A gasp echoed through the courtroom.

"Murder you say. Were you used to violence in your family then, Miss Brennan?"

"Not at all, sir. That is, I wasn't until drink got the better of my father."

"Where is your father now, Miss Brennan?"

"Still in York prison, I believe."

Mr Bowes had done his homework. Ruth was not on trial but it felt very much like it.

"While in the orphanage, did you gain a reputation as a troublemaker and of being, might we say, a very forward young woman for your age?"

Ruth kept her composure but he was beginning to get to her. "If you mean was I in trouble with the law then yes, I was, for stealing. They used to starve us in there and we stole so we could eat. I knew it was wrong but it was necessary."

"You went to prison, is that right?"

"Yes, sir."

He leant forward, hands on desk in front of him, eager to make her out as some kind of harlot. "I suggest, under such circumstance, especially at such a young age, you learnt other tricks as well, Miss Brennan. One of them," he stressed this point, loud and clear in the jury's direction, "was to manipulate weak minded boys and young men to do your bidding. One of these men happened to be the unfortunate Mr Henry Durville who, once you had no further use for him, you discarded. He, like a devoted lap dog, followed you to Gallows Howe where he almost met his death from an attack by another of your conquests, the accused, Joshua Thrall."

"That is not what happened." Ruth was appalled that such a man was allowed to twist the truth like this. "He attacked me in York and…" she was not allowed to answer as he turned arrogantly away from her and addressed the judge. "No further questions, my Lord."

"Please let me answer, sir. This is not…."

"That will be all, Miss Brennan. Please stand down."

Shaking with anger, Ruth bit her tongue, stepped from the witness box and took her seat.

"The defence call Joshua Thrall to the stand."

Joshua, face pale and drawn, managed a smile toward Ruth and his father before repeating the oath.

Mr Ingram stood, studying Josh for a second. You understand, Mr Thrall, you are accused of attempted murder and also, disposing of the body and you admit to this."

"I do." Josh's voice was shaky but he faced the courtroom with confidence.

"Miss Brennan has just stated, under oath, what happened that night. Is she correct?"

"Yes, sir, she is."

"Have you anything to say in your defence, Mr Thrall."

"I have. What Henry Durville was doing was wrong. This was the second time he had attacked Miss Brennan. It is well known he is a man that preys on young girls and women and…

Mr Bowes jumped to his feet. "Objection, your honour."

"Overruled. Carry on."

"And if this man is allowed to go free then someone, somewhere is going to suffer serious consequences. I do not condone my actions but it was done to save a person from a vicious attack. I returned from church to find Henry Durville on top of Ruth Brennan, with clothing undone after brutally throwing her to the ground. With no way of shouting for help because of my loss of voice, I panicked and picked up the knife, the first thing that I thought might save her, which it did. I might add that as Mr Bowes said earlier, I do love Ruth Brennan but as a sister, not as a scarlet woman as he

54

tried to convey earlier. Henry Durville should be locked away or put in a mental institution."

"Objection, your honour. It is not Henry Durville we are here to sentence but Joshua Thrall for attempted murder."

"Sustained. Please keep your observations to yourself, Mr Thrall."

"Yes, sir."

"Thank you. You may step down."

With an audible sigh of relief, Josh made his way back to his position by the prison officer.

Mr Ingram spoke. "We have one more witness to call on, your honour."

"Call Judge John Durville."

Heads swivelled as John Durville rose to his feet at the back of the courtroom. This was now his stage. He felt comfortable, at home in such austere and harsh surroundings as this. John knew this would have to be one of his best performances yet if it was to help Josh beat a prison sentence. If he was successful, it would also see his only son placed in a mental institution rather than prison. John knew there was no other possible outcome.

Dressed in his customary black attire there was a certain charisma surrounding him in these conditions, cutting a dominant figure as he strode purposefully to the witness box and repeated the oath.

Mr Ingram and John had met briefly when John asked if he be allowed to testify for the defence. Mr Ingram said. "The court is yours, Mr Durville."

Stating his name, occupation and place of residence, he placed both hands on the rail at the front of the witness box and surveyed his audience, especially the jury. His jet-black eyes rested on each in turn for a second or two before he began his statement in a strong clear voice. The atmosphere was charged with expectancy.

"I believe most of you in this room will have family. You understand how we all suffer when one or more in that family are suffering. I am no different." He paused for effect. "Henry Durville is my only remaining family. Miriam, my late wife, and I lost a daughter in a tragic accident when she was only ten years old. A beautiful child who we still miss to this very day. Miriam never recovered from that awful day. She did learn to live with it but the loss of a

55

child can destroy the will to live. It destroyed her. In the passing years we realized Henry had a problem but due to work commitments and also in view of what happened to our daughter, we turned a blind eye, believing it was something that would be kept in control. With hindsight, action should have taken place much sooner. The illness of the mind, because that is what it is, proved to be stronger than his will. Uncontrollable, like a cancerous growth festering inside his head, growing worse over the years." He paused again but not for effect this time. He was struggling to stay in control of his own emotions.

"It finally came to a head when I took Ruth Brennan out of jail to work at home as maid to my wife, Miriam." The court remained hushed, hanging on every word spoken. This was a speech directly from the heart. Each and everyone in the courtroom realized this.

"Unbeknown to my wife and I, our other maid, Bella was with child to Henry but she lost her life in an attempt to abort the child. Ruth was goodness itself to Miriam and was one of the reasons why my wife lived a longer and more comfortable life. Henry brought this amicable arrangement to an end, attacking Ruth with only Miriam at home, asleep. Ruth bravely fought him off. Then she fled, along with Bella, fearing she had killed him.

Henry learned of her whereabouts, doggedly tracked her down and tried to force his unwanted attentions onto her again. This time with serious consequences. For him, Ruth, and for Joshua Thrall."

John's eyes never left the nine jurors as he searched for small clues in their body language and facial expressions. Any sign at all that he was winning them over. He was, he could sense it, could almost taste it. A sudden surge of energy swept through his body. He carried on in the same vein.

"Henry recovered due to remarkable kindness and treatment from the two women who dragged him out of the river. He is now in Whitby hospital recovering." His eyes scanned the room. He did not intend missing anyone from this closing delivery which would make or break the case for Josh.

"He has since gained strength. So much so that he savagely tried to rape one of the nurses. She was saved only by the intervention of a very brave and able matron."

A chatter echoed around the hallowed room before the usher shouted for silence. John gathered himself for an emotional finale.

"There is only one thing you can do as fair minded and just people. Acquit Joshua Thrall of all charges." Again, a pause. "He is a good and caring person, from a loving, law-abiding family. Every effort should be taken in putting my son into a suitable institution where he can receive treatment. For all his wrong doings, I still love him dearly. Prison is not the place for him." John shook his head, before carefully stressing his last words. "Prison would do more harm than good. I hope to God these actions take place, which will prevent any more heartache. I do not want other families in the future to suffer as I have done." Gathering himself, he finished with the words, "and I would like to stress, I will not be pressing charges."

John pulled a handkerchief from his pocket and wiped away the genuine tears of grief that he had tried so hard to contain. He hoped they would not fall until finished but the emotionally charged atmosphere created by his closing speech proved too much for him. He sat in the witness box utterly drained and only faintly heard Mr Ingram call, "No more witnesses, your honour."

There was silence in the room for a full minute before Judge Strickland finally looked across to the prosecution bench and asked, "Have you any more witnesses to call, Mr Bowes?"

"None, your honour." Mr Bowes realized this final call from Mr Ingram had won the day. He could see it clearly in the juror's faces.

"Very well." The judge surveyed the courtroom, clasped his hands in front of him before delivering his final summing up. "I do realize this has been a very unusual case for all concerned. Now, I must ask the jury to take into consideration all the evidence presented by each and every one of the witnesses and stress that you must arrive at a unanimous decision that will not only satisfy the law of this country but also myself. Court is adjourned for the day. We will return at twelve noon tomorrow when I expect your final decision on this case." The Judge rose and walked out. Reporters rushed to meet their deadlines. The case had raised interest and alarm in the local area. This was a big story and most irregular. A father, a judge of law no less, asking leniency for the man who tried to murder his only son. Josh was led away and all anyone could do now was to await the jury's decision.

Chapter 12

⁙

Josh spent another restless night cooped up in his grey tomb. Today he faced the moment of truth and once washed and dressed, he waited for the click of the key. The prison officer entered and led him once again into the packed courtroom where he took his seat next to Mr Ingram. As noon approached the jury filed back to their respective seats. Solemn and expressionless, they looked neither right nor left, never a hint as to what the result might be.

The usher rose to his feet. "All rise for Judge Strickland." They rose as one. Judge Strickland entered and seated himself. Only when fully comfortable did he order, "Be seated."

Judge Strickland allowed the monotonous chimes of the town clock to subside before nodding to the usher.

Josh felt sick with fear. He dreaded the inevitable and his heart thumped in expectation. He was not sure if he would be strong enough. The clock chimes had sounded like a death knell to his ears.

"The defendant please rise, for the verdict." Mr Ingram assisted Josh to his feet.

The judge took over and addressed the foreman of the jury. "I expect you all to have reached a decision." It was a statement, not a question.

The foreman of the jury, an elderly man at the end of the bench, rose to his feet and confidently answered. "We have, your honour." The decision was then handed to the judge.

He studied the paper before addressing the foreman. "Could you please tell the court your decision."

The foreman of the jury, speaking clearly and with a voice crackling with the authority requested of his position, replied, "Not guilty on both counts, your honour." Again, audible gasps from the onlookers around the hushed room. Josh held onto the rail in front of him, legs unsteady. Mr Ingram eased him back down into the chair, where he sat and sobbed uncontrollably until the usher requested silence.

"Quiet please. For Judge Strickland."

Another minute of silence before the judge spoke and locked eyes with Josh. "Joshua Thrall, you have heard the decision of this jury. It is unanimous. You may leave the court a free man and put this unfortunate episode behind you with no fear of a stain on your good character. Thank you. That will be all."

It was over. Not guilty, and no stain upon his character. Josh, in emotional turmoil at the verdict was laughing and crying all at the same time. He thanked Mr Ingram for his knowledge and understanding and the testimony of John Durville proved pivotal. Family, friends and well-wishers crowded around. Ruth, face radiant with relief, was one of the first to throw her arms around his neck, saying, "Thank God it's over for you, Josh. Time to put this nightmare in the past."

After thanking everyone who had stood by him and offered their support, Josh returned home the very same day, a free and relieved man. Free and, hopefully, back to the ordered routine of his normal, working life and, as Ruth said, time to put it behind them.

In the weeks that followed, Josh still had plenty of work at Gallows Howe as Jacob took the opportunity to spend more time at the church. Also, close friend, Pete Eccles was often calling on him for help, especially with the sheep and Josh felt the horror of his confinement fading with every passing day. Even the unenviable task of tackling the bookwork, he was finding acceptable.

But now, after three hours sat behind a desk, he was ready for some company. A glance at the fancily carved time piece hanging above the fireplace showed four thirty. Time to knock off. After all it was Saturday and he'd arranged to meet Pete. Not that he expected much to be happening down in Castle Moor but there was definitely more chance of activity there than at Gallows Howe. Possibly he might meet up with a couple more friends and have a beer in the Buck.

Josh was excited but slightly nervous at the same time. The return of his voice had brought a dramatic change to his life and after coming through the stress of the trial unscathed, his confidence was growing. Now he must try to learn the art of socialising again in this beckoning new world.

Pete Eccles was sitting on the old stone guide post waiting patiently, idly flicking stones at an old tin can at the side of the road. Pete was a tall, gangly shepherd lad from nearby Conn House close by the railway station and he and Josh had become firm friends after many days working together over the past few years.

One of their favourite meeting places was high on the moor above the disused lime kilns, where they would sit and discuss life in general. Josh also helped him in the thick of winter when sheep could be lost in vicious snowstorms and die of starvation out on the moor.

Towering over Josh, Pete greeted him warmly, slinging an arm around his friend's wide shoulders. "Bang on time as usual, Josh." Pete studied his friend a little closer. "Bet you're relieved to be a free man, aren't you? God, it was exciting stuff, Josh. I listened in and even I felt the tension. What you must have felt like, I can't imagine"

"Well," Josh was smiling, "let's just say I don't want to experience anything like that ever again, Pete. Once is enough for me."

Pete took a step back, then slung both arms around his friend in a bear hug.

Josh said, "Another good thing to come out of it, Pete, was my voice stood up to the strain. The doctors were right. They said certain things could trigger a part of my brain into working again." He paused, remembering the trigger. "They didn't tell me it would have to be something dramatic for it to happen," he said grudgingly.

61

Pete let him go, a broad smile on his face. "Well, at least it proves you have a brain, Josh Thrall, cos meself, I didn't think there was anything in there." He clipped Josh across the top of his blond locks and they both broke out laughing at Pete's black humour.

Deep in thought, Pete remarked, "Hey, you know what this means, Josh? We'll be able to mix with the fairer sex a bit more now, eh?" His eyes lit up. "Y'know what, Veronica really fancies me, I can tell." Pete struck a manly posture and smiled. "Only one problem," he said, "she won't leave her mate, Freda, on her own."

"Freda from the mill, you mean?" Josh asked. He'd heard about her. Had also noticed her at the trial.

"You know full well who I mean, Josh. Oh, I know she's a bit odd." He thought for moment. "Well, it's not so much Freda that's a bit odd, it's more her mother, Winnie, that keeps such a tight rein on her. Never allowed out of her sight. Now, I'm sure if you were a really good mate and are man enough to take Freda on, I would have all on to keep Veronica off me. I know Freda's a bit older than you, but hey, what's a few years matter. 'Specially if it's for a friend."

At this, Josh doubled up with laughter. "Oh, come off it, Pete. Veronica? You're not handsome enough for her. Another thing, you'll not hold Veronica's attention for long if all you do is bleat on like one your old moor sheep. Or about how poor the weather is for hay making or sheep shearing and the like. I have more chance of going out with Veronica than you."

A feigned hurt look crossed Pete's features before he fired back. "Give over, Josh. No way would she ever look at a holier than thou vicar's son. Probably run a mile if she realized you fancied her." Then laughing he said, "you must have seen her old man knocking about the village lately? He's never sober and could start an argument in an empty pub. Definitely not a God-fearing family. No, it will have to be someone of strong character, rugged good looks with great physique." He sniffed, shoved his nose high in the air, a posture that he thought portrayed the gentry in such circumstances. "Does it remind you of anyone you know, eh?"

"Yeah, it does as it happens. Quasimodo springs to mind."

"Ah, that's cruel, Josh Thrall."

Their laughter and jokes continued as they neared Castle Moor, now one of the busiest trading villages in the valley. With its sheep sales, local dances, market days and occasional point to point races, it was beginning to attract a much younger crowd from the surrounding villages.

As they approached the school, a young woman was struggling to push through the wrought iron gate onto the road, as her hands were full with shopping bags. The gate was heavy and awkward and she appeared frustrated and tired. Freda was just leaving work after cleaning the school classrooms.

"Steady on there, Freda," Pete said, "you'll strain yourself, girl. You've far too much for one person to carry there. Please allow a couple of strong gents to escort you home with this little lot?" Pete gave a sly wink in Josh's direction. "We have plenty of time haven't we, Josh?"

Freda gave Pete a quick, cautious glance. She was in no mood for any of Pete's stupid ill-timed jokes about witches and quacks that he had often made in the past but this time he seemed quite sincere. Brushing the unruly bush of blond hair back from her face, she took stock of Josh for the first time. Her piercing blue eyes locked onto his for a moment longer than necessary and Josh felt as though his knees might give way.

Ignoring Pete, she spoke directly at Josh. "Hello, Joshua Thrall. I'm pleased you were acquitted. I saw you at the trial. I thought you did really well in front of those lawyers."

"Thanks. And thanks for coming to the trial." He smiled at her. "I know you were there. I recognized you."

"Did you? Did you really?" She smiled, the full lips widening. The smile of an angel, Josh thought. This was surely a time when he really wished he did believe in angels, like his father. But sadly, he didn't. A great pity, although this girl could possibly persuade him to think differently. Freda was older but that was no obstacle. Not to him anyway.

"Can I take your bags, Freda?" Josh said, pleased he hadn't stuttered and embarrassed himself.

Freda looked at him afresh. "Bet you're relieved your voice returned, aren't you? What brought this about, after all these years?"

"I am, really pleased. I think it must have had something to do with the shock. I can't quite believe it myself. All those wasted years. It means a new start for me."

He took the bags and she gently touched his hand. "I'm so pleased for you, Joshua. I really am."

"Hey you two, I'm here as well you know, or hadn't you noticed?" Pete jumped in to help with the bags and Freda turned her attention toward him. Josh, realizing he was staring, tore his gaze away from her.

"Sorry, Pete. I was just so glad for Joshua with all this good news."

Freda had a husky, slightly masculine voice that Josh knew he could listen to forever if need be.

"I can help Freda, Pete. Anyway, I thought you had business at the Buck tonight?"

Pete, a bit slow on the uptake, eventually took the hint. "Ah, yeah, you're right, Josh, I almost forgot. Right, will see you later on. Bye, Freda." But Freda had turned her attention back to Josh. With a laugh, Pete made his way in the direction of the Buck.

Now on their own, Freda said, "No, I can manage, honestly. Mother's not expecting me back 'til later anyway and you know what she's like. She's very cautious who I mix with." She hesitated. "On second thoughts, why not, if you do have time? It would be good to have company and a great help if you could take some of the bags, even just to the bottom of the village."

After years of sign language, Josh was not yet comfortable in company, especially female company. It was different with Ruth. She was more like family.

"Now, I do know you are Jacob Thrall's son from up at the Gallows, so you must know where I live, Joshua?"

Josh nodded. "Call me Josh, Freda. Everyone else does. Yes, I know it well. I used to fish on that stretch of the river above the mill." Josh hesitated then said, "I realize you and your mother saved Henry's life. If he had died, I would still be locked away in that damned prison cell now, Freda. The speech by Henry's father was a turning point. I owe many people my freedom," he said shaking his head.

"Good God, he was brilliant, wasn't he? What a frightening night, Josh, and to think Henry was this close to death." Freda put a bag down and held her fingers just an inch apart.

"Yes, I'm glad it's all over and with his father speaking up as he did, Henry might receive the specialist treatment he needs."

Silence reigned between the pair for a while before Freda broke it. "No doubt you'll have heard the old gossip stories about Winnie Grey and her daughter and their odd ways, right?"

Josh smiled, nodding in agreement. "Some, but she's proved her cures work. The doctors say so."

"Yes, but her remedies are odd, I'll grant you that and some of the stories you've heard could well be true, Josh, but the cruel and nasty ones are all false. Made up. Village tittle-tattle. My mother really is a gentle character, she wouldn't hurt a fly and has helped many in the past." Hesitating, Freda locked her soul-searching gaze onto Josh's again. She desperately wanted him to believe her. He did. With a passion.

"I've heard the gossip, Freda. I've also heard the good stories about your mother. Some people are quick to judge without full knowledge."

"My goodness, Josh, you sound like your father. Are you going to be a man of the cloth like him? If so, I better watch my language!"

"No, I'm definitely not cut out to be a vicar," they both laughed at the thought.

Arriving at the stone columns, Freda put her bags down. "So, here we are," she said. "Thank you for helping me, Josh, and if the stories you've heard haven't frightened you off, we might see each other again."

Josh, although his arms were aching, was disappointed the walk was over.

"I hope we do," he said as Freda gathered the bags and walked away. Before disappearing from view under the low avenue of overhanging trees, she turned and smiled. Josh waved goodbye, heart beating painfully in his chest, refusing to quieten down.

As darkness closed in, he decided to follow the winding footpath along the river and enjoy the solitude of the long walk back home. A stiff climb faced him as he took the little-used drover's road, a track soon to be lost in the mists of time as Mother Nature clawed back what was rightfully hers. On reaching the small garth which the road had once served, Josh tried to order his thoughts. A rowdy old pub held no appeal for him right now. Next time maybe, when he'd gained a bit more confidence. Staring heavenward, tiny pinpricks of light from the stars pierced the blue-black gown of night, adding to the eerie yellow glow from a crescent moon. As it flitted intermittently between the dull clouds, it occasionally lit the well-worn stones under his feet, as if leading him forward on a silver ribbon of opportunity towards a new life.

Freda had attended Castle Moor School but most of Josh's education had continued at home because of his loss of voice. All these years in the same village and he'd never even noticed her. Surely their paths would cross again. In fact, he would make sure they did. Somehow.

Over the next few days, Josh soon found out Freda's work days and then conjured up excuses to be in the vicinity when making her way home. Flattered by the younger man's interest, the relationship quickly blossomed but the secrecy proved harder than either imagined, as Freda did not want any arguments with her over-protective mother.

Reluctantly, Josh agreed to her wishes and they continued to meet in places free from prying eyes, both enjoying this new found freedom and excitement in their lives.

Chapter 13

Josh stabled the horses, then rushed inside and hurried through to the kitchen which housed the only mirror downstairs. Never a vain person before, it had now become important to Josh that he looked his best. The mirror hanging above the soapstone sink, Josh normally used for shaving, but now he smiled and preened in front of it even though the vertical crack across its face distorted his features. Splashing more water onto his unruly blond hair, he patted it flat as best he could. Choosing his smarter coat, he threw it over his shoulders and was ready to dash out when the door flew open and in walked Ruth.

"Oh, Josh, I'm glad I've caught you," she said, relief showing on her face, "Could you possibly run an errand for me tonight as I'm running short of time."

"Ah," he stammered, "er, I think that might be a bit awkward, Ruth. So am I. You see, I've arranged to meet Pete and I don't want to be late."

"I'm sorry, Josh. I didn't realize you were in a rush as well. Don't worry, I can possibly make it down to the old mill myself. I bumped into old Hannah Martin and she's running short on medicine. She asked if I could get a message to Winifred Grey for some more. She hoped Freda might call round with it."

"Oh well, I suppose in that case, I can make time for that. It's not much out of my way. Have you the list there?"

Ruth handed the message over, then studied him. "That was a sudden change of mind, Josh Thrall."

Josh looked embarrassed. Trying to appear nonchalant he smiled, making the excuse, "Well, your errands usually end up taking forever, so I thought I better tell you I was busy."

"Thanks so much, Josh. That can be your good deed for the day." Her face brightened. "It means I can make it over to Honey Bee and catch up with Jim." Suddenly she stood back and studied him afresh, noticing his slicked down hair for the first time. "What's with the tidy hair, Josh. And your best coat. In fact, over these past few weeks, I've seen quite a transformation in your appearance. Are you and Pete meeting up with someone and keeping it a secret from me?"

Josh coloured up. "Oh, for goodness sake, Ruth. You've been telling me to smarten up for ages and then when I do, you make fun."

"I am not making fun. In fact, if you weren't so much like family, I could possibly find you quite an attractive young man. Who's the lucky girl?"

If it was possible, Josh turned a brighter red. "I told you, I'm just meeting Pete and we'll mebbe go to the Buck."

Ruth giggled at Josh's embarrassment and glanced towards the clock. "It's a bit early for the Buck, don't you think?" She knew something was on the cards but didn't know what.

"Yes, mebbe a bit but we have things to sort out," and with that he rushed out, breathing a sigh of relief, glad to be clear of any more questioning.

Dropping from the high ground, he was soon clear of the slight breeze, the trees and landscape now changing to a russet brown. When days were sunny, everything around the moors appeared vibrant and tinged with gold. On dull dark days it was drab, lack lustre. The beauty of autumn was slipping away with each passing day.

Damn, he'd missed Freda by now, she would be back at home. But having the note gave him the excuse to call at the house. Josh walked quickly down the well-trodden track leading to the base of the valley before hitting the path tight by the rippling river.

Practising his words if Winnie answered, he strode up to the door and gave three loud bangs on the wrought iron knocker. He heard it echo down the hallway and waited. He was just about to knock again when the door creaked open a few inches. A small, pinch-faced woman with a hook nose peered cautiously from behind it but did not offer to speak.

"Hello, it's Miss Grey, isn't it?" Josh was nervous but not quite as bad as this woman. She appeared to be almost in a state of fright.

"Mrs, if you don't mind. Yes, I'm Winnie Grey. What do you want, young man?" Abrupt, cautious and jumpy.

"I have a message from Hannah Martin asking if Freda could possibly take her some more medicine as she is beginning to run low. If you are too busy, I could take it for you."

"No need for that, Freda will be able to take it. Wait here." The door suddenly slammed in Josh's face and he heard the key turn in the lock. She was not about to let him follow her in. Freda was busy clearing the table after their meal when Winnie bustled in.

"Keep this door closed, Freda. The vicar's son is at the door wanting Hannah Martin's medicine. She's running out. Would you be able to take it for me? I don't want him to come here thinking he can just call for everyone's medicine."

"Oh, mother, don't be so nervous. Henry's gone. We have nothing to be worry about."

Not wanting to alert suspicion in her over protective mother, Freda replied, "That's good really, I could do with a long walk. Yes, tell him I have time. It's not fair to bother others with our business."

Winnie returned to Josh. "I've had a word with Freda and she'll see that Hannah gets her medicine tonight. I have some already bottled up." Before shutting the door, Winnie eventually remembered her manners and had the good grace to say, "Thank you, young man and goodnight."

"Goodnight, Mrs Grey." Josh emphasised the Mrs. He turned and left, not only startled at the abruptness of Freda's mother, but the display of nervousness, as if she had something to hide. Strangely, even though living in the vicinity all his life, that was the first time he'd met Winnie in person. He had often seen her traipsing across the moor, or down by the river, scouring hedgerows and bushes for ingredients. He also knew she was disabled and a very private individual. As Len Bailes would say, "She nivver seems t' tire of her own company!"

When Freda related some of the cruel gossip spread about her, no wonder Winnie treated people with suspicion. Josh did not listen to hearsay. He preferred to make his own mind up, deciding Winnie was quite an eccentric character.

But for now, he would concentrate on the present, knowing this errand for Ruth made meeting up with Freda much easier.

Chapter 14

"You sure you'll be all right, mam? I've done all the tidying up necessary." Freda gathered the small bottles together for Hannah, adding with a wry smile, "D'you think the hospital will have adapted to some of your special ways yet, mother? Doctor Rourke explained, you know. I dread to think what they really thought when he told them."

Winnie laughed. "Well, I'm just pleased it is all over with and everything worked out for the best."

"Right, I'm off," Freda said. "I'll see you in a couple of hours."

"Oh, surely it'll not take you that long, will it?" She looked enquiringly at her daughter.

"No, I'll be as quick as I can, unless Hannah keeps me talking. You know what she's like once she gets going. I think she's lonely really."

"Don't forget, it soon comes in dark at this time of year, Freda honey."

Frustrated by her mother's persistent possessive streak, Freda snapped back. "Mother, I am not a child anymore. Please do not keep treating me like one. I hardly see more than these four walls and I need to get out occasionally, you know." Shocked at her own sharpness, she instantly softened her tone and pecked her mother on the cheek. "Don't worry, mam, I'll be back before you've even missed me." Pulling a coat over her shoulders, Freda dashed out, excited at this unexpected chance of seeing Josh.

Branching away from the track that led to Hannah's home, she struck out

71

up the moor side. Following the rough stone wall surrounding the small garth, a lone oak tree stood, bleak and bare of leaves, a clear silhouette against the darkening skyline. Josh was waiting in the shadows and her heart lurched. She rushed to meet him, breathing heavily, her face flushed.

"Steady on, Freda, you'd think the devil was after you. What's the rush?"

"Oh, I'm so pleased to see you, Josh. Also, I'm glad of the excuse to get some fresh air. When mother said you'd called, I hoped you would be waiting. Now, as you know, I haven't long as I have to deliver this package to Hannah as well, so if you'll…" Josh did not let her finish the sentence. His arms pulled her close.

"Well, if we haven't much time," he said softly, "we better make the most of what we've got," and kissed her firmly on the lips. After what seemed an eternity to Freda, Josh reluctantly let Freda take a breath.

"My God, Josh. You told me you were short of confidence. You hardly let me up for air." Freda was glad of the encroaching dusk hiding the flush of her cheeks. Was this what love felt like. Freda had no idea, never experiencing such emotions before in her entire life. Exploration, freedom, excitement, these feelings rippled through her body urging her to go further. But her response to the intimacy of the kiss also frightened her. Took her by surprise.

"I've been wanting to do that since I first met you in the village, Freda." He smiled and his blue eyes never left her. "Did I do okay? You may have to teach me how to kiss properly as I've not had the practice of your other boyfriends."

"Well, I have to admit, it was a real good starter, Josh." She giggled, trying to sound experienced. She licked her lips, smiling her approval. "But I think we can both improve if given the chance. By the way," her brow wrinkled, "which boyfriends would they be? What makes you think I've had more practice than you, especially with mother watching my every move. Oh, she means well but it can be a bit overpowering."

Freda's eyes sparkled as they searched Josh's. For what, she did not know. Reassurance? Confidence? Acceptance? It could be for any of these things, she thought. She could not find the right words to tell Josh that he was the first person to kiss her. To Freda, this moment was almost like losing her virginity. Or so she imagined. Even the thought she found sensual, sending a shiver through her body. How could it be that someone of her age had not experienced anything as simple and innocent as a kiss on the lips from a man. It just wasn't right.

Still with his arms wrapped around her, warding off the cool night air, Josh felt a tremor run through her body. "Are you cold, Freda?"

"No, I'm not cold, Josh. For the first time in my life, I feel alive with excitement at being so close to you." Freda hesitated, then lifted her gaze to Josh saying, "I don't want this intimacy to end although I know it must."

Josh was thoughtful for a moment. "It won't always be like this, Freda, having to meet in secret. Soon we will make our own lives, follow our own destiny with all the time in the world for each other. Just think of that."

Darkness had fallen and they wandered over to the jumble of rocks at the side of the track and sat down. Josh slid his arm around her again, felt the warmth of her body as she melted into him and he put both hands to her face and tilted her head toward him. This time, he saw stars as she hungrily returned his kiss. Freda was not starved of love at home. Far from it. But she needed a different kind of love, an all demanding, powerful love that only a man could give her. This man. Her body tingled with excitement, expectancy, but expectancy of what, she did not know, only a longing inside her so strong she wanted, nay needed, to find out. Finally, breaking from the embrace, Freda exclaimed, "Wow, you're a quick learner, Josh Thrall." Josh beamed at the praise, enjoying this whole new world beginning to take shape. And rapidly. He felt quite the lover boy.

Reality returning, Freda expressed the problems they faced. "You realize, Josh, if we keep seeing each other, it will be impossible to keep it a secret forever."

"You mean from your mother, don't you?"

"Yes. Oh, I cannot explain it at present but you must believe me, it is difficult."

Josh thought it best not to ask. He sensed she was close to tears.

"Well, let's not worry about that yet. A solution will arise in the future, Freda, take my word. And if it doesn't, then we make sure we resolve it ourselves. After all, it is our future and you only get one go at it."

"You seem to have a pretty definite attitude towards life, Josh. You certainly have not learnt that from your father."

"No, definitely not. Mostly from Ruth Brennan. When Ruth told me the full story of her suffering at such a young age, I couldn't believe it. She fought through insurmountable problems and eventually stumbled upon Gallows Howe, made it her home and rebuilt her life. It was that steely fighting spirit that made me vow to approach life like her." He shook his head. "She is such a strong individual."

"You speak about her with great affection, Josh." Freda felt a stab of jealousy, hearing Josh talk so honestly of his feelings for another girl. She noted the sincerity in his voice.

"Yes, she's certainly a tough character. I love her deeply." He glanced across at Freda, "but it is a brotherly love, Freda. Ruth is like the sister I never had. It is not to be thought of in the same way as I love you."

Freda took a breath of cool night air, relief flowing through her from hearing those last few words.

"Goodness me, Josh, I must be going. I still have this to deliver, then make it home."

Josh took her hand. "Have you enjoyed meeting up, Freda?"

"You know I have, Josh. I always will." She gave him a peck on the cheek. "That'll have to do until the next time. Bye, Josh." And the darkness of the evening wrapped itself around her departing figure, soon to disappear down the track toward Hannah Martin's home. Josh watched her go, then turned and headed homeward, still savouring the sweetness of Freda's kiss on his lips.

Chapter 15

R uth felt an overwhelming relief that the trial was over and had not dragged on for weeks. Josh was, luckily, a free man, back home working and Ruth was thankful that a semblance of normality was returning to their lives. Time still proved to be a precious commodity for her though, as she ran out into the morning light to see to the horses. The sky was brightening after a storm but a northerly breeze was already beginning to dry the dirt track leading to the main road.

Entering the stable, her spirits lifted further. Toby had already beaten her to it and seen to the horses. "Thank you, Toby," she whispered, "I owe you a favour." All Ruth needed to do was throw a blanket and saddle on Danny and she was away. Slowly, she warmed the little cob up before urging him into a gallop towards the open moor, hoping to make Roston around midday, leaving the afternoon free to help Jim.

It wasn't just the helping out that drew her to Roston. This way of life was becoming part of her. She loved being involved with the animals. Loved working alongside Jim, enjoying the occasional flirtatious glance that would pass between them. Or just the touch of his hand reminding her that he cared.

Approaching the highest point on the moor, Ruth brought the cob to a halt, admiring the beautiful sweeping valley stretched below her. She well remembered the teachings of Miriam Durville explaining how, over the centuries, the land was transformed by agriculture into these neat but irregular patterns of lush green fields and pastures.

Urging Danny forward, a grouse suddenly flew out from under his hooves. The raucous cry startled the horse but Ruth quickly settled him. In the distance she spotted the soaring swooping flight of a curlew, its plaintive call carrying clear to her on the slight breeze. These sounds of the countryside put her at one with nature and gave her the feeling she was part of it.

Before dropping from the moor top the sharp, clear air almost took her breath away. "Oh God, thank you for helping me find this part of the country that I didn't even know existed." The breeze blew a tangled mass of hair over her face and whipped the words clear out of her mouth to be caught and carried away, she thought, to circle this beautiful rugged landscape forever.

"You know what, Lord?" A questioning look crossed her tanned features, "There was a long time when I could not imagine a God allowing so much suffering. No one seemed to care for anyone, or anything. But once Jim came along, he told me straightaway that he would look after me. Would never let anyone hurt me. Well, I know it went a little bit wrong in the orphanage, but even You must admit, they were desperate times and it was Jim's strength that helped see me through." Brightening, she went on talking and Danny cocked his ears back as if he was listening as well. Maybe he was.

But in quiet moments such as this, in the peace and solitude of the ride, Ruth's thoughts would often return to her childhood. Images of walks to school with her mother, Sarah. The feel of a blanket wrapped tightly around her at bedtime. Images, so vivid and real, Ruth could once again hear her mother's soft comforting voice singing to her.

Danny suddenly lost his footing on a rough piece of ground and she was jolted back into the real world. "Steady, Danny boy, steady," she coaxed, gathering the reins tighter, realizing her imagination had left these valleys for a moment. Memories. They were just memories but the happiness of a moment ago vanished. A bitterness rose in her throat, like acid, as she fought against the nightmares of her past and of what she had lost. Love, security and a happy homelife snatched from her by drunken violence. Angry with herself at letting her mind wander, she pulled herself together and dried her eyes.

But Ruth knew, if she was ever going to be truly free, she must be allowed to grieve properly for her mother. Having this time and space on her own had strengthened her resolve that, sooner or later, she must open her mind to the past, accept it and move on.

She knew what must be done. Return to York, find her mother's grave and speak with her there, tell her that she still loved her and missed her. Would she be brave enough? "Yes," she said to herself. Her experiences in life had helped mould her and, hopefully, made her into a stronger person.

Jacob's advice came to mind. "It is good to remember the past but you do not have to live there!" Ruth realized memories could not be kept under lock and key forever. Feeling much more confident now a decision was made, she rode on. If Jim did not want to return, which she could understand if he didn't, she was not afraid to tackle the journey alone. She had done it before under much more difficult circumstances. She smiled at the thought.

The journey may have to wait until the new year though. Days were shortening and the onslaught of a hard winter beckoned. A shiver of excitement rippled through her as she urged her pony on.

Allowing Danny to pick his own way down the last of the difficult terrain and through the heavily wooded area above the farm, she marvelled at the animal's surefootedness. Bursting from the darkness of the wood into the bright sunlight, she shielded her eyes. From this high vantage point, Roston was just a huddle of small, red and grey roofed cottages clustered around the village green at the base of the valley. Many more were scattered around on the hillsides and more stood on the skyline, built to accommodate the influx of workers at the mines but as the iron trade declined, the vast labour force was beginning to thin out. Families were on the move, steadily drifting away in the relentless search for work. Roston would eventually, Ruth imagined, slowly return to its quiet, original way of life.

On arrival at Honey Bee, Ruth dismounted and called out, "Hello, anyone about?" She knocked on the door, opened it and peered inside. Martha appeared from the kitchen hands covered in flour.

"Come in, love. I'm just busy baking, as you can see. You've timed it just right to take Albert and Jim a bite to eat. Will you have time?"

"That's what I've come for, Martha. To help, if I can. Are they over on the reclaimed land?" Ruth went over and warmed her hands next to the glowing fire while Martha wrapped a couple of sandwiches up for the men.

That'll keep 'em going 'til teatime," she said smiling broadly. "My goodness, Ruth, you look the picture of health. Must be all this fresh air you're getting."

"I'm sure it helps, Martha."

Reluctantly leaving the fire, Ruth said, "right, must go. Will see if they want anything doing in the yard before they return." With that, she dashed outside and Martha watched in admiration as Ruth mounted once again and disappeared across the fields.

She found Jim and Albert dry-stone walling on the reclaimed land.

"Here you two. Martha sent refreshments. She said you're always thinking of your stomachs."

Jim caught her eye and smiled. "Have you come to help us, Ruth?"

"No, I don't think I'd be very good at that but I can start on some of the yard jobs if you want?"

Albert looked relieved. "That would be good, Ruth, because this young man is wearing me out."

"I'll do that. But before I go, I would like your advice." Ruth related her thoughts on visiting her mother's grave.

Albert was first to speak. "It makes sense, Ruth. Obviously, you'll find it hard but everyone needs to grieve, especially after losing someone close. You will certainly benefit from it." He paused. "Well, those are my thoughts on it."

"Thank you, Albert." She looked intently at Jim, keen to know what he thought. "What do you think, Jim?"

Jim shook his head. "Ah, Ruth, they were difficult times. I'm not sure I want to remember anything from back then. But it's strange, you know. Out here it gives you plenty of time to think." He settled onto one of the unwalled stones to take a breather. "Just this last year I've felt there was someone, somewhere very early on in my life that I have a vague, fuzzy memory of. A kind, older woman, more like a dream than a memory really.

It may have been someone at the orphanage. It certainly wasn't Miss Wade," he said with a rueful grin. "It could have been my mother early on. I'm not sure. I understand it's different for you and if you are up for it, then go." His face lightened and he beamed her a smile which almost melted her insides. She could see how happy he was. As if born to be here.

"Thanks for the advice. It's good to be able to talk to someone about it."

Shaking his head, he replied, "Not sure I would go with you though, Ruth."

"That's okay, Jim. I could go it alone. I've done it before under more difficult circumstances. Right," she glanced skyward, "I'm on my way, nights are closing in. I'll do the feeding up for you and if I've gone when you get back, I'll catch up in the next day or two."

This was where Ruth was at her happiest. Working outside, livestock milling around, made her feel as if she owned the whole world. Once finished she waved goodbye to Martha before setting Danny into the fierce rise up and out onto the moor top to appreciate nature in its truest form and enjoy the freedom which always meant so much to her. Another thing, Christmas was on its way.

Chapter 16

Edith Dent's heart rate quickened once she left the shimmering yellow pinpricks of gaslights behind and entered the unlit streets leading to her destination. All were eerily quiet, the heavy smoke-filled night air deadening any other sound but she was not about to turn back at this stage. Suddenly, the orphanage loomed stark and large before her. She appeared to be in luck as a small glow of light sliced through the curtains of a downstairs window and raised her hopes. Nervous to the point of shaking, Edith approached the front door and knocked, hoping it was not too late in the evening to make such a call.

John Durville sat at his office desk rubbing his eyes after a tiring day. Satisfying though, as he'd just heard that Bootham Park Hospital, York, had decided to take care of Henry. Formerly named York Lunatic Asylum, strong public opinion requested the name change at the turn of the century. The huge, classical style building with tall Tuscan columns supporting a very striking pediment at the entrance, had made a massive impression on John when he visited and he was sure Henry was in the right place to be well cared for.

He sighed. He was spending more and more time at the orphanage now. Darwin Court, his family home, which had once rung with the noise and laughter of young children growing up, had become a sombre, lonely place. If only he could dispel the sad memories that haunted his thoughts and remember the good, then the black cloud of depression would disappear. Even at this very minute, he was close to tears.

The faint tap at the door broke him from this mood. Pushing his chair back from the desk, he rose and strode to answer it. In the dim light from the hall, he was surprised to see a slim, petite woman standing there, features slightly hidden by the shadow from her wide brimmed bonnet.

"Yes madam, can I help you?" John asked.

"I'm sorry for calling so late but are you Judge John Durville, the owner of this establishment?"

"I certainly am, young lady. May I ask who do I have the pleasure of speaking to?"

"You may. My name is Dent. Miss Edith Dent." She took a deep breath. "It has taken all my courage to call on you, Mr Durville as it is a rather personal matter and I believe you may be the person who can help me." The lady was nervous for some reason, John noting the slight tremor in her voice.

"Please excuse my manners, Miss Dent." John immediately stepped back, ushering his guest inside. "You were lucky to catch me as I was just about to leave. Now, please be seated," he pulled another chair up to his desk, "and tell me about your request. I am at once intrigued. A personal matter, you say?"

"Yes, in a way." John thought Miss Dent appeared embarrassed. "I am trying to gain information on a small child, a new born in fact, taken into care, or for adoption. I am not sure which as it was many years ago."

While Miss Dent settled into a chair, John studied her carefully. Well spoken, dressed in a light blue jacket and skirt, piped with white, a matching bonnet which she removed to reveal a particularly pretty face. Slightly flushed, the pinched, worried features were accentuated by her long black hair, plaited and combed tightly back into the nape of her slender neck. John guessed her age around late thirties, early forties.

With depressing thoughts banished for the moment, not only was her request intriguing him, the lady was as well. He stole a quick glance at her hands, twisting nervously in front of her, the long slim fingers showing no sign of a ring. Now why did he do that? Force of habit maybe?

"A new born child you say." John dropped into deep thought for a while. "In my experience, Miss Dent, there were very few places willing to take new born children in. The Nunnery is a possibility, or maybe the workhouse if the mother was with the child."

"Are orphanage's such as this not a possibility, Mr Durville?"

"I wouldn't have thought so, mainly because of the care needed and also the facilities would not be adequate."

"Hmm, but it couldn't be ruled out altogether, could it?"

"No, definitely not. I suppose, depending on staff and other criteria, it could have been another option for the mother." He hesitated before adding. "Or whoever was trying to find the child a home."

Silence in the room for a few seconds and the ticking of the clock drew Edith's gaze to the clock on the mantlepiece. Suddenly, she appeared embarrassed and said, "I'm sorry, Mr Durville, I realize this is a really inconvenient time for you, as I was quite late arriving after losing my way. So, if I could call again, at a more appropriate time of day, as this may take some time."

"I think that would be a good idea. I will be here all day tomorrow. I have a meeting with the teachers in the morning, so we could talk after lunch. Would that be suitable for you?"

"That would be splendid, Mr Durville. Thank you so much for your time."

"Please, call me John. It sounds a little less formal."

She looked directly at John for the first time, then lowered her gaze as his black eyes searched hers. She knew from her enquiries that he was a well-respected judge and a man of strong personality, well-educated and very charming. He had certainly put Edith at ease immediately.

"Thank you, John. I bid you goodnight and I look forward to tomorrow."

"Would you allow me to call a cab? It is quite late."

"No, thank you all the same. I know my way now. Goodnight, John." He caught the hint of a smile in the dim half-light of the hallway.

"Goodnight, Miss Dent."

John retired to bed and slept soundly, even though thoughts of Edith Dent's enquiry were on his mind.

A sharp, bright morning greeted the early risers and John took to the street on foot. This regular, brisk one hour walk to work was beginning to take effect. A stone in weight had dropped away, putting a spring in his step and a feeling that he had a life and it was up to him to make it worth living.

No doubt the past few years had aged him. First the tragic loss of Tiffany his young daughter, then their maid, Bella, and finally the deterioration in health of his wife Miriam until death finally claimed her. It was a blessing when she passed. As for Henry, the vicious vendetta he carried for Ruth, he would never understand. Thank goodness, the court had listened and he was now in a safe place.

Work and involvement at the orphanage had truly been John's saviour and it was going better than expected. Also, finding Jim and Ruth again had lifted his spirits tremendously, bringing with it a fresh start. He was not about to let the opportunity pass him by.

Approaching the building, satisfaction spread through him, any morbid thoughts dispelled. The work was nearing completion, the building almost returned to its former glory and welcoming to everyone. There was no doubt he, the builders and the teachers, had transformed the place. On entering, the brightness leapt out, creating a massive impact on everyone who called to inspect, or enquire, the light colours pushing the former grimness of the old structure back into the dark ages where it belonged. This was the future, the way forward and the majority of the children were responding to these new methods of learning. Instead of the cruelty meted out in the past, their work, both academically and keeping the place clean and tidy was always noted and praised.

John was seated at his desk when William the headmaster entered. He was a no-nonsense sort of a teacher, strict but fair. He possessed the ability to reach vulnerable children in his care and spent time understanding their needs. Very much a father figure to them.

"Good morning, John. I can see I need to rise earlier if I want to beat you here."

"No need for that, William. I am naturally an early riser and this project, plus your enthusiasm for the work, has rubbed off on me. Given me a passion and a new lease of life."

"I'm glad to hear that, John, but I think it is more that you came to terms with your personal grief, then found the strength to dispel those black days of despair."

John rose from his chair, deep in thought, telling William of his previous night's visitor who was looking for information on a new born child placed in care many years ago.

William was also puzzled. "Did she give any idea of how long since, or who she is trying to find, John? Could it be her child, or one of her relatives that found themselves in trouble?"

"Either is a possibility, William."

"This is just a thought, John but as the builder cleared the rooms, he told me they stacked all the records in the loft. Boxes and boxes of them, so there could be information of some kind that would help. Mind you, it will be a devil of a job sorting through it."

"Hmm, could well hold the answer though. I will just have to be patient and wait to hear what the lady wants."

The morning passed quickly. John had meetings with the staff, all on improving education for these luckless children. Engrossed with the progress of work, he was on the point of making a cup of tea when the slim, unmistakable figure of Miss Dent passed the window. His heart lifted at the sight of her and he opened the door just as she reached for the bell push.

"Come in, please." Then realized he was slightly over eager in his welcome. "Perfect timing. I have the kettle on. Would you like tea or coffee, Miss Dent?"

"Coffee would be lovely, John. Black please."

"Please take a seat." John eased a chair out for her. "I shall be right back." A couple of minutes later, John returned with coffee and biscuits, settled back in his chair to face Miss Dent across the desk.

"Now," he said enquiringly, beetle brows drawn together in concentration, "tell me what is on your mind and who you are trying to contact?"

Edith appeared far more vulnerable than on their first meeting. "This is more difficult than I thought, John. Silly, isn't it?" She paused, breathing deeply. "I had rehearsed and memorised everything I wanted to say down to the last detail. So easy in the comfort of my own home. But now…" Edith stopped, unsure of herself, confidence draining, along with the slight bit of colour in her cheeks.

John did his best to encourage her. "Well, there is no need to rush. Once you feel comfortable, start at the beginning and let's see what happens. You must understand, even when all is said and done, I may not be able to help you."

"I do understand and I thank you for your patience." Edith waited a few seconds then, in no more than a whisper, the words came spilling out.

"I think my new born child may have been placed in this orphanage almost eighteen years ago. It was a difficult birth and I almost died. Two days passed before I regained consciousness and my aunt greeted me with the words, 'I'm terribly sorry, Edie, but your baby was stillborn.' Edith visibly relaxed. "There," a huge sigh escaped her lips. "I have actually told someone. I believe that could be the hardest part over, John."

Her eyes lifted, meeting his directly. Inner grief, guilt, all hidden behind her steady gaze that John could only guess at. He was shocked at this information. Why had she been misled? Many young girls have fallen pregnant due to ignorance and left to suffer the consequences. But if correct on her age, Miss Dent would not be a naïve, innocent young girl. More a confident young woman in her twenties who would surely have understood the risks involved.

Edith squared her shoulders and carried on. "I have lived these past years in total belief of those words spoken by my aunt."

Silence before John gently prompted her to go on. "Take your time, Edith, you're doing wonderful." She looked across at him searching his face for any sign of rebuke or reprisal, but could see only genuine concern.

Edith began again. "Then I received a letter from the hospital a few weeks ago. My aunt was terminally ill and could I visit soon as she was very weak."

Edith sipped at her coffee. "I rushed to the hospital and the sister led me to Aunt Grace's bedside. I didn't recognise the skeletal figures as my aunt. A scrawny, pathetic frame waiting for death. As I stood by her bedside, her eyes fluttered open. A few seconds passed, then a flicker of recognition reached her eyes. She asked if it really was me in a voice that was barely audible."

"Edie, I have something to tell you before I leave this earth. I'm ready to go but I must go with a clear conscience."

"Her bony hand reached out from under the sheet in search of mine. Gently, I took hold and in the same croaking whisper, she related how my parents had paid her to lie to me and, desperate for money, she agreed. As I lay unconscious, Grace told me she wrapped the child in blankets." Edith paused for a moment. "This is where she became confused, John. She told me she was frightened and hurried round to a large brick building and handed the baby over to a nun. I assumed it to be the school for Nuns in York, or the orphanage."

John stopped her. "As I said before, it is unlikely the orphanage would take a new born baby in. Certain nuns did work there but their facilities would not be suitable to cope with a new born child."

Edith thought for a moment. "Yes, it does sound odd. Aunt Grace was confused, so it could have been the nuns who took him in."

Edith, face deathly pale but quite calm, carried on. "Doctor and midwife were also coerced by money but it was far easier for them to walk away. Not so Aunt Grace. The burden of guilt must have eaten away at her, much like the illness was doing."

Edith fell silent for a while before continuing. "Once the ordeal of admission was over, Aunt Grace's head lolled to one side and her last few breaths rattled from her throat. I called the nurse but I knew she had passed on that very minute. She was now at peace. But what about me?" Edith looked up at John, holding his gaze, composed again.

"I thought we were a close family but my parents were more worried about the gossip and their damned, upper class lifestyle than about their own flesh and blood. They were not about to have shame brought into their tidy, uncluttered lives." Edith gave a rueful smile, shaking her head. "I know what you're thinking, John. Yes, I was utterly foolish, but I won't be the last woman to fall for a man's smooth talk."

A harsh laugh escaped her lips. "Oh, how damned gullible I was." Edith fell silent, remembering the shame and the wasted years and the memory fuelled more words.

"I loved my family, John. With all my heart. I knew they would be very hurt but I expected compassion and understanding from them." She shook her head. "They showed hearts of stone, as I was packed off to live with Aunt Grace, along with my few possessions." Edith sipped at the now cold coffee. "Once I regained strength, I never returned home and life proved hard to start with. Even though I had never seen my child or even held him, I still mourned his loss." John allowed Edith to talk.

"Luckily, credentials from my last place of work secured me a job at York Library, earning enough to pay the rent. Money proved tight, but I managed. I immersed myself in my work and it kept me sane, as I grieved for the loss of my child and also my family as well."

She paused, as if exhausted. "Now, you understand why I have to search for him. This is my starting point. It may prove fruitless. I may suffer more heartache but at least I will have tried. More importantly, if my child is out there somewhere," Edith spread her arms wide, "I can tell him that I did not forsake him once I learned the truth."

John was stunned at these revelations of her life. A secret withheld for all these years. Reaching gently across, he clasped her hand in his. So tiny and smooth in comparison to his own. Edith didn't snatch it away. In fact, she appeared to gain strength from such an intimate gesture.

A silence filled the room, each lost in thought. Eventually, John reluctantly removed his hand from her warm grasp and stood up, shaking his head. "A remarkable story, Miss Dent. Heart-breaking for you but remarkable all the same. After all this time. I am enthralled by it. It just so happens I explained your visit to William, our headteacher and apparently, stacked away in the loft, there are boxes of documents of what I do not know, but we can soon check." Edith looked up expectantly. "Do you think we could check now, John?"

"Come," he said eagerly, "there is no time like the present."

Edith quickly followed John through a long corridor and up a spiralling flight of stairs leading to where the school's accommodation rooms were situated. Passing through these they were confronted by another short, steeper flight up into the unused attics.

Pushing the door open, a damp, musty smell hit them. Cobwebs hung from the rafters and clung to their face and clothes as they wiped them aside. The two skylights allowed light into the room, enough to work with at present, John thought. Then he saw the shelves of files, coated in a thick film of dust, stacks and stacks of them, hundreds, maybe thousands. John turned to Edith who stood close behind him, smiling.

"As you can see, Miss Dent, it could be a monumental task. Look at the amount there is to trawl through."

"Don't worry, John. I told you this is my starting point. I have only just begun my quest. I have the time if you give me the authority. I know the date and I suppose it could vary a few years beyond his birth date, but it may not be too bad."

"Well, I wish you luck. In the meantime, I will get William to arrange for someone to bring a table and chair and give the place a good sweep out to make it a little more pleasant for your task. Help yourself to tea or coffee down in my office and I will see you later. If you want my assistance, please give me a shout. I will be around all day."

John smiled, turning to leave the room as Edith reached for his hand. "Thank you for listening, John. I do appreciate it. Now it's down to business. If you don't mind I will make a start this instant."

He admired her strength of spirit and courage, delving into the unknown. He left her to begin a checking system, hoping she would find information that would bring closure for her. One way or the other.

Chapter 17

A clinging, overcast mist covered the city next day as Edith arrived alongside the headteacher at the orphanage, eager to start work on the old records. Assuming there may be some cleaning to do first, she had dressed accordingly.

William turned and addressed her formerly, unlocking the door as he did so.

"Good morning, Miss Dent. John advised me you might be here early. I hope you will be happy with the children's efforts at tidying the attic for you." He crinkled his nose up. "It really was a mess up there."

"Thank you, Mr Hopper. Please pass my thanks on to the children." She smiled her appreciation. "This means I can start my search straightaway. Has John mentioned what I am hoping to achieve?"

"Yes, he told me. I spoke to John yesterday and he asked if we could tidy the room to make things a little more pleasant."

"That's very kind of you both. I do appreciate it." Edith entered as William stepped aside. "Now, if you don't mind I will go make a start, Mr Hopper."

"Very good. I'll catch up with you later in the day."

"I hope so." Edith made her way to the attic and, on entering, a complete transformation had taken place. Hardly recognisable from the day before, all clean and a smell of freshness. Also, much brighter, the mass of cobwebs hanging from the underside of the roof and obscuring the skylights had been cleared away. The files dragged out the day before were where she left them, the others left undisturbed ready for Edith's systematic check. A table, chair, inkwell, pencil and pens and blotting paper were all at her disposal.

Wiping the dust away from the first file with a cloth, she sat down, excitement and apprehension running through her at what she may uncover. If records were patchy or unkept, then it may prove futile. But there was no other option.

At least she had a starting date. With no identification on the boxes, Edith took a deep breath and opened the first brown folder. All in neat columns, children's names first, followed by parents if known or, Edith assumed, the person who brought the child here. So far, so good. But then exasperation. A set of folders with no dates recorded anywhere, names scrawled haphazardly across the page, almost unreadable. Edith's hopes plunged. Placing this to one side, she flicked open another file from further down the row and quickly looked inside. No different. Working methodically, Edith continued to open just the top file of each stack. Just when hope was fading fast, her heart thudded. A fresh signature was added. *Miss Rebecca Wade. Head Mistress. March 1ˢᵗ. 1890.* This must be a new beginning and a fresh start to the decade Edith was searching for.

Rebecca Wade appeared a very diligent and efficient bookkeeper. Every child noted. Day of arrival, age of child. Boy or girl. Name of dependant and signature and even a record of when they actually left. Gathering a heap of folders in her arms, Edith dumped them on the table, coughing as a cloud of dust caught in her throat.

At the end of a tiring day and numerous cups of coffee, Edith slumped back in the chair, face and hands covered with grime and clothes filthy. She was just about to call it a day when John entered the attic.

"How is it going may I ask?" He surveyed the enormous pile of papers on the table.

"Those are all done, John. I am close to the date now. If these papers are a true record, then another day I should be nearly there."

"I am about to lock up for the night now, Miss Dent. Is this a convenient time for you to stop work?" Edith looked relieved. "In fact, you look all in.

Let's start afresh tomorrow. I have more time to spare and can help you. Come on, you have done enough for one day. Now, how would you feel about eating at home with me tonight? I have a lady who cooks for me one day a week and I took the liberty of asking her to provide a meal for the two of us tonight."

"Thank you, John. That is very kind but I'm sure you have enough to do without feeding me as well."

"It would not be any more work. To be truthful I would welcome your company."

"Well, if you put it like that, how can I refuse?" Her eyes lit up. "Yes, John, I would love to eat with you."

"Splendid," he said. "Right, we'll lock up, hail a cab and return home to enjoy our meal."

Escorting Edith down to the front entrance, John made sure all was secure before taking her arm and calling a cab. "10, Darwin Court, please cabbie."

"Right you are, sir." Once seated, a sharp crack of the whip and they were away enjoying the ride on such a beautiful night. The mist had lifted and darkness had fallen by the time they arrived. John paid the driver, then hurriedly opened the door, ushering Edith into the hallway and took her hat and coat.

"We're home, Mary," he shouted. "My goodness something smells good. What have we on the menu tonight?"

Mary appeared at the dining room door, curtsied to Edith and said, "I have a lovely cut of pork with sage stuffing, potato and veg. Hope that meets with your approval, sir."

"If it tastes as good as the aroma coming from the kitchen, it will be wonderful. We will eat in the dining room, Mary. But first we will wash some of the grime away from today."

"That'll work splendid, sir. The table is all set for two. When ready, just pop through and be seated. I will serve then."

"Excellent, Mary. It has been a tiring day. It will be nice to relax." He showed Edith to the washroom. A few minutes later they entered the dining room, John holding a chair out for her to be seated. Edith studied her surroundings, the quality, the elegance, the subtle décor and furnishings. All the trappings of a successful business man. John sat down opposite her.

"Would a glass of wine be suitable with your meal, Miss Dent?"

"Please call me Edith, John. The position we find ourselves in, Miss Dent sounds a bit prim don't you think? And yes, a glass of wine would be lovely."

John reached for the bottle and there was silence in the room, while he poured. Then their eyes met.

John was first to speak. "I do realize the uncertainty for you in this search, Edith but whatever happens, it will bring conclusion. Who knows, if you were to find your offspring… well, no one can foretell what the outcome will be." They touched glasses across the table. "Here's to your search. May it be successful."

"I'll drink to that." Then thoughtfully she said, "John, I don't know why but I have a feeling right here," she clasped a hand across her heart, "that I will find him, wherever he is."

After enjoying their meal and Mary had cleared away, they sat discussing the future. Not only if they found her child but also the many pitfalls if they didn't.

Relaxing for the first time in months amidst these sumptuous surroundings, Edith suddenly glanced at the ornate clock as the chimes struck 10 pm. Rising from her chair, she said, "My goodness, John, look at the time. I must go. I have taken up all your evening and we both have a busy day tomorrow. But I must thank you, and Mary, for a lovely meal and your company. Today I have turned a corner and can see the way ahead."

"That's wonderful and you have brought a new enthusiasm into my life, Edith, so I shall look forward to helping you." When John finally walked her to the door and hailed a cab, Edith reached up on tiptoe and gave him a peck on the cheek. After her departure, John realized that was the first feminine touch of endearment he had experienced for a great number of years and his heart began to beat just a little faster as he watched the cab disappear into the darkness. It had also taken his mind off his own troubles.

Chapter 18

A s Ruth rode back from seeing Jim at Roston on Christmas Eve, the weather worsened on reaching the high moor and winter storms could be ruthless as Ruth well knew. The full force of a bitter north wind clutched at her clothing as if trying to rip them clear from her slight frame.

"You fool, Ruth Brennan. You should know better than be caught out in these conditions." This was the first harsh sign of winter, the strong wind whipping the black clouds down from the head of the valley that Ruth could not outride. Darkness closed in rapidly. Digging her heels hard into the soft flanks of the little horse, she urged him on to greater efforts in the hope that the flickering lights of Gallows Howe would soon emerge in the distance. The fine snow peppered her unprotected face, blinding her vision and the fierce wind sliced through her. She cursed herself for being so stupid. All because she could not summon up the will power to drag herself away from Jim at Roston.

Ah, but it was worth it. She flicked her tongue over frozen lips to savour the taste of him once again, the feel of their last passionate parting kiss still sweet upon her face. Warmth flooded her body at the thought of his strong arms wrapping around her. God, how she loved him. With all her heart. With every fibre of her being. What lay ahead or what life had in store for them both, she had no idea but knew full well she would do her damnedest to see that they spent it together.

The bone chilling cold forced her back to the task in hand. The surrounding black-brown moorland was quickly changing to a world of white. Shielding her face against the driving peppery snow that threatened to rip the skin from her cheeks, she pushed Danny hard. Scurrying, twisting drifts of snow lashed by the ever-increasing wind, spiralled in all directions obscuring her vision. She was thankful of Danny's sure-footed gait and the knowledge that he could find his way back to the comfort of his stable whatever the conditions. All the same, Ruth heaved a sigh of relief once she reached the comforting shelter of the low moor. Suddenly, the welcome orange glow of the house lamps, spilling out onto the now white wasteland, came into view.

Quickly dismounting, Ruth slapped her hands hard around her, forcing circulation and blood back into them, knowing the pain would bring tears to her eyes. The warmth from the other horses in the stable hit her on opening the door. Leading Danny in she untacked him and placed a forkful of hay at the front of the stall before laying fresh bedding down, then dried him off.

"Now you should be comfortable for the night, little fella." Patting the horse's head, she spent a few minutes talking to him before closing the stable door and dashing through the deepening snow. Relieved to be out of the cold, she hoped Jacob would have a blazing fire going. That is if he had arrived home.

Thankfully Jacob was there, stood with his back to the fireplace, flames already dancing up the fireback, relief spreading across his face. "Goodness me, Ruth. Where have you been? I was beginning to think something had happened."

"Sorry, Jacob, I didn't mean to worry you. I just stayed a bit too long at Roston. The weather wasn't too bad there but once up on the rigg the full force of the blizzard really hit us. I had to shield my eyes from the storm but once off the high moor, it wasn't too bad. Luckily, I'd gone on Danny." The affection she held for him was clear on her face. "He could find his way back from anywhere, blindfolded if need be, to get to his stable, come hell or high water."

"You have great faith in your animals, Ruth." Jacob had always admired the girl for the work she put in to caring for any animal but her passion for every one of the horses was remarkable.

"Now go change out of those wet clothes, you look absolutely frozen. When you come down, I'll have the kettle on and get you thawed out." He became stern, adding, "and let this be a lesson to you, young girl. Do not treat these moors lightly. There have been numerous deaths recorded locally due to losing direction on nights such as this."

He peered out of the window. "Let's hope the storm eases and people can make it for tonight's service." Jacob threw another log on the fire. "If it's only the weather we have to contend with, we'll not take any harm. We are well stocked up with food and logs."

Rushing upstairs, Ruth ran a towel over her hair and found a change of clothes. The small window overlooking the church was already plastered white with snow even though the blizzard was beginning to lose its bite. But Ruth knew the storm had done enough to cause a dramatic change to the landscape in the morning.

No one could ever be certain how bad conditions would be, not even Len Bailes and it would often become a fight against nature. If frosts were severe, there would be some cold mornings ahead to endure with the thawing out of frozen water pipes and troughs for the animal's water.

But although hard, it also held a certain kind of magic for her and this year would be even more significant as she would be involved in the children's Christmas party at school. Ruth well remembered her first Christmas here. Returning from church with a group of friends, the first featherlight tickle of a snowflake rested upon her cheek. Laughing, she tilted her face heavenwards and a myriad of dancing diamond lights littered the blue-black night sky. In those few moments the silence became surreal, as if entering an entirely different world. The carpet of pristine whiteness covering the old stone path even muffled their footsteps that not a sound was heard.

Suddenly, Jacob's voice from below brought her back to reality. "Kettle's boiled, Ruth. I'm on my way. Will see you there later. Bye."

Ruth answered. "Yes. I won't be late, Jacob. Bye."

Outside the wind had dropped and the snow was light. Nothing to bother his congregation too much. Enjoying the solitude of the walk, he'd allowed himself more time to prepare for this service, one of the most meaningful of the year. Once certain all was ready and everything in place, Jacob heard the outer door swing open and in rolled Mrs Peters, the organist, always one of the first to arrive.

"Ah, good evening, Isobel. Lovely to see you. Hope you are in good health?"

"Oh, I'm in excellent health, Jacob. You should know by now, never a day goes by but what I thank the Lord for looking after me so well." Isobel Peters was a rather plump lady, well in her fifties but still retained the cherubic features of her youth and a certain bouncy charm that Jacob, and many others, always found refreshing. Isobel checked everything was in place, before settling at the organ, her practiced fingers rippling over the keyboard with a surprising suppleness, showing the dedication of many years following the faith.

Jacob, smartly dressed, his collar and long white hair standing out in stark contrast to his customary black garb, he took his position behind the carved eagle lectern, bowed his head in prayer before the congregation filtered in. All were well wrapped up against the cold and after a stamping of feet, greetings and handshakes the small church was suddenly alive with the goodwill of Christmas.

Lifting his head, Jacob's eyes scanned his packed congregation and felt a pang of anxiety when noticing Winifred Grey and her daughter, Freda, seated near the door. There was no reason why they should not be there. Normally he was glad of newcomers to his church but their appearance put him a little on edge. His sermon did not go quite as well as normal. Not so smooth or confident in his delivery and was relieved when the service was taken over by the organist, the old building ringing out in celebration of the virgin birth.

As Ruth was now working at Castle Moor school two days a week, her enthusiasm for the festive period was infectious and Charlie Haigh, the headmaster responded by helping with the decorating of the church. A small holly tree stood at the entrance and light from the flickering candles glinted pleasantly on the decorations made by the children.

With service over, Jacob noticed that Josh had already left his seat and was in deep conversation with Winifred and Freda at the back of the church. Jim had actually made it over for the service for Ruth's sake and also found it rough going on the high moor. Ruth, sat close, whispered in his ear. "Do you think Josh has got himself a girlfriend, Jim?"

Jim took a quick glance to the rear of the church, then flashed the gap-toothed smile at Ruth that so captivated her. "Mebbe so," he said. "If he has, he's not wasted any time, has he? How long has that been going on?"

"Not sure. I have noticed a change in him but I put it down to his voice returning. It seems there was more to it than that."

Jim stole another look over his shoulder. "Well, it looks as if Freda's just as keen. First time I've ever seen any kind of life in her."

"Jim, that's an awful thing to say." She scowled at him. "It can't be easy for her, looking after Winnie and the mill, as well as working at the school. She's really nice. I've got to know her a lot better as I meet her at work occasionally."

"Only joking, Ruth." Jim got to his feet. "Right, let's walk back home, eh? I'm not much into religion. It never did me any good from what I remember. Anyway, I only came to see you really, and I have a hard ride back home yet." Putting his arm around her, he guided her outside to spend a few minutes together before facing the cold ride back to Roston.

As Jacob made for the door to say goodnight to everyone, Josh said, "I was just saying it was nice to see Mrs Grey and Freda attending the service tonight father, don't you think? Hopefully, if they didn't find it too boring," a quick smile passed between himself and Freda, "we might see them at church again?" His eyes locked onto Freda's. Jacob did not miss it. A frown, hardly perceptible, crossed his brow. A shy smile flitted across Freda's face but Winnie appeared nervous, uncomfortable and began edging steadily towards the door, trying to drag a reluctant Freda with her.

Jacob replied. "That would be nice. As you know everyone is welcome in the house of God." With that he turned to shake hands and wish everyone a happy Christmas.

Although Josh was pleased to see Freda and her mother there, the coolness he detected in Jacob's manner to Winnie and Freda preyed on his mind and was determined to bring it to his father's attention when the time was right. But this was not the right time and he decided to accompany Winnie and Freda back home.

Chapter 19

A fter enjoying a white Christmas for once, the weather eased into the new year as a thaw brought a welcome release for a few weeks. But harsh frosts returned in February creating images that took the breath away. Len Bailes from the village, forever telling anyone willing to listen, usually Toby, "Mark my words, lad, these frosts are a sure sign we are in for another rough spell. Lot o' snow 'll follow this."

Toby chuckled, as he brushed the horses down. "Well, you're on a pretty safe bet wi' that information, Len. After all, it is only February."

"Ah, you young 'uns mek fun," Len said with a shake of the head, "but you'll see. Next few days 'll prove me right."

A few days later, Len was proved right. Ruth, waking early as usual, did not jump straight out of bed, the sharpness of the morning making itself felt on the end of her nose again. She buried her head under the bed covers for a few more precious minutes of warmth before flinging them back to brave the cold. Pouring water into the bowl, she splashed her face, the iciness causing her to gasp but once washed and dressed, felt quite refreshed.

Drawing the curtain back, the window revealed the severity of the night. Spidery patterns of frost glittered across the glass in the morning light and, childishly, she huffed a hot breath onto the window and with a finger, printed her name into the melting patterns. Finally, scraping the window clear, she blinked at the change outside, the vast expanse of moor now cloaked in a shimmering white. Only the bare straggling branches of trees and the occasional monolithic rock high on the hillside stood out black and stark from this cap of whiteness. Even the rough stone walls and hedges were covered in drifts or plastered with snow. The severe cruel beauty of winter had taken over the ruggedness of the dale, sculpting the moorland into a vista of smooth rolling hills, spectacular in every sense.

Ruth shivered at the sight before dashing downstairs to find Josh already eating breakfast and the fire sending flames shooting up the fireback.

"Oh, I'm sorry, Josh. I intended being first up this morning but you beat me to it." In truth, she appreciated the heat already spreading across the room.

"That's okay, Ruth. I couldn't sleep anyway and I have a lot to do today. I'm pretty sure Pete will need help out on the moor with his sheep. That is, if we can find them."

"Well, I think the school will be closed today, so I can look after the horses for you." Taking the cup of tea Josh offered, she seated herself next to him and smiled.

"By the way," she asked, a devilish twinkle in her eyes, "how is Freda?"

A look of astonishment crossed his face before he gathered himself. "Quite well, as far as I know. I only saw her briefly at church and she was with her mother."

"Is there something you want to tell me, Josh?"

"Er, not just yet, Ruth." He took a quick look across to the stairs. "It's a little delicate at present. You know how possessive Winnie can be."

"I'm not prying, Josh. I just want you to be happy and I can see you are."

They sat in comfortable silence for a while before Ruth said, "I'm glad we're alone, Josh. I've made the decision to visit mother's grave as soon as the weather picks up." Josh waited for her to go on.

"Well, you know, with Christmas and family gatherings and such, memories of home returned and I need to bring closure to this vast hollowness I feel right here." She placed a hand over her heart. "You see, I've never really grieved properly for my mother. Or for my father, either, but that is quite different. I do not know whether he is alive or dead. And what of Aunty

Moll who took me in for a while? Will she still be living? And where? I'm not sure my home will still be there. Could be my memories are all buried under a mountain of rubble by now." The coming of tears hurt her eyes but she was not about to break down in front of Josh just when everything seemed to be going right for him.

Josh spoke softly. "You know in your heart what you have to do, Ruth. You have known for a long time but the timing had to come from you. From within." He spoke with a touching sincerity. "Everyone must go through the grieving process, Ruth." He hesitated, before adding, "You must also understand that it is not a sin to remember the past. All it means is that times change, lives move on and you must adapt to whatever life throws at you and act accordingly."

Ruth allowed a smile to break through. "You're right, Josh. I believe the time is right for me and I know I'm much stronger now to cope with whatever happens at York." Josh could immediately tell by the set of her chin and her determined manner that she still possessed the steely will that he so admired. "I will write to Aunty Moll and ask if she could help."

At that very minute, they both turned to acknowledge Jacob as he came down the stairs.

"Morning, father. A cup of tea on the go if you want one."

"That would be lovely." His eyes flitted to the clock. "I'm sorry, I must have slept soundly. Never heard a thing all night."

As Josh brought his father's tea, Ruth said, "That's all right, Jacob. I'm just about to do the horses and wander down to the village for a few things. It doesn't look like I'll get to see Jim for a while if this weather keeps up."

"Maybe not Ruth, but Jim will not be able to keep away from Gallows Howe for too long knowing you are cooped up here." He smiled at her and settled in his favourite chair by the fire.

Leaving him in peace, Ruth realized the harsh winter was hitting Jacob hard, spending more time at the church than normal. Ruth didn't know his correct age, had never asked but assumed he must be at least sixty as he married late in life and Josh was almost eighteen. Age takes its toll on any man and although God fearing, life had not been easy for him.

In the comfort of her bedroom, Ruth decided to write a letter. But to who? Sat at her desk, a blank sheet of paper stared back. I must make my mind up. She knew John Durville would be the better choice and she had his address at York. But her conscience told her it wasn't right to ask him after the troubles he had suffered.

Ruth stared out across the distant hills, desperately searching for inspiration from the bleak white landscape. She was not only missing Jim but also the excitement of her rides to Roston. For how much longer she didn't know. And what about Dan at Folly Cottage? How would he be managing?

Eventually, Ruth decided on Aunty Moll, understanding she may have passed on, or might not even live in the same house but the only way to find out was to send a letter. She began to write.

Ruth Brennan
The Stables
Gallows Howe
North Yorkshire
March, 1912

Dear Aunty Moll

I hope this letter finds you in good health and I hope you remember me. I understand you are not my real Aunt but you were a very good friend to us all, especially my mother Sarah, when we lived next door. I am writing to ask if you were present at my mother's funeral and if so, could you possibly tell me where she is buried as I was placed in the orphanage. If this letter finds you and you can help, it would mean I could visit her grave.

Also, and again I'm not sure if this is possible, if you know what happened to my father. It is not that I have any feelings for him, whether dead or alive, but I need closure on certain things so I can lay some of my many demons to rest.

I would appreciate your help in these matters. I would also understand

if it is not possible, or you would rather not be involved.
  Yours sincerely
  Ruth Brennan

Once finished, she folded the letter and addressed the envelope to what she hoped was the appropriate number in Lady Peckitt's Yard. Rummaging in the small desk at the side of her bed, she luckily found a stamp. Deciding not to waste another minute in case she changed her mind or forgot to send the letter, she ran downstairs, grabbed a coat and scarf from the rack, pulled on her boots and walked out into the snowy world. The vicious cold nipped at her cheeks and lips as she ran along the pathway dug out through the deep snow to the main road.

Feeling very much alive, the sharpness soon brought a flush to her cheeks and also freed her from any previous worrying thoughts. The school was shut and a group of youngsters were out with sledges of all shapes and sizes. She spotted Toby showing the younger ones how to go faster. "Aren't you too old for that sort of thing, Toby," she shouted across to him, secretly wishing she could join them.

"You're never too old for sledging, Ruth Brennan. Come on, are you brave enough to jump on wi'me?"

"Not likely. I've seen the speed you ride horses."

Running down to the village, Ruth had to jump into the deep snow at the side as Toby, showing off, whizzed past, laughing so much he almost crashed.

"You wait, young Toby. I'll get you back," shaking her fist in mock anger as he disappeared in a flurry of snow.

As the letter slipped through the narrow slot, apprehension shot through her. Had she done right, or would it just revive old wounds and sorrows best left hidden?

No, it was done. She must be patient now and await a reply.

Chapter 20

W ith the troubles of the previous year behind him, John Durville fervently hoped a much more settled future lay ahead. Although January had proved cold, there was very little snowfall and February had started clear and bright.

With a lot on his mind, John rose at the crack of dawn and once washed and dressed, walked to the orphanage. When William and Edith arrived, a whistling kettle and a cup of coffee welcomed them to work.

"You two must have a busy day ahead?" William asked, studying the pair carefully.

"Yes, I worked things so I have a free day to help Edith and I thought we can take our cups up to the attic and begin."

Climbing the stairs, they entered the room. John turned and asked with a smile, "Now how can I best help you?"

"Well, if it's true what Aunt Grace told me, that she came straight here after the birth, and I have no reason to disbelieve her, that date was March 3rd, 1893. But," she frowned, "as you rightly said, neither the facilities or the necessary people would be able to cope. I suppose it is possible that an experienced nurse or teacher was on hand at that time but if not, then we could be poring over every record for the next few years."

While talking, Edith showed John which folders to check and he began to wipe away the dust.

"Well, it appears Miss Wade was a better book keeper than teacher, because apparently, she was a cruel and ruthless woman, ruling the school with a rod of iron."

Searching each file thoroughly, the date of March 3rd, 1893 passed with nothing of significance coming up that year. Approaching midday and well through the files, John was now into 1895 and beginning to think the search futile. Then opening a fresh folder, words in the left-hand column leapt out at him, bold and clear. *Boy, parent's unknown, taken into care. Friday, 8 p.m. January 10th, 1895. Special care by Nurse Britton.* This was followed by two signatures, but more specifically, under notes in the centre, *approx. d. o. b. March 5th, 1893.*

John snatched a deep breath in a bid to remain calm before uttering, "Edith, I think you better read this folder. It might be the one."

Edith immediately stopped what she was doing and stared at John, hardly daring to accept the file as he handed the aging paperwork over. She sat, placing it on the table in front of her and, trembling with anticipation, began to study the pages. A few minutes passed before she paused and reached for her spectacles to study the neat, hand written text in the columns.

Edith slumped back in her chair, lost in thought. This is my child, my son. Must be my son. After all these wasted years, I have found the first trace of his existence. Good God, where will he be? Will he still be alive? If he is, what will he be doing? He'll be a young man.

John watched carefully, allowing Edith time for the information to sink in, before venturing over and laying a hand gently upon her shoulder. Her face lifted to his, eyes moist but voice steady, said, "We have found him, John. After eighteen long years of suffering, pain and guilt, we have found him."

John settled beside her his dark brooding gaze serious. "No, we haven't found him yet, Edith, but by God, we are on the right track. This is an amazing start and our next enquiry is right in front of us, Nurse Britton. Now be warned, there could be a long, tortuous road ahead with possibly many disappointments, but we have a name and if we have a name, we can trace her for sure." John looked directly into Edith's troubled eyes, "and if we trace Nurse Britton, we have a chance of finding out more information on the early years of your son's life."

Edith rose shakily from the chair and John helped steady her. "I think I am in shock, John? My whole body is trembling. I feel quite faint." Carefully easing her back into the chair, John shouted for William to bring a tot of brandy up and bring a glass for himself.

Within minutes and puffing slightly, thinking something had gone drastically wrong, William appeared with glasses and bottle on a tray. "Is everything all right, John, you sounded worried?"

"I assure you everything is fine, William. I'm sorry if I startled you but we have struck lucky. We have found an approximate date of birth that corresponds to being Edith's child. Also, the name of the nurse who actually took him in. Nurse Britton." John showed William the file. "It came as quite a shock and Edith felt faint. I thought the brandy might help." John splashed a mouthful into each glass, adding a drop of water and handed one to Edith.

"Thank you both. I'll soon recover. It was beginning to look like a lost cause and John had worked through to a folder two years hence and there it was, on the first page." She looked up at the two men, a smile on her face, the colour returning to the pallid complexion of just a few minutes ago.

"What great progress," William exclaimed. He was as pleased as they were. "In such a short time. And her name is Britton?"

"Yes. Her signature and everything."

"Nurse Britton." William's brow wrinkled, deep in thought. Silence, both Edith and John studied him, waiting for him to go on.

"This is difficult for me, Edith. I do not want to raise your hopes too high without good cause, as I could well be wrong. But I feel I must mention this. If proved right – and I stress if – this could be your first port of call for information." William drew a chair up alongside Edith, took a sip from his glass before carrying on.

"As you well know John, my wife, Harriet, suffered health problems many years ago now and while visiting the hospital so frequently, I got to know the nurses very well who tended to her. Now, I must admit, I did not meet this lady personally, but I do know there was a nurse on that particular ward called Britton. It came to my notice when studying the duty rota for their shifts. But, more to the point, the spelling of the name Britton was exactly the same."

After letting this news sink in, William reached for their glasses and quickly poured another drink. "I suppose this is a little premature, but I do think we should all drink to the success of Edith's search." The clink of glasses echoed around the attic room and in unison, they said, "Here's to the search."

A restless night followed for Edith, as she knew a return to York hospital was inevitable, the recent death of Aunt Grace still vivid in her mind. But bravely, the very next day, Edith walked hesitantly through the wrought iron gate in front of the tired looking, three story building again. This was York's main hospital for the city's mounting number of sick and dying patients. A large brick-built frontage surrounded by iron railings and featuring stepped stone quoins at windows and doors it dominated the whole street. A flat stone-flagged area led to the front entrance and a plaque alongside the door, announcing your arrival at York County Hospital. Main Entrance.

Taking a deep breath, Edith swung the huge door open and entered the impressive hall. A plan of all rooms and wards hung on the wall but Edith well remembered matron's office. A light tap on the door and a voice shouted, "enter." Edith entered. Behind a large desk sat a tall, middle-aged lady with sharp chiselled features, a woman Edith did not recognize. Approaching the desk, Edith asked, "Could I possibly speak to the matron, please?"

The lady lifted her head and surveyed Edith carefully, before replying. "Of course, dear. I'm Matron Dennis. How can I help you?"

Matron listened to Edith's story and sympathised with her plight. She told Edith that she would check the records and find out if and when a Nurse Britton worked there.

"As you see, I'm new here, moved to this hospital just two weeks ago. If you could come back tomorrow, I may be able to help more."

Edith, although disappointed, was glad of the offer. About to leave, she decided to ask if it was possible to question some of the staff. Someone might remember her.

"Of course, my dear. No problem, but please try and catch them when on their break as we are extremely busy. Their rest room is at the end of this corridor." She nodded in the general direction and Edith noticed staff dashing up and down and disappearing into certain wards allotted for differing illnesses.

"Thank you, matron. I promise I 'll not stop them working." As Edith passed wards and waiting rooms, she heard the hacking coughs of the elderly, mingled with screaming cries from babies and infants. Tempted, she snatched a look into one of the wards and a painful stab of envy hit her when seeing a young mother holding and rocking her child in an effort to quieten him. Motherhood. Taken from her, never once experiencing the warmth and comfort a small bundle of flesh and blood could give. A bitterness welled up inside her but her resolve remained strong.

On finding the canteen, Edith found the nurses helpful but only two of the staff had been employed there longer than four years. They could describe Nurse Britton from the many stories told by some of the long-term patients who remembered her. A formidable woman by all accounts, with a head of short grey hair, often tied back in a short plait. Kind hearted and particularly good with children.

"Well, thank you so much for your help, ladies. I must think of another route to follow. Before I go, could I leave my address so that if anything springs to mind you can contact me."

The nurse pinned it up on the notice board. "Just so we don't lose it," she said with a smile. "Best of luck, Edith." And they rushed back to their patients.

That night, sitting quietly in front of a slumbering fire at 10 Darwin Court, Edith kicked her shoes off from her aching feet and asked, "What do I do now, John? Where do I go from here?"

Edith had recently taken up John's offer to rent a room at Darwin Court to make it a little easier. It did make sense. It was more central and much more comfortable than her flat at the other side of York. Although her flat proved adequate, it paled in comparison with John's abode. But Edith found having someone to return home to and share her thoughts with was comforting.

John thought for a while before answering. "Well, it appears you've gone as far as you can at the hospital, Edith. I think the way forward will be to make enquiries at the council offices." He rose from his chair. "Yes, that's it. First thing in the morning, I shall ask Jonathon for his contacts there. I'm sure they will carry records that can help us."

A smile appeared across Edith's previous solemn features and John realized just how beautiful she really was.

"Thank you, John. You always seem to have an answer. A way forward. Your life must have been much less stressful before I knocked on your door with my problems."

John's heart lurched in his chest as her eyes locked onto his. He knew he must tread carefully after so many lonely years and not let false emotions lead him astray. After all, what had the pair in common, apart from this search. Also, he was much older than her and the new school had become his life's work, an obsession almost and he kept telling himself he was only helping Edith out at a very emotional time in her life. Once Edith accomplished this mission, they would go their separate ways.

The doorbell rang. They exchanged worried glances. It was almost ten. This could only mean trouble. John hurried to the door. A young woman stood in the dim light reflecting out from the hallway.

"I'm sorry to bother you so late, Mr Durville, but I have some urgent news for Edith Dent."

Instantly recognizing the voice, Edith rushed to the door as John ushered the lady inside. It was Ann from the hospital. Apologising again, she said, "I'm sorry to call at this time of night, Edith, but I had to work late, we were so busy. I have come straight here to tell you."

"Tell me what?" Edith asked. "Have you remembered something?"

"No, but Charlie the caretaker did. He's been there years. I needed his help with a patient and took the chance to ask him about Nurse Britton, thinking he might know where she moved to."

"And did he?" Edith could barely conceal her excitement.

"Yes, he even remembered the address." Ann handed the torn piece of paper over on which Charlie had scribbled it down. "This is the last information Charlie had on Nurse Jessie Britton." Ann hesitated. "I suppose she could have moved on by now, he did say it was quite a few years ago."

"Ann, this is the best news ever." Edith, face flushed and radiant, gave Ann a big hug. I'll never be able to thank you enough. Will you come in and have a drink with us both."

"No, I can't. I would love to but I'm back at the hospital at six in the morning, so it's back home and straight to bed." With a wave of her hand, she turned and was gone, disappearing into the darkness of the night. Edith rushed to the door and shouted after her. "I will let you know how I get on, Ann."

Returning to the comfort of the fire, Edith showed John the address and he dropped into deep thought for a while.

"Anything wrong, John? Is there a problem?"

"Not sure, Edith. You see, I think this part of York was, or is, definitely due for regeneration but development may not have begun. I know it is a very deprived area but we can soon check if the properties are still standing." Edith flopped into a chair next to him and reached for his hand.

Smiling up at him, she said, "Well, there is only one way to find out. I shall go check it out tomorrow."

"No, I can find out much quicker in the morning. Then, if still standing, I will accompany you. It is not a place for a woman to go alone."

"I would appreciate that, John, if you have the time. Now, early start tomorrow, do you think?" Her eyes sparkled with a new optimism at this progress.

"Definitely," he replied.

John realized this was just another step along this difficult winding path that Edith had undertaken in the search for her missing boy. Raising his glass and clinking it with Edith's, his admiration at her courage and commitment was rising every day.

Chapter 21

J ohn rose for an early breakfast, then placed a call through to Solomon who was already at work. A brief discussion and summary on the solidarity of the business before John enquired on the rebuilding programme. "Not as yet, sir. As it happens, I had a similar enquiry on the area the other day and nothing has gone ahead so far. They do take their time." After a few more pleasantries, John finished the call and turned to Edith.

"We are on our way. Are you ready for this, Edith?"

"More than ready, John."

Donning coats, they were greeted by a wet, miserable morning, the acrid smell of smoke hanging thick in the air. John hailed the first cab that passed and eased Edith into her seat shouting the address as he jumping aboard.

Although John had lost weight and was quite trim, the confined space of the small cab meant sitting in close proximity to Edith and the warmth of her thigh against his own did not go unnoticed but Edith soon put him at ease with her new found optimism.

After leaving the opulence of Darwin Court, the slum conditions of Samuel Street shocked her. Edith really believed she had suffered, having to survive on meagre earnings over the last two decades, but she now realized her situation was far removed from the extreme deprivation experienced here.

It was not only the state of the dwellings or the rubbish lining the streets, it was the sheer, beaten acceptance of the inhabitants living here. Their expressions mirrored their thoughts. Eyes, dead to the real world, stared out but saw nothing. No work. No hope for the future. Shoulders slumped, they trudged through the rubbish, or hung about on street corners with no other place to go and with nothing else better to do.

The cab pulled up at the head of Samuel Street and the overwhelming stench from the middens drifted toward them, catching in Edith's throat which she tried to hide. John paid the driver "Thank you, driver. No need to wait. We'll find our own way back."

The driver quickly doffed his cap in John's direction. "Thank you, sir," and was relieved to drive away from the area.

As the sun broke through the clinging mist, roofs and cobbles shone slick and bright on the long lines of brick terraced houses on either side of the street. Luckily, as most numbers were missing, John and Edith tried the left-hand side first.

Surveying the shabby, tumble-down state of the houses for a second or two, John stepped up to the door and before knocking, turned and said to Edith. "Right, Edith, brace yourself for a shock."

"I'll be quite alright, John. Don't worry." She gave him a reassuring smile. Initially, she was shocked at the squalor, never having experienced anything like this in her life before. She felt an overwhelming sympathy for the families living in such terrible conditions. But it was not sympathy they wanted. It was help. She hoped it would not be long in coming.

Rapping loudly to rouse anyone inside from slumber, John breathed a sigh of relief when the handle turned and the door swung open, revealing a very smartly dressed woman. In her sixties, John assumed, with a certain air of authority about her. Short grey hair framed an oval face and she was dressed in a tweed skirt and jacket with sensible leather shoes as if ready to go walking.

John was quite taken aback, not expecting such a woman to answer the door. Regaining his composure, he asked, "I am terribly sorry to bother you but we are searching for a lady by the name of Nurse Britton? Nurse Jessie Britton?"

"May I ask who wants to know?" For such an authoritative lady she spoke quietly.

Edith stepped alongside John. "Good morning, madam. My name is Edith Dent and this is my friend, Judge John Durville. I am searching for information on my son. We think he was taken in and looked after by a nurse who possessed the heart of an angel called Nurse Britton. We are trying to trace her to see if she can add any details that would help us find him." Edith stopped for breath, then added, "the only problem is, it was more than eighteen years ago."

A trace of a smile appeared on the woman's face. "Well, you are a very fortunate couple." Edith's heart missed a beat. "You are at the right place but whether Jessie can help you or not is another matter. You see, her memory is not all it used to be." She leant forward peering up and down the street before saying, "I'm sorry. I should not keep you out here. Please step inside." She opened the door and welcomed them into a short narrow passage which showed signs of damp and peeling wallpaper. On entering the living room, they were both surprised at the tidiness and the décor, the smell of the freshly painted room a pleasant relief from the putrid outdoor smells.

"You look a little surprised. I must admit, Jessie has fallen on hard times but we try to keep the place habitable. Shame we cannot say the same for the outside mess. Let me introduce myself. I'm Jessie's younger sister, Mary, and I help out when I am in the area." Mary turned to the huddled figure hunched in the easy chair in the corner who was carefully studying the two strangers standing in her front room. A bulky shoulder cushion offered support to a small wizened head protruding from a thick knitted shawl draped across stick like shoulders. A black dress and button up boots gave the impression that Jessie was in mourning. Her thin pointed nose hardly appeared big enough for the large pair of thick spectacles balanced upon it.

"You have visitors, Jessie."

"I can see that, Mary. I am not completely senile yet you know!" Mary gave a patient smile as if used to such abruptness. "Now," Jessie looked directly at Edith, "what can I help you with?" Edith settled herself in the chair next to her and explained everything.

"My goodness, you are going back a long way, my dear. Eighteen years, you say." The wrinkles deepened as she frowned in thought. "Well, my memory isn't as good as it was but by Jove, I'm still sharp on things back then." She took a deep breath and carried on. "You say it was your aunt who dropped the boy off, newly born. Well, in all my working years, there was only one new born baby left with me but that wasn't at the orphanage, that was when I worked at the nunnery. Your aunt must have been mistaken, or forgotten."

Mary looked worried, as if the old lady might just be leading them astray. "Are you sure Jessie? After all, it is a long time ago." Jessie gave her a look that could have withered a normal person on the spot but Mary said nothing.

"I'm quite sure, Mary and I'll tell you for why. The lady who dropped him off with me left in a rush with never a name for the little one, so I named him James after my late husband. Eventually, the Mother Superior and I had a difference of opinions over the methods of treating these unwanted children and I left my employ there and began work at the orphanage taking the child with me. If they still have records there, my name will be on it and the year."

Settling back in her chair as if enjoying the memories, she heaved a big sigh. "I took to that little fella and looked out for him as much as I could because he was a sickly child, a poor start in life for him. The bigger children were a cruel lot, especially to the little 'uns. I was sorry when I left but I couldn't stand the hard-faced lady that came in to run things. Evil she was. Cruel as well, the beatings that went on."

Edith stopped Jessie's flow of words as she began to reminisce. "How long were you there, Jessie?

"Oh, about four years. Long enough to see that the little chap would pull through and be okay. Once I made sure he got good food, he came on a treat, turned into a real tough 'un. Not frightened to stand up for himself even at that young age."

Edith's heart was hammering hard against her rib cage, this knowledge making her dizzy. Finally, to meet someone who had looked after her child for the first years of his life. "Do you remember anything about him, Jessie?

What did he look like? Was he fat, skinny? Did he have black hair? Was he…
, you know, was everything as it should be with him?

Jessie gave her a similar withering look. "Why, of course. Didn't I just say
he was a fighter in more ways than one. Terrible temper on him for one so
young, though. Although small and skinny he was always fighting. In fact, I
remember him hiding away from me one day after an older boy knocked
him clean over with a blow to the mouth. Split his lip, damaged his teeth
terrible. But he didn't back off. Took knocks that would have older boys in
tears. "Aye, a real survivor that one."

On hearing this, John's heart suddenly lurched in his chest. Surely not.
Far too much of a coincidence. He shot a quick glance at Edith. The earnest
expression, the lively, dark dancing eyes, the mannerisms. Good God, how
could he have missed such tell-tale signs? Keeping his composure and
remaining outwardly calm, he realized there was a distinct possibility that
he may hold the key to her son's whereabouts. Problem was, how could he
broach it to Edith without building her hopes up too high.

Before leaving, Edith bent and gave Jessie a hug. "Thank you so much for
your help. You and Mary have been so kind allowing us into your home
like this. It means a lot to me, to actually speak to someone who knew my
son. I now have some idea of his early life and I will carry that picture in my
mind."

Having bade farewell to Mary and Jessie, once out on the street the squalor
and smell hit them again and John hastily called a cab. Edith, face flushed
with excitement said, "I can't believe this, John. Jessie's mind was as sharp
as a pin, wasn't it? Now we have the first five years of his life. I can picture
him in my mind, even how he will look now. The big question is, where do
we go from here? What is the next step in our quest, John?"

"Correction, Edith. In your quest, my dear."

"Not so, John. You have been with me every step of the way. Yes, he is my
flesh and blood but it is our quest now." And Edith slid her hand into his in
the confines of the cab.

Back at Darwin Court and settled in for the night, John decided to tell
Edith his thoughts.

"Edith, I have given our recent findings much thought. After meeting Jessie today, there is something I must tell you. I may just be able to shed light on your son's whereabouts." Edith was instantly awake. John raised a finger. "Please, do not get your hopes up too high. It is a long shot and maybe too much of a coincidence but I feel we should organise a visit to my friends out in the North York moors. I admit it is only a hunch but it's worth a try."

With that, John related all his knowledge on Jim and Ruth and where they were now living.

"John, it does sound too good to be true but we must follow it up, our next step. If it proves futile, we carry on. But it is a step we must take." She stopped. A smile lit her face, adding, "in fact, I can't wait to visit that part of the country."

Chapter 22

Post arrived early for Molly Turner, having moved in with her friend, Dorothy. A light sleeper, Molly heard the click of the letter box as the postman made his rounds. This was her alarm clock. 'Come on, Moll,' she said to herself, easing stiff and aching limbs into action. The cold weather didn't help any but now rehoused, life was far easier and much warmer than her old home in Lady Peckitt's Yard.

Pulling her dressing gown tight, she shuffled into a pair of slippers to enjoy the luxury that Dot's small bathroom offered. After washing and pulling a comb through her head of snow-white hair, Molly felt ready to face the world.

It proved heart wrenching when forced to leave her old home behind but there was no other option as it disappeared along with the whole street. Molly had ventured into the area only once since the demolition and was so upset vowed never to visit again. She missed the streets and the alleys of her childhood years. Years of laughter and excitement. Moments of joy and sorrow. Later, the experience of secret furtive meetings enjoyed in the dark recesses of the street with her boyfriend who became her husband. Now, all those precious memories just buried beneath mountains of rubble.

Old bedsteads, picture frames and furniture poked out through the heaps of bricks and broken timber. Stark reminders that time waits for no one. These were once people's possessions. Part of their lives, discarded now. Unwanted. Memories, her memories of childhood and married life, destroyed along with the falling masonry. Not a sign left that she had ever been on this earth. Well, they'd mebbe knocked 'em down, she thought, but they could never erase the memories. With tears in her eyes, she had turned away, never to return.

A couple of letters poked through the letterbox, one from the church asking for donations. A wry smile passed her lips. That was a bit of a liberty. As if she could afford to give anything away. It was still very much a hand to mouth existence every day but as long as she was careful, life was manageable.

The neatly handwritten address on the other letter was crossed out and replaced by this one where she now lived. Popping through into the kitchen, she put a match to the fire before preparing breakfast but while waiting for the kettle to boil the letter intrigued her. So much so, her impatience built and the urge to open it became stronger.

It couldn't be from family. All were dead and gone, along with most of her friends. This is when old age can be so cruel. Sometimes you can live too long, knowing your only companion will be loneliness. Damn the grim reaper, she thought.

Appreciating the comforting warmth spreading across the room, Molly slipped a knife from the drawer and slit the letter open. The name in the top right corner immediately triggered long forgotten memories. "Good God, Ruth Brennan!" she exclaimed, her voice appearing loud to her own ears in the confines of the small kitchen. "I can't believe it. After all this time." She slumped into a chair, breakfast forgotten as she recalled wrapping her arms around the hysterical young girl and carrying her away from the dreadful scene of her mother's murder.

Molly shook her head as if this would erase all memory of the incident and tried to concentrate on the letter. She noted the address. Ruth had somehow made it into the countryside and the more she read, the more her heart lifted.

"Oh, what an absolute joy to hear from her." Molly realized she was talking aloud, talking to herself. "Damn, I don't care if I am going a little batty. This is wonderful. I'm so pleased she remembers me. What that poor girl suffered." With tears of emotion blurring her vision, she searched for a pen and ink, paper and blotting paper. She would reply instantly. Then doubt crept into her mind. She couldn't remember how to write a letter. It had been so long since having anyone to write to. Nowadays, she didn't even bother with Christmas cards.

Reproaching herself for being so stupid and lazy, she said aloud, "Of course I can do it. All I have to do is follow Ruth's neatly written letter." After pouring a cup of tea, she reached for her glasses on the mantelpiece, laid everything out on the table and began, very carefully, to write.

Chapter 23

Back in Roston, Jim and Albert had all on to keep up with their workload of taking stock to the market and the mine contracting work. What little spare time they had was spent repairing the farm buildings. Jim's enthusiasm had rubbed off on Albert and Martha, as they could see Honey Bee thriving once again with the new energy of youth at the helm.

Roofs were retiled, doors and windows painted and instead of the farmstead appearing run down, it began to show signs of prosperity. Where the trees had once stood, the reclaimed land had been brought into use and Jim could actually see a good living eked out here just as Albert and Martha had done before him.

Chatting after tea, Jim outlined his plans for the future and hoped to keep the contracting work going at the mines as long as possible, which brought in better money. Albert nodded in agreement. "Best thing we've ever done, Jim. Not sure how long it'll last but let's make the most of it while it's there." Martha sat quietly stroking the old cat that had jumped up on her lap for a little comfort.

"While on the subject of the future, Jim, this is a good a time as any to mention it. Martha and I have first chance on a small property coming up in the village. The couple are not ready for moving as yet but as work tightens up at the mines, they'll be on their way. I've spoken with the landlord and he's promised us first chance to purchase." Albert lit his pipe and soon the familiar curling smoke and smell of tobacco filled the room.

"You think you have enough put by to see you and Martha through, Albert?" Jim asked.

"Yeah, I'm pretty sure we can manage, Jim. We have everything we want, really."

Jim was quiet for a while, then smiled. "You know what, Albert, I'm going to ask you a question and if you don't want to answer, I would understand. I know you and Martha own the farm as it was handed down but how the devil did your parents manage to buy it? There was no money about, you've said so yourself, just poverty and hardship. I also know you weren't born here." He looked enquiringly at Albert for a response.

Albert placed his pipe on the mantlepiece and said, "No, I don't mind answering. In fact, only too glad to tell you." Albert loved to reminisce and settled back in his chair. "We were very lucky really and it was all down to my father's good nature. He was the type of man who would help anyone out if he knew they were struggling and it was due to this he eventually inherited Honey Bee."

Warming to his task, Albert related the story. "When we first moved here as a family, like many others we had nothing apart from the clothes we stood up in and a few work tools. My brother Harry and I were just youngsters. With a stroke of luck, father landed a job as gardener-cum-handyman for a Mr Joseph Langburn. Joe and Agnes didn't have a family and they took to my father as if he was their own. Well, Joe ran a successful building business in Pickering and had bought Honey Bee as an investment for his later years but a stroke left him partly paralysed."

Albert recalled the story as if it was yesterday, clear as a bell in his mind. "Father, kind-hearted man that he was, helped Joe with everything right up until his dying day. He'd even tended the grave of Joe's wife, Agnes, placing flowers there at special times. When Joe's time came and his last will and testament was read out it stated that if my father would keep tending their graves, not only would Honey Bee Nest Farm be his but he would also receive a small pension for the rest of his life." Albert paused to study

Jim and Martha. "You two haven't dropped to sleep, have you? You're still listening."

"Yep," Jim nodded, "we're still listening. Go on, Albert."

Albert didn't need prompting. "Well, this was a blessing to my parents, they had security for the first time in their lives. They moved into Honey Bee and raised us two kids there. As Harry got older, he wanted nothing to do with farming and went his own way and on my parent's death it became mine. Well, you know the rest. I met and married Martha but we had no family until God saw fit to bring you into our midst as the son we never had."

Quite misty-eyed with memories, Albert stopped but Jim was still listening intently. Albert carried on. "You see, Jim, even if we have to borrow money at the bank, we have enough behind us for collateral and can manage to buy this house. With a rent coming in from yourself, this means we can take it a bit steadier."

Albert rose from his chair. "Now, if this couple do move on, well, it could be in the next couple of years."

Jim knew the reality of the situation. Had known from the beginning but hearing it from Albert brought it home. Responsibility, bookwork, taxes. God, how would he manage with his education? Ruth was patient and bringing his writing on a treat but lack of a proper education would be a problem. Then he thought, well Albert did it. If he was brave enough as a young man to tackle it, then so must he.

"Daunted by the thought are you, Jim?" Martha could see the troubled expression cloud the young man's face. "There is no need to be. You'll soon be pushing twenty and a long time in front of you to learn. We've not run off yet and will always be here for you as long as we live, you know that. So, settle yourself down and take things as they come. You never know what's around the corner."

Martha was trying to break the news gently of John Durville's visit. A week earlier a letter had arrived from John asking if he and a lady friend could visit. He explained the reason and also asked if it was possible to pre-warn Jim on what might lay ahead.

"While we are in talking mood, did Albert mention that John Durville would be calling to see us?"

"No, he hasn't but that's good news, Martha. It'll be good to see the big fella again." Jim then studied the worried look on her face. "Is there something more you want to say, Martha?"

Martha nodded slowly. "There is as a matter of fact." She hesitated and tried to sound brighter, "John is bringing a lady friend with him. They met in York."

Jim was shocked but delighted for John. "Well that's good news Martha. It'll be really good for him. Just what he needed after the troubles he's suffered, don't you think?"

"You're right Jim, it is good news. Now, the reason I'm telling you this is to prepare you for his visit so it doesn't come as a shock." Struggling to find the right words, Martha said, "John thinks his lady friend might well be your real mother." Martha waited for Jim's reaction. Apart from a slight hardening of the tanned features, no other sign registered.

Eventually, Jim raised himself from his chair, went over and gave her a hug. "You know in my heart you're my mother, Martha. I think it's mebbe a bit too late for someone to turn up in my life expecting a warm welcome from me." Deep in thought, he carried on, an earnest expression on his face. "I missed out on a hell of a lot as a kid. No parents to stand up for me, no mother or father there when in trouble. It might have kept me in check. Who knows?" He shrugged.

The gap tooth smile appeared. "There are certain memories that sometimes try to fight their way into my head. Vague fuzzy pictures rather than memories. Such as when I first came here and I felt the comfort of your arm around my shoulders, or a hug, or when you would just run your fingers through my hair. Little things like that and I would suddenly see a picture of a grey-haired lady, talking to me, calming me down. But that's all. Nothing else."

He settled back in his chair as Martha lit the lamp which sent a warm glow flitting to all corners of the room.

"Well, that's certainly a nice thought to have, Jim. But promise me, please try and keep an open mind until you have heard this lady's side of the story. It won't have been easy for her either, I can tell you that."

"I promise, I'll listen Martha. But I'll not promise any more than that."

"Thank you, Jim. If proved right it is a big moment for the pair of you."

"Also, for you and Albert," Jim replied, knowing someone would suffer heartache, one way or another after this meeting.

"Just be sure Jim, you can never guess what the Lord has in store for any of us."

Jim broke out laughing at this statement. "I'll never get used to you and your blind faith, Martha," and he shook his head in disbelief.

"Now don't you make fun of it. Look how you happened to come here. Who would have thought o' that, young man, a few years since, eh?" Martha cocked her head on one side waiting for an answer. There was no reply forthcoming from Jim. He did not want to condemn Martha's passion for religion. She carried on. "It's possible John might have found out there was mebbe more than that evil old witch at the orphanage early on when you first went there."

A comfortable silence reigned for a few minutes before Jim asked Albert's opinion.

"Listen carefully to everything that is said, Jim, then make your own mind up on what to do."

"Thanks Albert." Turning to Martha, he said, "thanks, Martha. I'm pleased it's not going to be dropped on me unexpectedly."

Albert changed the subject. "You know Jim, if we can get another couple of years work out o' the mining contract, that money will help set you and Ruth up for a life together."

"Hey, not so fast, Albert." Jim's head jerked up. "Martha has me catching up with me long lost mother and in a couple of years, you'll have me running a farm, married and settled down with a couple o' kids before I'm twenty."

Albert rocked back in his chair with laughter. "Well, there's nothing like getting a good start wi'things, you know."

After a moment of quiet, Jim spoke. "Have you heard about these recent thefts, Albert? When Ruth came over the other day, she tells me there's some sheep stealing going on."

"Yes, I'd heard but I don't know how true it is. If it is going on, they'll soon find out who it is because there are only a few sheep strays on these moors and all of 'em marked."

"Suppose so." Then Jim asked. "Didn't you ever fancy keeping a few sheep, Albert?"

"We could do. There is a stray with Honey Bee." He stopped, looking thoughtful again for a moment.

Jim was ahead of him, knew what was coming. "Don't even think it, Albert. We have enough on our plates at present."

"Perhaps you're right, Jim. Possibly in the future, eh?" he said with a glint in his eye.

Just at that minute a light knock at the door and Albert glanced up at the clock. "Now who can...?" He didn't finish as Ruth breezed in.

"So, this is where all the work is going on," she said laughing and planting a kiss on Albert's bald spot on the top of his head. She went swiftly over to Martha and gave her a hug.

Jim held his arms out. "Don't I get a kiss?"

"Whoa, you are getting brave Jim Styles. In front of other people, you mean?" said Ruth flirtatiously. "Yes, there is a kiss for you. Later on. Now how are you two keeping? It must be at least a week since I've seen you all."

Albert answered. "We're doing well, Ruth. I was just saying about the future for you and Jim..."

Martha silenced him. He stopped immediately. "Albert, these two have more to do than chatter to us. They need to catch up with their own lives. They hardly see each other."

"Well, it's not that we don't enjoy your company, Martha but you're right," Jim replied. Rising, he walked to the window and looked out. "There's a bit o' daylight left. What about a walk up onto the railway, Ruth?"

"That sounds good."

"Won't be long, folks." Taking Ruth by the hand they walked out into the lengthening shadows.

"By the way, which horse are you on tonight, Ruth?"

"I'm on Pal. Toby said to exercise him if I had the time. Why?"

"Well, I just thought all the stock are fed and watered, what about making time for a bit o' socialising?" As he said this, the urge to place his hands either side of her soft warm neck and pull her close was too hard to resist. Ruth responded instantly, her skin tingling as the rough stubble of his unshaven chin brushed roughly against hers as their lips met. Jim did not want the kiss to end but Ruth eventually pulled away from him. "Wow, I sometimes wonder why I run after you so much, Jim Styles but when you kiss me, I understand why." Then she grabbed him again to savour the moment once more.

Ruth's face was a picture of health. Her body, lithe, graceful and her movement more feline than ever. There was no need for fancy clothes or dresses. She could even make an old jute sack from the barn look good. Jim often wondered how she could ever have fallen for a scruffy street urchin like him.

"Tell you what, Ruth. How about a ride down into the village on Pal for a drink tonight? I have a few shillings in me pocket. We could grab a couple of hours before you have to ride back home. What d'you think?

"But Jim. I'm not dressed for going out to the pub and what will Martha and Albert say if they think we're squandering hard-earned money on beer? Another thing, I've never been in a pub. In fact, I'm not sure I would be allowed in?"

Jim took her by the shoulders. "Ruth, you look better than anyone just as you are and, believe me, Martha and Albert will enjoy their own company for a change instead of us hanging about home all the time. It isn't as though we are going on a pub crawl, is it?" As for not being allowed in, we can always sit outside." Jim decided not to mention the impending visit from John, in case things didn't work out.

Ruth looked doubtful. Her only experience of alcohol or drink was of her father's decline but swiftly put it out of her mind. The thought actually excited her, never having seen the inside of a public house.

"Okay then," she said, lowering her lashes and holding the pockets of her skirt out to show them empty. "If you are going to treat me to a wild night out in Roston, just remember I am only a poor home help. I'm not used to the bright lights of these villages."

Jim clasped her hand and they entered the kitchen where Martha was making a pot of tea for Albert as he struggled through the bookwork.

"Cup o' tea, you two?" Martha asked.

"Not tonight, Martha. It's Friday night and we're just going down to Roston for a beer. Give you and Albert a bit of peace and quiet."

Martha couldn't believe her ears. "Jim Styles, you going out for a drink and taking a young lady with you? What is the world coming too?" She stared across for a response from her husband but none was forthcoming, Albert kept his head buried in his books. Not to be deterred, Martha carried on but with advice. "Now you be careful down there, young man. Don't be getting in any trouble. Either of you."

Albert finally looked up from his paperwork, peering over the top of his spectacles like a wise old owl and spoke up. "You go and enjoy an hour. It'll do you both good. Remember the saying, Martha, all work and no play…"

Martha's brow creased as she still looked doubtful. With a sigh, she added, "Aye, you're mebbe right, Albert. I'm getting to be a bit of a worrier. Must be my age." Smiling, she wagged a finger at the pair of them. "But don't be too late in."

Running out of the door, they shouted back in unison, "Don't worry, we won't be."

A few minutes later Albert shuffled his papers together and settled by the fireside, even though no fire was lit and looked enquiringly at Martha. "Well, we better accept it, Martha, those two wayward kids of a few years ago have suddenly grown up." Shaking his head in disbelief, "and what a fine couple they make, don't you think?" And he said this with such pride in his voice it brought a lump to Martha's throat. She felt exactly the same.

Chapter 24

Two up on the back of Pal, Ruth wrapped her arms tightly around Jim. Although enjoying the closeness of their bodies, she realized she was much more confident when holding the reins than being on the back like this. Thick black ribs began to cut across the darkening sky, the best of the daylight gone, and only the rhythmic plod of Pal's hoofbeats broke the stillness of the night. On nearing the blacksmith's shop, a few implements waiting repair, or ready for collection, stood outside the double doors as the strong smell from the dying embers of the forge drifted slowly away in the night air. Now hitting easier going they were soon into the village and Ruth was beginning to have second thoughts as she surveyed the front of the Tavern.

Ruth always thought a pub would be welcoming, but surrounded by tall oaks as it was and almost hidden in the dull light of the evening, it held a more sinister look. A shiver ran through her and it wasn't just the cool night air. The building, set back from the road and constructed from a finely dressed stone had matching bay windows either side of the entrance and a glimmer of light escaped through the open door. A stone flagged area at the front allowed plenty of room for the horses and carts.

Dismounting, Jim threw Pal's reins over one of the low-slung branches, noting a few other horses eating from nosebags. "Looks like some are aiming to stay most o' the night," Jim said, smiling, trying to put Ruth at ease as she appeared apprehensive.

"I'll go in and see if there's any women inside. If there isn't, I'll bring the drinks out, eh? What would you like to drink?"

"That's a good idea, Jim. A lemonade 'll be fine. You see, I don't cost a lot to take on a night out, do I? I'll wait here with Pal."

Jim disappeared inside. First impressions were not good, the only light came from a door at the far end of a passage, slightly ajar. Edging through the gloom, he gave an expectant glance into the interior from the half open door into what, for him, was a totally different world.

Quite a few customers in, mostly in their working clothes but there was a couple of better dressed men over in the far corner seated at a small table. Plucking up courage, he entered. The talk and laughter died and Jim felt, rather than saw, several pair of inquisitive eyes scrutinising him. With a confidence he didn't feel, he strode to the bar and tapped the large brass bell. While waiting for the landlord, he acquainted himself to the surroundings.

The walls were stained a nicotine brown, whether by decoration or neglect it was impossible to tell. The flickering light from the old-style carriage lamp, swinging from a centre oak beam, glinted on the shelves of polished silver jugs and tankards behind the bar. On the opposite wall stood the old inglenook fireplace, a peat and turf log fire smouldering away in the open hearth. Occasionally a ribbon of smoke would slowly spiral out into the room, adding to the thick, hazy atmosphere. The witch post, obscure carvings etched deep in its face, was positioned just to the right of the fire and from there ran a short-cushioned seat to the wall.

Jim risked a quick glance around and was relieved to see the landlord sauntering back behind the bar after exchanging gossip with his customers. Although appearing to be a large jovial looking character, the bald, bullet type head gave the impression of a man who could keep his establishment free of any trouble that came his way. Wearing both belt and braces, he sported a less than white shirt with buttons strained to breaking point in a bid to contain his ample girth but he greeted Jim warmly enough. "Good evening, young man, what can I get you to drink?"

Jim breathed sigh of relief as things appeared to be going okay.

"Err..., good evening, landlord. Could I have a beer please and a lemonade to take outside if that's okay?"

"Of course, coming right up. While expertly pulling the pint, he said, "Now, I think I know where you are from, young man. Correct me if I'm wrong. Heard you were working for Albert at Honey Bee. Is that right?"

"Yep, right first time. Lemonade's for my girlfriend, Ruth. She lives at Gallows Howe and works for Jacob Thrall."

After taking pay for the drinks, he held out his hand. "Pleased to meet you, Jim. I've heard of Jacob. Well respected throughout this area, both for his doctoring and preaching. I must say, I've benefitted more from the former rather than the latter," he said with a laugh. "Tony Henton's my name, landlord of this house for the past twenty-five years. Seen it through the good times and the bad, along with the customers you might say. Well, enjoy your drinks the pair of you," and Tony turned to serve more of his regulars.

"Will do. Thanks."

Gathering the drinks, Jim returned outside where Ruth stood with her arm around Pal's neck.

"There were no other women in, Ruth, so I didn't ask. Anyway we're okay out here for a while, aren't we?"

"Course we are. It's a lovely night to be out." As they settled onto the seat on the green, three youths walked slowly past, eyeing them intently before entering the pub.

"What was it like in there, Jim. Was it as you thought?"

"Well, I didn't really know what to expect. The bit I saw appeared old fashioned but trade seemed good. It quietened off as I went in. I don't think they're used to many strangers just walking into their pub." He laughed. "The landlord was friendly enough though, which helped." He sipped his beer and smiled. "Can you believe it, Ruth, this is the first time I have ever tasted beer in my life."

"What does it taste like, Jim?"

"Here, try it. Tell me what you think?" He handed the glass over. She took one sip and screwed her face up.

"Urrgh, it's terrible, Jim. How do people manage to drink that stuff?"

Laughing, he took the glass from her. "Mebbe it just takes a while to get a taste for it."

"Maybe so but it's not for me. I'll stick to lemonade." Then, as the cool of the evening closed in, with Jim's arm draped over her shoulder, Ruth nestled her head against him and whispered, "I can't believe how lucky we are, Jim. I know we have come through some tough times and we don't have a lot of money but we have each other. That's important, don't you think?" She lifted her head for reassurance.

"To me it's the most important thing in the world." With that, Jim took her in his arms and they kissed. Eventually they parted.

"What a lovely way to finish our first night out, Jim." Ruth's eyes shone bright, even in the dim light as she hugged her coat tight around her.

"Come on, Ruth, we better be going, it's turning cold." Jim had noticed one or two leaving the Tavern and knew it was time to make a move. "I'll just return the glasses and then we'll head off."

"Fine by me, Jim."

As Jim returned to the bar and put the glasses down, he noticed the three youths. One a gangling, skinny youth, the other two, rotund and ruddy faced. They cast a glance in Jim's direction then sauntered over and stood behind him as he turned to leave. Jim instinctively sensed trouble, the skinny, rat faced one really putting him on edge.

Sure enough, they were up for a confrontation of some kind.

"The skinny one said, "You'll be Jim Styles, are you?"

"I am that," Jim replied confidently. "From Honey Bee just up the dale." Jim proffered his hand.

The youth refused to take it. "You don't need to tell me where Honey Bee Nest is. I know well enough where it is."

"Well, that's okay then. A lad like you could soon get lost up there." There was a snicker of laughter from the customers within earshot. Rattled by such biting sarcasm from a city boy that made him look foolish, he fired back.

"You'll have heard there's bin some stealing goin' on, have you?"

"Yes, I've heard." Jim's skin was on fire, prickling with anticipation.

"You been a city boy 'll know nothing about it then, eh?" Taunting, confrontational. "Some o' them sheep 'at went missing were ours."

"You'll have to look after 'em better then, won't you?" Supressed laughter again. Jim stood his ground, dark eyes full of fire, excitement surging through his veins. A feeling he had not experienced since his early years growing up in York. He confronted the youth head on. "Now, I suggest you, shepherd boy, and your mates back off before you get into something you can't handle." He was goading the youth into a fight, a slight smile flicking at the corners of his mouth. The gangly lad became unsure, turned to see where his mates were. They had moved in close behind him. He appeared relieved.

The three of them stood barring Jim's way, no backing off. The silence descended once again, the regulars watching, waiting, expecting trouble any minute. Jim's heart thumped in his chest but he was actually enjoying himself, a slow smile breaking across his features, his eyes pin sharp, staring the youth down. Who would back off first, he wondered? It definitely wouldn't be him.

Then from the far side of the room, a voice, sharp, gravelly. "D'you lads happen to know who you're speaking to?" Sat alone on the old settle and staring into the depths of the fire, he had listened, taking everything in. Instinctively, he turned to the three youths, shoved his cap back from his forehead and a wisp of unruly white hair fell across the furrowed brow. Gnarled, arthritic hands and fingers grasped the smooth, horn handle of his shepherd's crook like a bird of prey hanging onto its kill. The shadows from the swinging carriage lamp continued to play tricks with the old man's craggy features.

The gangly one spoke. "You keep out of this, Jed. This is our argument."

The tension was not about to ease, slowly creeping back into the room as Jed, not to be quietened, replied to the leader of the three trouble makers. "I'll keep out of it once Dave, your mate there, knows what this lad did." The one named Dave stole a quick glance toward Jed.

"What'd he do that was so special, Jed?"

"Only saved your dad's life, Dave. In the mine accident." It was news to

Dave. He studied Jim for a second or two then strode forward and grabbed his hand. "I'm sorry, Jim. I didn't know you'd done that. That was real bravery."

"Not really, Dave. It's one of those things that most people would do on the spur of the moment. I just happened to be there."

The confrontational attitude of the skinny one evaporated on learning the truth and the atmosphere in the bar changed from tense to a room full of excited chatter.

Dave now took charge. "Right, let me buy you a pint, Jim. A quick drink with us before you go in way of an apology from us all. We're a bit too quick to judge out here sometimes. I'm Dave McCloud and, well you know I live in the cottages at Bank Top. He nodded to his mates who held their hands out to shake on it. "Jack. Jack Lawton." The skinny one was more reluctant but had no option. "Wally, Wally Simpson. Sorry, Jim."

Eventually, Jim explained Ruth was waiting for him outside and after suffering jokes about a 'petticoat government' he took his leave, thanking Jed for his intervention and invited him to call in if he happened to be passing.

"Thank you kindly, young fella. Keep a look out for me this next week or two." And he waved him goodnight.

Ruth had already mounted. "Where were you, Jim? I was beginning to worry something was wrong."

Jim jumped up behind her and explained his encounter as they rode home. But in a strange sort of way, he'd made new acquaintances and felt as if he had entered into the community of this small dale. Maybe he would be accepted and fit in eventually, as Ruth had at Gallows Howe.

As Jim wrapped his arms around her, Ruth said, "God, Jim, I'm glad I didn't go in, it would have frightened me. I hate violence. Weren't you frightened?"

"Well," that old bravado and confidence returned, showing off again in front of Ruth, "I was pretty sure the one called Wally didn't have it in him on his own but the odds changed when his mates arrived. Then I began to get a bit excited."

"Jim, how can you say that. Fighting is no good to anyone. It proves nothing."

"You think I should just have stood there and taken it. If you think that Ruth Brennan, you don't know me well enough."

"That's the trouble, Jim. I know you too well. I know you wouldn't back down." Just at that moment, Jim eased her hair back and began to kiss the bare flesh of her neck while his other hand crept inside her coat. Ruth took one hand off the reins to halt his roving hand from going too far, as she tried to concentrate on riding the rough track. She was thankful when the lights of Honey Bee blinked out a greeting in the distance.

Jim leapt off and Ruth leant down for a goodnight kiss. When their lips finally parted, Jim whispered to her. "Hope you don't get into trouble with vicar Jacob, Ruth. He may think I'm teaching you bad habits that 'll lead straight to the devil's door." The trade-mark grin lit his face as he gave Pal a tap on the backside. "Ride steady, Ruth."

Easing the horse up through the first tortuous, twisting climb, Ruth soon disappeared from Jim's view. Once on the hard moor track, she urged him into a gallop and the drumming of Pal's hooves in the cold night air were like music to her ears. They were also her only company in this isolated part of the world. Still savouring their final kiss and the speed of the ride, exhilaration ran through her body. Approaching home, she began to hope that Jacob had not worried unduly.

Chapter 25

꧁ᏻᏻ꧂

A t the very first opportunity, John and Edith arranged a couple of days away for a trip to the coast. More importantly, their trip would include a visit to the North Yorks moors, and in particular, to Honey Bee after receiving Albert's reply. Glad to hear they were all in the best of health, Albert asked that they be tactful on confronting Jim with his findings. John understood his concern. If his hunch proved correct, there were some difficult issues to talk through. For everyone.

Early morning sun glistened like silver on the damp roof tops surrounding Darwin court but the temperature was still low. Once loaded, expectancy was high on what this journey may hold as it could affect them all. He realized, apart from their occasional night together over a glass of wine, this was the first time in each other's company that did not involve gathering information. Hopefully, if the meeting proved amiable as well as successful, then surely an enjoyable break in the open countryside would follow.

Edith, enjoying the experience of motoring, sat enthralled as they left the Vale of York behind. They passed through picturesque villages, some with odd sounding names, before hitting the steep climbing road that cleaved its way through to the remote villages.

"Who could believe such a vast expanse of wild moorland could be so powerfully beautiful as this, John?" Excited at the journey but also pensive and apprehensive on the outcome of what lay ahead, Edith lapsed into

135

silence. John gave her a few minutes to put her thoughts in order, before saying, "You like it then?"

"I find it invigorating," she said as they swept past the isolated roadside hostelry but deep down, she was wondering how on earth anyone could earn a living in such an isolated area. There was not another building or house in sight and she could see for miles. Then the stark silhouette of a stone cross came into view and John related the story of the kind hearted farmer who stumbled upon the body of a homeless, destitute man who had died in a ferocious storm. So moved by the experience, he had the cross erected with a hollow carved out on the top so the gentry could place a few coppers there for the more unfortunates of this world, ensuring they would have a few pennies for a meal.

Intrigued by the story, Edith said, "I suppose that means us, John, doesn't it?" Both stepped out of the car and Edith opened her purse and stood on the base of the cross but even at full stretch, could not reach the top. John quickly came to her aid, placed his hands on her waist and hoisted her high enough to ease the pennies into the hollow. As John put her down, Edith turned toward him, still close and said, "I do not want to spoil things, John Durville, as this is the happiest time of my life but I do believe I have fallen in love with you. If you find this stupid, or I am misreading your kindness for something else please correct me before I make a bigger fool of myself." Her expression was serious, earnest, as she scanned his face for a true answer to her feelings.

John smiled, lowered his head and kissed her. Out on this bright, bleak moor next to the cross that had been placed there as a symbol of hope and love.

"They are the most beautiful words I have ever heard, Edith." He studied her. This beautiful woman stood before him. Radiant, sparkling. "Words I never thought would come my way again. I believe I loved you from the first time you arrived on my doorstep."

She reached up on tiptoe and kissed him again, full on the lips. John savoured the taste and the moment.

"What a romantic setting for a couple of our age to pour out heartfelt feelings to each other," Edith said. "Surely, we can face anything now, John. Let's go and meet Albert and Martha," she paused before adding, "and Jim."

Jumping back in the car they took a right turn and were soon descending the steep, twisting incline to Roston. Pulling to a halt in the farm yard, Edith couldn't help but admire the idyllic setting of the old farmstead. Cut deeply into the rising terrain and surrounded by trees, the land fell quickly away to the front but the house remained well sheltered in the lee of the moor behind it.

Martha rushed out to greet them and John introduced Edith.

"I'm pleased to see you again, John and pleased to meet you, Edith. Now, come inside the pair of you. Kettle's boiled and we'll have a cup o' tea before the men get back, cos' I would like a chance of a word on our own if that's possible. I know you are searching for your son and John believes it could be Jim. I really hope it is." Martha was worried and it showed.

Once they were settled, she tried to explain to Edith not to expect too much from Jim, to take it gently as it was a lot for the young man to adjust to all of a sudden.

"I do understand, Mrs Styles."

Martha put her hand on Edith's. "Please, call me Martha."

"You're absolutely right, Martha," she said, a smile breaking through. "I do realize it will be a shock for all concerned but I am prepared for rejection or acceptance. Whichever way it goes, if it is my son, at least he will hear my side of the story and know that I didn't abandon him."

The clatter of hooves in the yard brought silence and a feeling of apprehension spread through the room. Albert was the first to enter, quickly shaking John's hand followed closely by Jim, whose face lit up on seeing John.

Trying her hardest to keep calm, Edith's heart felt as if it would jump clear of her chest as Jim strode over and John gave him a bear hug, then Jim turned to Edith and shook her hand. God, she was shaking, unsure if she could handle this situation. Edith knew instantly this was her child. There could be no mistake.

John did the introductions. "Albert, Jim, this is Edith Dent a friend of mine who appeared on my doorstep one night and explained to me her mission in life. Over time, we have become close friends."

Edith was relieved John had taken charge as she was unsure if her voice could be trusted at present, such was the state of her nerves.

John carried on. "Now I think it best, if you are all agreeable, for Edith and Jim to be left on their own for a quiet talk." All nodded in agreement. "Shall we retire to the other room and catch up on old times?" John gave Edith and Jim a reassuring nod of the head as they left the room.

On their own, the tension escalated.

"Hello, Jim." Edith held out her hand. Jim remained seated, making no move to take it again. Her mouth had suddenly dried like parchment, words stalling in her throat and her face paled.

"Hello, Mrs Dent, or is it Miss?" He emphasised the word, Miss.

"It's Miss Dent, Jim. I was never married."

Jim studied Edith, his dark eyes sharp, but cautious, taking all in. Smart lady for her age. Quite well dressed, spoke with a correctness showing a good education and middle-class upbringing. Jim let the silence run again, leaving Edith no option but to somehow try and break down the formidable psychological barriers. Edith understood that Jim would have many years of resentment due to his belief of being abandoned as a child. But if she could only tell her story things may change.

"Did Albert and Martha explain my visit, Jim?"

"Albert told me the news a week ago." Cool, off-hand answers, as if it made no difference to him.

"Jim, I am so sorry for what has happened,…"

"You stop right there, Miss Dent." His voice had taken on a hard edge. "You're sorry. For what? That my birth ruined your life? That your man left you on your own and now for some stupid reason, you pick me out as your long-lost son. Eighteen years down the line after I suffered years of squalor, beatings and shame at the orphanage. Anyway, disregarding all that for the moment, whatever makes you think you have the right to walk in here and assume that I might be your abandoned son?" A look of loathing swept across his features, cutting deep into Edith's heart. He turned away, struggling to control himself.

"Please believe me when I say that with John's help and the research done it is a distinct possibility that you could be."

"So could any number o' those kids I were in the orphanage with, or any other establishment for that matter. Any of 'em could be your off-spring." He threw this back at her over his shoulder, refusing to meet her gaze.

Edith was desperately trying to keep her composure against such an unforgiving onslaught from him. Speaking quietly, Edith said. "No, I don't think so, Jim. Not by the dates that we found in the records."

Jim had risen from the chair, unable to contain his anger. His aggression had startled her. Frightened her in fact. He suddenly turned to face her, his eyes locking onto hers.

"Please, Jim. Please give me the respect of listening to my side of the story. If you are still angry and don't believe me, I will walk out of your life and you will never see me again. I promise you that. Will you promise to hear me out?"

Her composed attitude had the desired effect. It made Jim feel uncomfortable with his abrupt abrasive manner. After a brief silence, which to Edith seemed like an hour, Jim said, "D'you mind if we go outside and talk. I'll feel better outside."

They walked outside, crossed the yard and Jim leant on the gate overlooking the fields that ran down to the edge of the village. The descending sun was casting a golden hue to the very tip of the high moor, as if setting it alight as it steadily dipped below the horizon. In the quiet solitude of the evening, a few hens were scratching about in the grass and the two horses, Pippen and Farmer sauntered up to the gate to see what was on offer. The minutes ticked by, the atmosphere tense.

Edith stood next to Jim as they both gazed upon the natural beauty of the valley. Risking a glance sideways at him, she realized just how handsome he was. Not film star handsome. Just a rugged outdoor look.

"Are you angry with me, Jim?"

"Yes. Very angry. But I promised Martha that I would keep it in check and listen. And I will." He stared straight ahead, eyes on the valley base but actually seeing nothing.

"Do you promise to listen to my side of the story now?"

"I've already told you I will listen." Impatient. No softening of the voice. Emotion high within him. He was only just being civil.

"I thank you for that."

Edith began and her story poured out, as it had done with John. Jim listened intently, neither butting in, asking questions or showing any emotion at all. When Edith stopped, Jim asked, "Is that it?"

Edith was drained. Her legs felt like lead, her heart heavy. If this was her boy, he had an edge of steel in him that she felt may never be broken. But she had completed her quest.

Finally, she turned to face him and noticed his eyes wet with tears. He brushed them away on his shirt sleeve. Eventually Edith said, "I'm sorry, Jim. I didn't mean to upset you but you had a right to know. We both had a right to know."

"Edith," a softening of the voice as he turned his head toward her. "I apologise for giving you a hard time. But I have to admit, through the hard times I hated you. I didn't ask to come into this world. I held you responsible for every damned thing that happened to me. For abandoning me, ruining my life, not wanting me. The early years were hard, Edith. I had to fight, steal, beg and be selfish just to survive in a cruel world. It wasn't until I picked this job up and came here to live with Albert and Martha that I began to understand what real caring was. What love actually felt like. I didn't know of any other way to survive in life, apart from fighting." He sighed heavily, his eyes showing compassion, an understanding of what Edith had gone through. Her own fight and loss of family.

He carried on speaking softly. "It is too soon to say if I can accept you as my mother because Martha has given me all the love a mother could ever give. But that doesn't mean I don't respect you. I do. Very much. But what we must do now is try and make up for all these lost years and get to know each other. This has affected our lives far too long."

Jim took her hand in both his, squeezing gently. Edith almost collapsed into his arms, tears flowing freely as they stood together by the field gate.

The sun had already set and they had not noticed.

Eventually, Jim spoke again. "Come on, Edith, there comes a time when the tears have to stop." His tone was gentle, understanding. "We both have a life in front of us, cos' I'm no mind reader but I can recognise signs of affection when I see it and the big man's fallen for you in a big way, don't you think?" Edith blushed. Jim laughed at her embarrassment but placed an arm around her waist and, turning away from the valley, guided her back into the farmhouse. Edith had found her son.

Chapter 26

Ruth could not read the future but it did not need a fortune teller to see that Gallows Howe had had its day as a trading village. The drop in custom over the last couple of years was drastic. Why, only a short time ago cottages were being repaired, now many were standing empty again, the younger inhabitants moving out, keen to experience a larger world.

This barren landscape offered nothing but hard work and poverty. The older generation were happy that Castle Moor was now a thriving community, with more facilities. Even the stone for the new church had been led to a new site at the base of the village and Jacob's hopes of the old tin tabernacle being replaced on the moor were in ruins. Like the church would soon become.

Ruth, lucky to have plenty of work herself was optimistic, shaking off these worries as she hurried to school. It was only then she realized her birthday was almost upon her. This thought and the golden glow of the rising sun bathing the hilltops helped dispel all her former gloom. She had to be positive with such a lot happening in her life.

Remarkably, Jim was reunited with his mother and Ruth was surprised at how well he had responded. Maybe a sign of responsibility and maturity, she thought. Josh's relationship with Freda was still ongoing but there was definitely a problem there. She did not want to become involved in a conflict between father and son and hoped it would soon be resolved. Her own relationship with Jim was strong, just short of time together at present.

Ruth was finding it quite an exciting time, meeting new acquaintances, enjoying the social side of life and even attended a couple of local dances together recently. Surprisingly, Jim admitted enjoying them but there had been a few drinks flowing as well. So much was beginning to open up for them, both here and at Roston.

One matter that did bother her though was there had been no reply from Aunty Moll in York. Not surprising really. Moll could have passed on, or even been rehoused. So, it seemed the hope of visiting her mother's grave had disappeared. She could never ask the judge for help after what had happened. It would not be right. But while out riding later in the day, she remembered Jim telling her how Edith had traced him through searching records. Her face lit up. That was it. Why hadn't she thought of this before? There must be records kept on everyone's death somewhere. People needed to know where relatives were buried otherwise how could graves be tended and kept tidy. That's the answer. Ruth brightened, vowing to ask Jacob his advice for contacts or addresses to write to. He would know of authorities who could help. But she must be patient and wait until the tension and atmosphere lightened between the two of them.

A fortnight later, when arriving home from work, Ruth saw the letter on the kitchen table with her name on it. A surge of excitement ran through her and with expectation rising, she drew out a chair and sat down. Studying the envelope, the address was in a very spidery type of handwriting, but still readable. Sliding a knife from the drawer, she sliced the letter open and with thumping heart began to read.

Moll Turner
2 Walmgate.
York.

Dear Ruth,
So good to hear from you. I often wondered what happened to you, if

you survived or if you were one of the many that got trodden underfoot in the years that have passed. It broke my heart to let you go, little one, but I couldn't afford to feed myself let alone another mouth. Please forgive me, Ruth. I did my best but it wasn't good enough.

Also, please excuse the writing, my hands are a bit shaky but receiving your letter made me realize I must try and write to you. I am living with a very dear friend at the moment who has taken me in. Life is still a struggle but if we are careful, we can manage.

On the question of your mother's grave, I visit once a month if I can, place a few flowers and keep it tidy and would gladly visit with you if you can make it to York. If you would rather visit on your own, I understand. The church is St Catherine's, Eden Close, York and the vicar is the Reverend Simmons.

Hopefully, if this letter reaches you, would you be kind enough to reply. Before I sign off, I must tell you how much happiness I felt on receiving your letter.

God bless with love and hear from you soon.

Aunty Moll

Tears slid down Ruth's cheeks but they were tears chequered with joy and sorrow as she read and reread the letter. A link with her past and a way forward. As she studied the letter, she tried to bring Aunty Moll into focus in her mind but the terrifying moment of her mother's death became startlingly vivid and she instantly shut it out. Aunty Moll would have to remain an indistinct figure for now, unable to face the trauma of that terrible day again even after all these years.

There was no date on the letter and the postmark was unreadable. Ruth quickly gathered pen and paper to write a reply. No time like the present. Buzzing with excitement, now knowing the correct address, she wrote a short note asking to meet the first chance available, on a weekend, if possible.

A shiver ran through her. Finally, the time had come to lay the demons of her past to rest.

Chapter 27

In a matter of weeks, Ruth's visit to Molly was arranged. Apprehensive, but also excited at the prospect, Ruth gathered a few belongings together for the trek.

Toby arrived at the stables early to help Ruth prepare. It was already agreed Pal was the stand out choice for the journey, Ruth just needed to make certain Toby was still happy with the arrangement.

"I'm sure, Ruth, the journey 'll do him good." His young features took on a serious look and he was full of questions. "You think you'll be okay, Ruth? It's a long way, you know? Will it be done in the day, or will you stay overnight somewhere, d'you think?"

"Yes, I'll be fine," she said, with more confidence than she really felt. "Not sure how long it will take me though, Toby. A lot depends on how good Aunty Moll's memory is. Hopefully, I'll make it back the same day. If not, I'll sleep rough. I've done that before."

Always full of admiration for her, Toby said, "You would as well, wouldn't you?"

"I surely would," Ruth replied with a laugh. "But let's hope it doesn't come to that."

"Well, good luck. Are you going today?"

"This very minute, Toby."

"Always in a rush, aren't you." He began to gather the tack together. "Just hang on a bit and I'll have him ready by the time you come out of the house."

"Thanks, Toby. You're a gem. I couldn't manage without you, you know." She put her arms on his shoulders and pecked him on the cheek."

Toby blushed. He was in love with this girl. She always made him feel special. Damn it. If I'd only been just a few years older, he thought, I might have stood a chance.... Ah, well, he wasn't but it didn't stop him from dreaming. Embarrassed, he said. "Aw, give over, Ruth," and continued getting the horse ready.

She couldn't have picked a better day. Bright and sharp, the sun in its ascendency as she stepped out to mount Pal as Toby held the reins for her. Stuffing a few necessities into the saddle bags, her heart beating a little faster than was comfortable, she blew Toby a kiss as he stood waving her off. It brought to mind her epic journey in such different circumstances just a few years ago.

But she was optimistic about the ride. Nothing could dampen her spirits on such a beautiful morning as this. As the old stone cross came into view, it brought to mind the stories of these dales, all handed down by the men and women who created these hill farms centuries ago.

Passing Roston turn off, the railway line snaked its way around the rim of the valley, the towering black chimney still spiking into the vivid blue of the sky but, recently, it had become almost redundant. A sign of the times.

Along either side of the road, the grass sparkled with heavy dew and the splashes of brilliant yellow gorse shimmered in the early morning sun creating a kaleidoscope of colour. To her right, a stark, sentinel-like stone marker came into view, a reminder of the brutal sport of cock fighting days which took place on this very spot. Ruth shuddered. Pushing such morbid thoughts away, she brought Jim to mind and the familiar warm glow entered her chest unbidden. Although he'd now met and accepted Edith as his mother, he had no intention of recalling anything else of his past.

Dropping down from the high moor, Ruth recognised some of the stone built thatched cottages from her first journey, the road following the route of the small winding stream. Lush green banksides either side, dotted with sheep, dipped toward the river's edge. Oh, this return trek, older and wiser now, would certainly do her good and answer many questions

On she travelled, hitting easier going, through the busy market towns and beyond, the day beginning to offer more warmth. As the steady rhythmic beat of Pal's sure footed gait offered Ruth reassurance every stride he took, the companionship between horse and rider was complete and her uncertainty about the journey disappeared.

Pal made good progress, Ruth allowing him to make his own pace. They were as one with the world. Pal had become just that. Her best pal.

On the outskirts of one of the villages, Ruth spotted a stone bridge with a narrow walkway down to the gentle flowing river. A good time to give Pal a break, so Ruth dismounted and led him down to the water's edge. After taking a good drink, he came and nuzzled against her in search of the nose-bag he knew she was carrying. Laughing, she drew it from the saddlebag and placed it around his head, talking and stroking him gently all the while as if to an old friend, which indeed he was.

Once Pal was fed, Ruth rummaged in the saddlebag for her own drink and sandwich. Easing down on the sun-kissed grass, the solitude and gentle warmth of the day washed over her as she happily watched the ever-changing rippling patterns of the stream reflect up onto the rugged stone arch of the bridge. The throbbing note of birdsong all around mingled with the satisfying chuckle of the river was relaxing and Ruth knew they had covered a good distance, possibly no more than an hour's ride left before arriving at York. Hopefully, this would leave plenty of time to find Moll and visit her mother's grave.

With horse and rider fully rested, Ruth mounted and they set away on the final leg of their journey. Agriculture was noticeably further ahead in this area than the hill farming that she was used to. Although harbouring a close affinity with the moors, Ruth, albeit grudgingly, had to admit there was also a certain beauty in such a vast expanse of openness.

Once passed the small dirt tracks of the villages and onto better roads, Pal kept a good pace. Shielding her eyes against the strong sun, Ruth spotted the outline of the city in the distance. The first motor vehicle that sputtered past, had Pal prancing sideways, but a few soothing words soon settled him.

The rest of the road traffic was mostly horse drawn, or pedestrian.

Nearing the river, a shiver ran through her as she recognised the small plantation of trees which had offered cover when making her escape from York. This was where her journey to the coast had begun. Bitter sweet memories from now on, but this is why she had returned. Riding on, they were soon among the small streets and back alleys where she and Jim ran wild as a couple of uncared for waifs. Orphans. Forgotten children that had somehow, with good fortune, emerged from the bowels of this great city to find a place in life.

Ruth could not see much change. Poverty still gripped the area. Men loitered on street corners, shabbily dressed, hacking phlegm from congested lungs. Gaunt faces, etched deep with the wretchedness of their lot, watched her furtively through hooded eyes, not through having any particular interest but wondering why a well-dressed young girl on horseback would want to visit this particular vicinity at all.

The streets and alleys all came vividly back. As did the stench, as it gradually wormed its way into her stomach. With great determination, she kept the feeling of nausea at bay and kept her mind busy trying to find Walmgate.

Scouring the many signs, there it was, right in front of her eyes. What a stroke of luck. A sigh of relief escaped her lips and, on dismounting, a scruffy ragamuffin of a boy maybe ten, eleven years old, immediately appeared from nowhere. "Want your horse looking after, miss? I can do that for ye, fer threepence?" Goodness me, charges have gone up since Jim and I were roaming the streets, she thought with a wry smile.

"Just give me a minute, young man. I'm not sure if I'm stopping yet."

"Well don't take long, miss. I don't want to be spotted here or I'll be in trouble."

"I will be as quick as I can, I promise. What's your name?"

"Everybody calls me Pete, so that must be me name."

"Hold Pal for me will you, Pete, while I see if Aunty Moll is ready for me?"

"Okay." He reached up, grubby hands tightly grasping the reins. His sharp blue eyes shone from thin, dirt smeared features and he studied this young woman in disbelief. Eventually he asked, "how long you bin riding, miss?"

Ruth, already knocking on the door, turned to the boy and replied, "Oh, since I was about your age, I guess."

"Gor, you lucky thing."

Suddenly the door swung open and there stood Aunty Moll in real life. No longer a smudgy image in Ruth's imagination, a real person. Moll immediately reached out for Ruth, not a word spoken, and flung her arms around her and they hugged and hugged it seemed forever. They broke free, tears of joy coursing down their cheeks. Moll pulled a hankie from her sleeve and wiped her eyes. She held Ruth at arm's length to take stock of the beautiful young lady standing in front of her.

"Oh, my goodness, Ruth Brennan. I can't believe my own eyes. Dot. Dot, come quick," she shouted over her shoulder into the house. "It's Ruth Brennan come to see me."

Dot shuffled down the narrow passage and Moll moved aside as Dot introduced herself. A shout from the young boy suddenly broke the spell and brought Ruth back to reality. "Hey, miss. Will you be long? I can't stand here all day, I've fings to do, you know."

"I understand, Pete." Turning to Moll, she asked, "Moll, are there any buildings handy for stabling Pal for an afternoon?"

Pete piped up. "I know where there's one, miss. Follow me. It's just up this road."

"Won't be a minute, Moll. I'll just get Pal comfortable then I'll be back," and off she walked with young Pete leading Pal.

"My, I bet you grow up to be good with animals, Pete. Have you any pets where you live?"

"Nah. Don't be daft. You think they'd let me keep a pet in the workhouse? By, but Pal's a lovely horse, in't he?"

"He is that," and Ruth told Pete the story of how Toby saved the young horse.

"Just a bit older than me you say? He must be brave. I daren't do that, miss. I'd a bin frightened o' the dark."

"It's surprising what you can do when called upon, Pete. Always remember that."

On arriving at the old building, Pete shouted into the interior darkness. "I've brought you a new customer, Wilf." His voice echoed around the empty passage but Ruth had noted the smell of stables. Wilf finally approached from out of the gloom, a heavy-set man with muscular upper arms, grimy appearance and wearing a leather apron. Ruth spotted him slide a few coppers into Pete's hand.

"Thanks, young fella. Now, what can I do for you, young lady? Is it a bit o' stabling you're after?"

"Just for the half day if that's possible?"

Ruth fished in her purse for a threepenny bit and handed it over to Pete. "Thank you for your expert help, Pete. It is possible we may meet again sometime in the future. And remember, keep out of trouble, won't you."

He looked at Ruth through fresh eyes, as if seeing her for the first time. "I will, miss. Honestly, I will. I do try me best, you know." He then gave an exaggerated bow to her before running off down the narrow alley. She smiled after him, with an understanding of the boy's way of life.

Turning her attention to Wilf, she asked. "This is an odd question sir, but if I do not finish my visit today, could I possibly sleep in your stable with the horse? You see, I have travelled a long way and I would like the horse to rest up overnight." Ruth noticed the shock on Wilf's face. "Oh, I'm willing to pay. I won't pinch anything." she added.

"It's not that I'm worried about, miss. But there isn't anywhere for a young lady to sleep in here."

"What about next to the horses?"

His eyes widened, amazed at such a request. Wilf replied, "Well, if you are willing to do that, I'll throw the overnight stay in for free and just charge for the stabling."

"You are very kind. I will settle up with you before dark. Do you live close by?"

"Just come through the stable and it's the door facing you."

"Thank you once again," she said as Wilf walked Pal through to the stable. Once Ruth knew Pal was settled, she grabbed a few things out of the saddlebag and returned to Walmgate. Molly already had the kettle on for, as she put it, "a cuppa after your long travel, me dear."

"Thanks, Aunty Moll." Moll was a small slim woman with sharp eyes that missed nothing. Lines creased her brow and a shock of white hair was tucked tidily under a hairnet. A wraparound pinafore with front pocket completed the picture. Dot, on the other hand, was more of a roly-poly sort of woman. Jolly in her outlook and a smile never far from her lips. Ruth took stock of her surroundings. The small kitchen where they were all seated, the table and chairs placed under the tiny window where a drab lace curtain hung. Washing hanging from a rack above the black leaded range and a brass faced clock in pride of place on the high mantel shelf.

At that moment, Ruth's insides quivered as she was transported back to her childhood. The scene, the smells. The tiny but cosy kitchen reminiscent of her own home. It was like peering through a window into a past life. She shook her head in a bid to quell such thoughts.

"You know, I can't really believe I've found you alive and well. You see, to me as a young girl of nine, and I do not mean this disrespectful, you appeared much older back then than you are now."

Moll laughed. "I will take that as a compliment, Ruth Brennan. No, we are not doing so bad, are we, Dot? Both in our eighties you know and if it hadn't been for Dot's love and friendship, I would o' been dead and gone long ago. Isn't that right, Dot?"

Dot was savouring her cuppa. Between sips she replied, "Don't you believe that, Ruth. Moll's a fighter, a survivor. We both are and we look after each other, day and night. And that's how it will be until death tears us apart."

"Dot's right. Everyone needs a true friend in life and I've found mine." She looked across to Dot with admiration in her gaze. "Now, when would you like to visit Sarah's grave? I usually manage to walk there, so if we have a quick bite o' dinner we can go after that."

"That would be good and it would leave me time to ride back home, although I have made other arrangements with Wilf at the stables if I need to." Ruth did not mention that she would sleep alongside the horses.

Moll looked aghast. "What, you aim to ride back today? You must be mad, young lady."

Ruth broke out laughing. "No, it's not too bad at all, Moll. Pal and I are a bit like you and Dot. We make a good team and we both enjoy exercise and the freedom of the open countryside. If we do happen to run out of time, I'll soon find somewhere to lay my head."

Dot prepared sandwiches and they sat down to eat and caught up on days gone by. Soon, Dot called a halt. "Come on the pair of you, time's passing. You haven't got all day, you know."

Shrugging into their coats Moll, now needing a stick, stepped gingerly down the steps into the street, Ruth trying hard to dismiss the smell and the rubbish infested alley. Taking Moll by the arm they walked steadily to the graveyard. Apprehensive but excited all at the same time, Ruth hoped she would be strong enough at the graveside and not become too emotional.

Moll appeared glad to be out of the house and also enjoying a change of company. Ruth explained about her journey to the coast and how she stumbled upon the small hamlet and by some kind of miracle met up with Jim again. With a smile on her face, Ruth added that maybe in the future, marriage was in the offing.

"How marvellous." Moll could hardly believe the young girl's tale. "How brave you were, Ruth Brennan. Oh, I'm so glad you got in touch." Moll's emotion once more rising to the surface.

Ruth kept the conversation light-hearted, asking how such a firm friendship had developed and how well they were managing. Then, Moll halted and lifted her gaze. In front of them the huge spire of St Catherine's Church speared into the clear blue sky. Ruth's heart jumped in her chest at the realization that the small bunch of wild flowers that she had picked by the riverside could now be placed on her mother's grave. Her own personal sign of remembrance and love.

Moll studied Ruth closely. "You okay, love?" she asked, sincerity clear in her voice. Ruth nodded but did not risk a reply, tears not far away. She hoped in her heart she would be strong enough for this moment. They opened the small gate and entered the sombre, peaceful setting of the graveyard. The smell of freshly cut grass eased the stench of the streets away and the solitary song of a bird rang out, as if in welcome to them both. They continued along the stone flags until Moll halted. "Here you are, honey," she said quietly. "Your mother's resting place. The lady that brought you into this world. A remarkable woman but a life cut far too short."

Ruth's breathing deepened in a bid to stay calm but her emotions were surfacing, out of control. She dropped to her knees and ran her fingers gently over the beautifully engraved words on the rough stone.

Sarah Brennan

Born 1875 Died 1904

Dear Lord She is Thine.

And the words were instantly carved upon her heart. As if chiselled there by the very mason who carried out the work.

"I'm so glad my mother has a resting place, Moll. Especially in such peaceful surroundings. I dreaded her buried in a pauper's grave with no marker but the headstone is beautiful, isn't it?"

"The burial and stone were paid for by a private donation, Ruth. We think, but we don't know for sure, that it was Doctor Evans who helped Sarah so much when she was ill."

"How kind, whoever it was," Ruth replied, staying on her knees. She sobbed quietly by the side of her mother's grave. Moll retired to a nearby seat to let Ruth grieve alone. Finally, after reciting a short prayer, Ruth placed the flowers in the small trinket close to the headstone, wiped the tears from her eyes and turned to face Moll.

"Thank you so much, Aunty Moll. You don't realize it but this means the world to me. All these years I have kept thoughts of my childhood locked away. I know now I will be able to look back without fear and remember my mother as a sincere loving person who gave me as good a start in life as possible." Breathing deeply, Ruth rose and went to sit alongside Moll. "Also, thank you for keeping the grave so well-tended."

"Aw, don't mention that, honey. I enjoy doing it. Another thing," she said with a little smile, "Me and Dot are real good friends and get on well but even the best of friends need their own bit o' space sometimes and this gives me my own personal talk with your mother."

They hugged tightly for a while before Moll said, "There is one other thing. You asked if I knew what happened your father, Patrick. Well, I can tell you now, as I received a letter from him before I moved in with Dot. Possibly trying to ease his guilt or conscience, or maybe just turning over a new leaf. He escaped the murder charge which should have seen him hung and was given a ten-year sentence which he is still serving at York gaol. In his note he asked if I knew where you were living but as I couldn't help him, I never replied." Moll cast her gaze to the gravestone. "If you look at the date carved there, he must be due for release anytime soon.

A troubled look crossed Ruth's face. After a few minutes silence, she answered. "You know, Moll, I feel guilty at having no feeling at all for my father but there is nothing there." She touched her heart. "Nothing at all. It is empty."

"That's not surprising Ruth, after what you went through. Now, there is nothing more you can do about that. If I was you, I would leave that be and get on with your life, because if you aren't careful it'll pass you by and be gone in a flash. Come on, let's head home before I get too tired and you have to carry me there." Laughing the recent sorrows and tears away, Moll placed an arm around Ruth's waist and they began to retrace their steps back to Walmgate.

Chapter 28

Josh's secret romance with Freda was now common knowledge around the village. As expected, complications followed, from both Winnie and Jacob. Josh knew Winnie's problem was her possessive nature but could not comprehend why Jacob was so against it. Could not even hazard a guess. While just the two of them were at home, Josh decided to confront his father on what the problem could be.

"Father, you appear to have a grievance with Freda and I seeing each other. Whenever the conversation turns to the Grey's, you change the subject, or become curt and offhand. I must know the reason why, because Freda and I intend to marry whatever the circumstances."

Jacob's face turned ashen, stunned into silence by this information he was dreading. Again, he proved reluctant to discuss the matter but Josh pressed him hard, leaving Jacob no option.

He answered bluntly. "I see many problems Josh. For one thing, you are far too young for marriage. Another, Freda is much older than you, and lastly, neither of you have ever ventured out of these dales." Jacob spread his arms in exasperation. "You need experience in the real world before making such important decisions as marriage."

Anger began to rise within Josh but he controlled it well, remaining calm, confident and reasonable in his manner, realizing this was not as straightforward as he thought. "In answer to your first objection, I am going on twenty years old and Freda is only twenty-four."

Jacob shot back, "almost twenty-five, Josh, and she will never leave her mother whatever promises are made."

"I can see you are always going to put obstacles in our path, for some reason, father. You say we need to get out in the real world, I don't see much chance of that happening around here. Unless I look over the hill into Roston at the mining jobs, and there is no guarantee they will be available much longer. That leaves shepherding and farming."

Jacob pushed his chair back, a scowl on his face. "End of conversation, Joshua. You are not marrying Freda. I forbid it." He turned to walk away.

Josh's anger spilled over at this unexpected show of authority by his normally complacent father. There was something far more important in this decision his father had made and Josh intended finding out. This was his future they were talking about. He grabbed Jacob by the shoulder.

"Do not walk away from me father when I ask you a perfectly civil question about my future. If these are the only stupid reasons that you have against us marrying, well, I shall tell you now, I will defy you and go against your wishes whatever you say."

Jacob glared at his son but Josh's gaze did not falter. A minute passed, which seemed like an hour, before Jacob's shoulders dropped in defeat. The determination shown by his son was not to be beaten. Eventually, Josh let his hand drop away from his father.

"You better sit down, Josh. This will come as a shock." Jacob slumped back in his chair. "I hoped and prayed it would never come to this." A sickly feeling filled Josh's gut, like a vicious kick to the stomach. It was nothing to do with age or him seeing the world.

Jacob was struggling to speak, how to say what he had to say. Eventually he uttered the words, "Freda is your half-sister."

It was Josh who was now speechless, the loss of voice terrifying him again. But this time it was only temporary.

"Surely this is not true, father. This cannot be happening to me." He rushed back to his father still slumped in his chair and grabbed him by the shoulders once again, shaking him violently. "Tell me. Tell me this is not true."

"I'm afraid it's true, Josh, I have asked for God's forgiveness over the years, but…"

"You've what?" His face was red with rage, his voice rising, as the truth finally overwhelmed him. He spat the words out. "You've asked your all-loving God for forgiveness. What about me? What about Freda? You have the audacity to wrap that white collar around your damned neck as a symbol of righteousness and goodness, stand up behind that pulpit and preach the supposed word of God every Sunday and this is what you are telling me. You had a dirty, sordid affair with Winifred Grey."

"No, Josh, no." Jacob was pleading for understanding from his son. Forgiveness maybe, for all the years of guilt suffered. But Josh was in no mood to forgive. "Please listen to me, Josh, it was just a moment of madness."

Josh was on his feet now, eyes ablaze with unashamed anger. "Hypocrite. You bloody, shameless hypocrite. I no longer want to hear anything you have to say."

"Josh, please? You have to listen. At least, let me try and explain how it happened."

Josh put his hands over his ears. "Damn you. I don't want to know any details. Just believe me when I say you have just brought my world crashing down around me with this one statement. To Hell with you, Jacob Thrall. Damn you to Hell. Your God may forgive you but I never will!" Josh stormed out of the room slamming the door hard behind him.

Jacob was stunned at the fury of Josh's onslaught, the silence of the room deafening. Filled with regret, he could not think of a way he could have told Josh any better. He sighed, always hoping the truth would never surface. How could he explain to Josh that a lonely woman, clinging to life by a thread had misread sympathy and treatment as a sign of love?

The love he felt for his fellow humans somehow got confused with kindness and suffering, boiling over into an uncontrollable hour of passion. The vision of Winnie's face, all those years ago, as her eyes searched his, haunted him. She did not need to ask. She offered herself and in a moment of weakness, he had not been strong enough to ward off the sins of the flesh.

Slowly climbing the stairs, he undressed for bed. But a troubled mind cannot claim the freedom that sleep offers. Instead, he lay awake listening for the return of his son. For once, Jacob did not offer a prayer to his Almighty God.

Chapter 29

With much to talk about, Ruth left the comfort of Dot and Moll's front room much later than intended. But she was in contented mood walking back to the sanctuary of her stable, the dull shimmer of the street lights a satisfying guide for her.

Creeping in from the street she heaved one of the huge double doors open and counted six horses stabled for the night. Through the back, she noticed a flicker of light from Wilf's abode and knocked on the door.

"Sorry I'm late sir but we had a lot of catching up to do. Now, what do I owe you for your troubles?"

Wilf shook his head in amazement. "That'll be sixpence, m'dear. You sure you'll be okay?" he asked.

"I'm sure. I've slept in far worse places than this when I was younger, believe me."

"Well, all I can say is it must have been an important meeting, so good luck on your return journey, young lady."

"Thank you for all your help. Now I shall retire to sleep with my friends, the horses. I shall most likely have gone when you rise in the morning."

With another shake of the head, Wilf retired inside to the comfort of his armchair.

Pal was already well fed and watered and settled on clean bedding, the smell of the stable bringing thoughts of Gallows Howe to mind. Placing a saddlebag on the heap of straw for a pillow, she lay alongside Pal, content with the outcome of this momentous trip back to her childhood days. With her arm laid across Pal, the warmth and steady breathing of the animals was somehow comforting and as soon as her head touched the makeshift pillow, sleep took over.

Next morning as a glorious dawn broke, Pal nudged her awake. "Goodness me Pal, morning already and my first night free of nightmares." She couldn't quite believe it. Splashing water out of a bucket over her face to wash the sleep from her eyes, she then dried herself on some spare clothing. Fully refreshed and wiping the straw from her clothes she quickly tacked Pal up and made her way out onto the street, happy in the knowledge that the two of them could now spend the day together.

A beautiful, steady ride back, plenty of time to halt once again at the bridge by the river to give Pal a rest and a drink. Lost in happy thoughts, Ruth couldn't believe it when they hit the long, steep climbing road unwinding over the moor. It appeared to her like a welcoming ribbon drawing them closer and closer to home.

Finally turning into the familiar pot holed track to Gallows Howe, Ruth stabled, fed and brushed him down. Only then did she notice there were no lights on in the house. She didn't think it was that late but crept up to her bedroom, quiet as a mouse, trying not to wake anyone. Undressing, still with a feeling of exhilaration rushing through her from the challenge of the ride, she knew full well sleep would not come easily. She felt so alive, her mind so active from the thrill of the return to the city of her birth.

Ruth knew for certain that a new beginning beckoned. Her decision to retrace her steps had been the right one. Finally shedding the troubles of childhood, she somehow felt older. Not older in age, but older in experience, much more able to face the future with confidence. With the lamp emitting just a soft glow by her bedside, Ruth settled to read for a little while. Then from below came the familiar click of the kitchen door. She smiled. Josh having a late night apparently. Closing her eyes, she drifted off to a night of peaceful slumber.

On rising, Ruth reached out and pulled her bedroom curtain aside at the first sign of daylight. She watched as the spears of early morning sunlight peeped over the horizon, steadily breaking onto the craggy moor-side to expel the heavy dew silvering the distant rocks.

Keen to face the new day, Ruth ate breakfast alone before walking across to the stables where Toby was already watering the horses at the stone trough.

"Morning, Toby. You've got a good start to the day. Horses all okay?"

"Yep, all looking good. Did Pal do you well on your trip, Ruth?"

"He was wonderful, Toby. You really do have him in good shape. What are you feeding him? We had a full day's riding and he was still far from finished after trekking such a distance." Ruth wandered over and wrapped her arms around Pal's neck.

"Josh and Jacob not about yet?" Toby asked.

"No, not yet. I'll go and prepare breakfast in a few minutes for them."

"You spoil 'em, y' know." His face split into a grin. Toby was growing into a confident, handsome young man. Ruth could not believe the change in him. Work had given him a new found confidence. But even though his job left him very little time, he would never forsake looking after Pal.

After helping Toby with some of his chores, Ruth returned to find Jacob and Josh both up and about but silent. The strained atmosphere hit her on entrance. Something simmering beneath the surface, as if it could break at any minute.

"Morning, Jacob. Morning, Josh. I'm surprised to see you up and about as early as this, Josh. Hope you both slept well?" Josh was quiet, sullen, making it clear he was not in a talking mood. Jacob answered for the pair of them, trying to break the icy coldness. "Yes, quite well, thank you, Ruth. And you? How did your journey go?"

"The best sleep I've had in ages and after meeting Moll and visiting my mother's grave, I can see the way forward." Ruth looked worriedly toward Josh, who remained indifferent to them both as he continued to rush his breakfast down.

"Josh, what's wrong? Have I upset you?"

The piercing blue eyes held hers, never once acknowledging his father's presence. "No, you have not upset me, Ruth. Now, I must be going."

"Please, Josh, this is unlike you. Please tell me what's wrong. The only way to put things right are by talking. Isn't that what you always tell me?"

"I haven't the time right now, Ruth. Father can explain better than me. I'm meeting Pete, so I must go."

The bitterness in him was clear to see. Ruth was baffled. Hurt, in fact. She had left a close comfortable household and returned to a family in conflict. The slamming of the door brought her back to reality and the image of Jacob at the table, breakfast uneaten and his head in his hands, crying softly.

"Jacob, whatever has gone on while I've been away. Please let me help, if I can. And if it is a family matter and I need to keep out of it, please tell me. But don't shut me out. You at least owe me that."

"I do not know how to tell you."

"Well, Jacob, the advice you gave me, I remember, was to begin at the beginning and talk. A trouble shared is a trouble halved." Ruth settled quietly beside him, taking his hand in hers. "I have the time if you have."

After hesitating for what seemed an eternity he began to speak. Softly at first, then with more confidence, Jacob finally opened his heart to her, as Ruth had done with him in the church that day. He had proved a pillar of strength for her then and she would try to be as strong for him now. Just as he had difficulty believing the story of her young life, Ruth experienced the same from this man of the cloth sitting before her, relating such intimate details of a long-gone episode of his life. But she was not in a position to condemn anyone after suffering her own personal nightmares. Experience had at least taught her that each and every one of us, often carry their own particular cross.

Jacob, story finished was a beaten man. He had suddenly aged in front of her eyes. Ruth let silence reign until he felt like speaking.

"I've lost my son, Ruth. Through one moment of madness, weakness, I have lost my only son."

"No, you haven't lost him, Jacob. Love does not die with just one mistake. Josh will never stop loving you, I can guarantee that. But he will be angry with you because you have caused his world to collapse. Freda was, and maybe still is at present, his first true love. Maybe she always will be, but

I doubt it. There will be others in the future and as the hurt dies, the love he feels for you will surface again. Because love does not die, it just lies dormant for a while."

Jacob studied this young girl, who talked so much older than her years, preaching words of wisdom to him that he himself could never match. Drying his eyes, he held her hand gaining comfort from her words and the warmth of her compassion.

"You think he'll ever forgive me, Ruth?"

"There is no doubt on that, Jacob. But we will never know when. Just be ready for him when he does. He will go on to make his own way in life, as you did. This was a huge shock for both of them and they have to come to terms with it in their own way. He may yet flee the family home, and everything he holds dear, in a search to find his true self. Sometimes this only comes about by necessity."

"As you well know, young lady," he sighed.

She smiled at him. "As I well know, Jacob."

Jacob took her in his arms and whispered, "Thank you, Ruth. Thank you so much."

Chapter 30

J osh headed for the high moor where Pete Eccles waited for him,
kneeling among the heather, his arm around his sheepdog, Bramble. A
strong west wind tugged at his clothing as he reached the highest point
and a smile broke out on Pete's face as he watched the familiar gait of his
friend draw nearer.

"Morning, Josh. Bed too comfortable this morning, was it?"

Josh glared at him. "Not in the mood for jokes this morning, Pete. What
do you want me to do? Are we just gathering today?"

Pete stared at his friend. This was unusual. Very rarely snappy, especially
with him. "Oh, like that is it. Sorry I spoke but I think it's going to be a long
day, Josh old mate, if you are in a bad mood. Why not get it off your chest
first thing? If I do sometimes upset you, you usually let me know why in no
uncertain terms."

"Honest, Pete, it's not you. Let's do some work and I'll tell you about it as
we go."

They set off across the moor and Josh unloaded all his troubles from home
upon Pete, who listened with a sympathetic ear. No jokes, no butting in. He
just let Josh tell the whole story. When finished, he said, "Good God, Josh, it
takes some believing. I can't even begin to understand how you feel. How
are y' going to tackle it?"

"I'll have to tell Freda first. Not sure how she'll take it but I've set my mind on joining the army, take the King's shilling and fight for my country. I've had enough of this place, Pete."

Pete glanced across at his friend, read the seriousness of the situation and thought he better try to talk him out of it. Yet at the back of Pete's mind, a seed of doubt was already forming about his own future.

"I know what you mean. You're right, there's no real prospects out here for the likes of us. I've even considered it lately, meself." He stared out toward the far horizon as if studying it with a fresh pair of eyes. "You've thought this through have you, Josh? It's a big step, all the bloodshed and killing. You might come back minus limbs, shell shocked. Or worse." Pete hesitated, then looked Josh direct in the eye. "You might not even return at all!"

"At present that would be no bad thing for me, Pete."

Pete suddenly realized this was serious, just how far down his friend's spirits were. "Hey, come on, this is not the real Josh Thrall I'm used to hearing. Rid your mind of talk like that. I know, just at present, it'll feel like the end of the world but things change." Pete was doing his best, hoping he was saying the right things in this situation. Even though not really sure of himself, he went on. "There are loads of young girls out there, Josh, just crying out for young handsome studs like you and me. But it might take a while before you feel like that, I suppose." Pete thought it best not to joke about it just yet.

"I'm not sure on that score, Pete. Freda and I were very close over the last year or more and it's hurting, right here." He placed a hand across his chest. "But it's not only the thought of losing Freda, it is the sickening thought of having a father who is such a hypocrite, spouting off about love and doing the right thing, everything all milk and honey, then finding out he's done something like that." He shook his head, as if trying to shake the awful thoughts clear from his brain.

"Aw Josh, come on now, everybody makes mistakes in their lifetime. You'll o' made plenty already, I bet. Just don't be so judgemental about people. Sometimes, it can be bad luck, or just circumstances, who knows? Things happen in life that we have no control over. I know they shouldn't but they do. After all, we're only human."

Pete's words instantly brought back the night of the stabbing to Josh. He glanced across at the gangling figure beside him, his best friend and suddenly saw him in a different light. Smiling, he said, "I never expected you to come out with such sensible views as this, Pete."

"Ah, you should know by now, I'm a man of many talents."

"I hate to admit it but you could be right, Pete. I do act hastily sometimes, although I have definitely made up my mind about going to fight. But, first things first, I have to face Freda."

"Yep, that's going to be hard. I don't envy you that job, mate."

They both settled down into the springy softness of the heather for a rest, then Pete changed the conversation to stop Josh dwelling on Freda. "Well, about joining up, Josh, you might not have to go alone as Barney Stopes and I were just talking about it recently. Your decision might just persuade the two of us to be brave enough and join you."

Josh looked astonished. "Really? You mean, you've been thinking about it already?"

"Too true, have we. Just the other night, we decided there had to be more than just scraping a living out here. Barney gets the odd day of work here and there but that's it. No future, no night life, no girls, no money. We must all be idiots." Rising to his feet, Pete exclaimed, "So, lead on, young Josh Thrall. Let's find out where we go and sign to fight for King and Country, eh?" Pete pounded his chest in playful mood and let out a hollering call that rang out across the open countryside. "Lord Kitchener has no idea what he is about to get from outta these rugged old hills."

They both broke into laughter, Josh's spirits higher than they had been for some time, lifted by the humour and support given by Pete. Soon they were running across the wild open moor, sending Bramble dashing back and forth through the deep heather to gather the wayward flock together.

Chapter 31

The very next day, Josh decided to tell Freda the bad news. It was close to mid-day when he arrived at the school waiting for her to finish work. He really had no idea what he was going to say. Slouched against the railings and lost in his own thoughts, she was suddenly at the gate.

"Hiya, Josh. Missing me that much, eh? Couldn't wait to see me, I bet." Lively, happy, the blue eyes bright and sharp with expectation of a few hours together with Josh. But then she noticed his mood. This was not the usual Josh Thrall she was used to meeting. This was a sullen, despondent man stood in front of her. She studied him a while longer then lowered her voice. "Josh, what's wrong? What has happened?"

Josh looked quickly around. "Wait until we get clear of the school, Freda, then we have to talk."

"Okay, if that's what you want?"

They walked down through the village and it wasn't until they reached the steep winding hill towards the station that Josh broke the silence.

"We have to stop seeing each other, Freda."

Freda laughed, incredulous at this suggestion, believing it to be a joke. Then her face turned serious as she could see the hurt in Josh's eyes. "What do you mean. Have you tired of me already? You can't just treat me like that, Josh. How can you just drop me like it doesn't matter? I love you Josh Thrall.

Don't you understand?"

Josh suddenly blurted it out. "Jacob Thrall is your father, Freda." Josh looked at Freda and watched the puzzlement in her eyes, the colour slowly draining from her face as the realization of these few devastating words sunk in.

Her voice no more than a whisper. "You mean..." she left the sentence unfinished, unable to hear the truth out loud.

They sat together on the green by the river, the steady burble of the stream the only sound. Josh put his arms around her, the shock too much for Freda to take in. He broke the silence. "It came to a head when I confronted my father with the fact that we intended to marry. That's when he told me we had no future. It breaks my heart, Freda but we must part."

Rising together they hugged and with great effort, refrained from a final kiss.

"I want you to know my feelings for you will never change, Freda. I will love you for always and I will never forget the time we have spent together. It will always be special, but this has to be goodbye."

Tears streaked her cheeks as she asked, "but what happens now, Josh? You were my whole world. How do I pick up the pieces?"

"I've made my decision, Freda. I'm joining up to fight for my country. It is the only solution for me. You must also try and move on from this heart-breaking news. I will be terribly jealous as I know there are plenty more young men out there who will be eager to step into my shoes." Then, holding her at arms-length and shunning the urge to comfort her, he stared into those piercing blue eyes for the last time, then turned and walked away, never looking back.

Sat alone in her bedroom, Freda mulled over what would become of her. It was over a week since she learned the truth but her mind was still tortured by the thought of her future torn to pieces but the tears and recriminations were over now. It would be hard but this was the only solution.

Strangely, Freda had always thought Winnie would be the biggest problem in her and Josh's relationship but believed, given time, she would eventually accept it. Never in a million years did she expect the truth to be so devastating. Since meeting Josh, the short times they'd spent together had been the happiest days of her life. For once, she could see a future. The daily grind and chores of work and the long lonely nights spent alone would not be forever. She had dared to dream that a door of opportunity was opening up onto an exciting world for her.

It was not to be. Her hopes and plans were in tatters. She could not bring herself to speak to Winnie since. Closed her out completely.

Freda had never felt anger surge through her like this in her entire life, especially against her mother. Her anger was also aimed at Winnie and Jacob's self- righteous, tight-lipped attitude, assuming it would never ever be discovered. Well, it had been and with disastrous consequences that affected other people's lives. She knew Josh had already disowned his father and she was close to doing the same with Winnie. But with nowhere to go, she could not avoid living under the same roof.

Freda tried to persuade Josh from going to fight. She understood his anger and the tension at home but the thought of him injured, maimed or worse still, killed in action and lying among the dead in some far-off foreign field was too hard to bear. So, she accepted his decision and tried to make the best of it.

It was now almost two years since she and Winnie had hauled Henry from the river and saved his life. Following all the publicity in the local papers about the attempted rape and Josh's subsequent acquittal, things had quietened down and people's attention had turned to other things.

Surprisingly, Doctor Rourke still called round to keep them up to date with information on Henry's progress, even after his admission to York. He even asked Freda if ever she fancied a trip to the city just to let him know. Admittedly, she had thoroughly enjoyed her few visits to Whitby, found them quite exciting but it was more about the feeling of freedom, much like how a tethered animal must feel, she thought. The trips out had meant fresh scenery out on the open road, the fishing boats in the harbour and the smell of the sea. Even just sat on the quay side eating fish and chips was an exciting time for her. This was the reality of her enjoyment rather than keeping in touch on Henry's well-being. She was also unsure of what Doctor Rourke's real intentions were. He was becoming more and more attentive as time went by.

In fact, it came as a relief when Henry was moved. This gave her an easy opportunity for opting out of visiting. Once the trial was over, she realized just what a sick and depraved man Henry was. No wonder she had always felt nervous in his presence. That was why she finally made the decision not to visit again.

Ah well, it had to come to an end sometime, she thought. At least no one could take away those days of freedom in Whitby.

Chapter 32

The tension in the Thrall household between father and son gave no sign of a quick ending, Josh stubbornly refusing any discussion about it. Ruth knew he was battling with the invisible enemy, which was his own mind and conscience. The longer this bitterness festered, the deeper the wounds would be. Her persistent efforts at polite conversation to try and break the deadlock, fell upon deaf ears and, eventually, even her patience ran dry, finally accepting the fact that Josh would only speak when ready. Surprisingly, the very next day, it was Josh who brought the matter to a head when he and Ruth were alone in the house.

"Ruth"..? then a long pause. The questioning tone in his voice helped break the stilted unease between the pair of them since the argument. Ruth raised her head from the books she was working on, hoping for a solution to spill from his lips. She knew Josh regarded family unity significantly higher than any religion could ever reach. In his eyes, it was the bedrock of human endeavour, motivation and inspiration to achieve, often against all odds, not just in his own life, but throughout the world. The dilemma he now faced had thrown these beliefs to the four winds. The close-knit family unit had disappeared and, because of it, he was a restless, unsettled character pacing steadily back and forth across the dimly lit room.

Patiently, Ruth replied, "Yes, Josh? Carry on, I'm listening. But if you have something to say please stand still and tell me what is on your mind."

Josh studied her, a slow smile twitching at the corners of his mouth. Maybe a breakthrough, Ruth thought, the first sign of civility shown since the conflict began. The iron mask of stubbornness, a formidable shield in front of him, began to show signs of weakness.

Josh spoke quietly and deliberately, making sure that Ruth grasped the enormity of what he was about to tell her. "Jacob will have told you his side of the story no doubt and it will have come as a shock to you as much as it did to Freda and I. I have no more appetite for going over what happened. I am only interested in a solution. Having discussed it at length with Freda and also having had time to reflect, I have decided on what I am going to do."

Now the ice was broken, Ruth tried to help him by keeping the conversation going. "I think I can read you pretty well, Josh Thrall," casting a questioning look in his direction. "I know recent weeks have proved a tremendous strain but dwelling on it will not help. Nothing anyone can do about the past. Let it be and move on. Now, tell me what you are thinking of."

Once more a heavy silence hung in the room. This very room where they had laughed and joked together, talked of each other's future. Now, at best, it could only be described as an uncomfortable politeness. Eventually, Josh grabbed a deep breath and blurted out, "I've signed up for the army, Ruth. Along with Pete Eccles and Barney Stopes."

Ruth expected a decision but nothing like this bombshell. Her controlled calmness of a moment ago left her completely. "What?" Ruth almost screeched the word, her voice sounding harsh even to her own ears and jumped up from the chair as if bitten. Reaching out, she clutched him by the shoulders as if trying to shake some sense into him. Impossible. He remained solid, steadfast, like a mighty English Oak standing before her. Exasperated, she gave up. The slow smile once again spread across his troubled face.

"Please, don't do this to us, Josh," she said, pleading with him. "You cannot leave us. How do you think Jacob and I are going to manage without you? Your father is not getting any younger and it is impossible for me to do your work." She kept her hands clenched on his shoulders, willing her words to be more effective so he would see sense.

Tears misted her vision of this broad-shouldered young man with the solemn features. The honest ice blue eyes were still the same but it was a mature adult who stood before her now. So pre-occupied with her own life, she realized just how much Josh had changed. Over the years, he had always been there for her, every step of the way, a shoulder to lean on in troubled times.

"I've thought of that, Ruth." he said earnestly, "but you've seen young Toby coming on a treat. He can do all my work, easily." It was Josh's turn to take Ruth gently by the shoulders, the smile warm and caring again. "You have to understand Ruth, there is nothing for me at Gallows Howe anymore. You and Jim have found each other again, for which I am truly glad." His face brightened. "A new job teaching in the village means more security and a forthcoming marriage must be in the near future and all of us will look forward to that very much," before adding, "and maybe a farm to move into, your own home."

He let this sink in as Ruth remained silent. "Who would have imagined that just a few short years ago, eh?" He stood thoughtfully for a moment before continuing. "Jacob still has the building of his new church, even though on a new site at Castle Moor. This will drive him on, especially with his loyal flock of believers to care for. This is why I need to make my own way in life. Something for me. Who knows, the army may give me the life I am searching for. Having lost Freda, I am no longer committed to live here. The shackles of family ties and the responsibility that went along with it are shattered. It is time for me to break free from this life."

"But Josh, why the army and fighting? You've heard the news. The war is going badly. You may not return. You have no idea how dangerous it is. There could be a thousand things go wrong. You could be sent anywhere, especially with the fighting. You should read the newspapers more. Ask yourself why they are pushing for new recruits? Because it's to replace the soldiers already lost in battle. For what?" She held her head in her hands as if the thought was too much to bear.

"Ruth, listen to me. For once, I will be doing something of my choice. Also, there will be three of us to start out together. Don't forget, Barney and Pete will be alongside as well."

The look of shock had disappeared from Ruth's face, to be replaced by a sadness as she realized that Josh would never be swayed. She well knew the stubbornness within him. Finally, her voice hardening, she said, "Have you spoken to Jacob about it? He'll not let you go, Josh. You are all he has left."

"Jacob and I have nothing in common anymore. He will understand why I have to go." This said with a conviction that Ruth found hard to believe.

"How can you be so sure, Josh?" she asked.

Josh lowered his voice, becoming even more serious as he explained. "Because my father confided in me many years ago how he came to leave home, although not for the same reason I am going. In fact, he was younger than myself, only sixteen, the calling of Jesus even then, far too strong to resist. Even with the wrath of his parents ringing in his ears, he strode toward a new life to follow what he believed to be his calling, to spread God's word."

Josh went on. "Believe it or not, Jacob was from a money family, his father, a well to do shipping merchant. He gave Jacob the ultimatum of following him into the business or face banishment from the family home, his will, everything, if he were to pursue the ridiculous dream that God Almighty would provide for him. Well, as you know, Jacob has a stubborn streak. Must be a family trait." Josh smiled ruefully and carried on. "He walked out of the family home never to return, making his own way in life from that day on. A very brave and committed man who even after what has happened, I still admire for such strong beliefs and love for his fellow man."

Ruth was shocked at this revelation. Speechless in fact. At that very moment the door opened and in walked the tall, stooping but still assertive figure of Jacob Thrall. He eyed the two of them quietly before speaking. "I get a distinct feeling that you two were possibly discussing me. Am I correct?"

"You are correct. We cannot, and will not, hold any secrets away from you." His father did not fail to notice the stress on the word secrets.

"Is it important or can it wait until later?" Jacob asked.

"If you have the time, it would be better discussed now."

Jacob eased his long frame into his favourite chair, making himself comfortable before saying, "I have the time. Go ahead."

Josh hesitated as Jacob waited. "Come on. Do not keep me in suspense any longer. I assume you have told Ruth." They were cool in their manner to each other but at least they were communicating.

"Yes, I have, and I hope you can take the news as well as her. I have joined the army, along with Barney and Pete."

Jacob's features paled. The sparkling eyes dulled and the lines on his tanned face appeared to deepen. Joshua hurried on. "I do not need to explain why I have to go. You should understand."

Jacob sat quietly for a few minutes and let the startling news sink in. And it was startling. Jacob realized Josh's world had crashed around him when learning that Freda was his half-sister but assumed he would eventually find someone else. This was not the case. He had misjudged the depth of feeling his son held for the girl. He studied Josh closely before saying, "I must ask if you have thought this through, Josh, and not just a hare-brained idea dreamt up on the spur of the moment after a few beers with your pals? Bravado and foolhardy talk of fighting for your country to return as all conquering heroes. Because if it is, that only happens in story books. Very rarely in real life."

"No, we have talked it through and I intend to make my own way in life. I have no reason to stay here. This place will die in a couple of years as trade and custom is moving fast to Castle Moor. And then what? Toby will easily manage my jobs and with Ruth working at the school, it just leaves me to find a job and it'll be one less mouth to feed."

Ruth had heard enough. Running over to Jacob she pleaded with him. "Tell him Jacob. You must tell him how dangerous this is. He will not return from the fighting. More and more are being killed and maimed. It's on everyone's lips, you read it in the papers every day. Violence is not the answer. You preach this every Sunday, Jacob. Please, make him see sense."

Jacob raised his gaze to this girl who had blossomed into a beautiful young woman and clearly thought the world of his son. She also understood the suffering that humans brought on each other. A victim of violence herself.

Jacob vividly remembered his own heartbreak when forced to part from family without their blessing. Well, at least Josh would leave on speaking terms with his father, which had seemed unlikely just a few days ago. This was a huge step into the unknown for Josh but knowing his families love and prayers were with him would mean a lot in the coming months.

"No." Jacob's voice was soft but firm. "I'm sorry Ruth. I cannot stand in Josh's way like my parents did with me." He raised himself from the chair and proffered his outstretched hand to Josh saying. "We will certainly miss you Josh but you will go with my blessing. All I ask is if you can keep in touch, then do so. I know it may not be possible depending upon where they post you. You will have much to learn and no doubt, training will come first, so I hope it will be quite some time before you see any action."

Deep in his heart, Jacob was pleased the barriers between his son and himself, due to his own foolishness, had been broken. He was proud that Josh was strong enough to take this step into the unknown.

Hesitantly Josh took the proffered hand. His father moved forward to hug him but Josh moved away. He was not ready to forgive that easily. Not yet. Instead, he held his arms out towards Ruth. "Please Ruth, if I can walk out of this door with your blessing also it will mean everything to me in the long days ahead as I will miss you and home."

Wiping her eyes dry, Ruth said. "You have my blessing, Josh. I'm being selfish, I suppose. I know I am going to miss you so much and I fear for your safety. If it is what you want to do, then like Jacob, I will pray for your safe return."

"When do you leave, Josh?" Jacob asked.

"Early next week. We'll be transported to Ripon for training first and then who knows? It could be months before we know anything."

"As Ruth says our prayers will be with you every step of the way. We do have a few days left before you go, so let's make the most of them."

Josh nodded curtly and retired to bed. Ruth sat with Jacob a few minutes, asking if he was okay with Josh's decision. "No," he replied. "Although I am happy that we are on speaking terms again. That is a start. Hopefully, forgiveness will come later."

Ruth kissed Jacob on the forehead and went to bed. Heavy of heart, she tossed and turned into the early hours before drifting off to sleep.

Chapter 33

Always an early riser, Ruth rubbed the sleep from her eyes and peered outside towards the distant gallows. She watched, fascinated for a few minutes, as the leaden sky grudgingly gave way to a strengthening sun trying desperately to break through the heavy clouds to lighten the drab landscape. Heavy overnight rain pooled in the potholed road but as the morning progressed, strong shafts of sunlight began to transform the lead grey rocks on the hillside into shimmering silver-black diamonds the length of the valley.

After washing and dressing, Ruth prepared breakfast. It was Saturday and with some free time, she could make the journey to Dan Parkes homestead. Spare time was a scarce commodity, what with work at Gallows Howe, Dan Parkes and her new job at the school. It left very little time to help Jim at Roston. Days were just not long enough at present.

Slinging a coat over her shoulders, she shouted across the yard to Jacob that she would be back for tea. She bridled a young cob in the stable and not bothering with a saddle, threw a blanket on his back and set off at a gallop along the narrow moorland track and headed for Dan's cottage.

These were her precious moments of freedom. She loved the thrill of the ride, the wind whipping through her hair and the sharpness of the morning making her feel more vibrant and alive than anything else in the world. How things had changed for her these last few years. Never in a million years could she have imagined the life she was experiencing now. Finally, she pulled the cob up outside the cottage, both of them breathing hard after such an exhilarating ride and just caught Dan leaving for work.

"Goodness me, what have you been doing all morning, Dan Parkes? Half the day gone already and not a thing done." Dan scowled at her. He didn't mean to. Deep down, he really thought he had half a chance with Ruth but mornings were not the best part of his day.

"Now don't start that. You know I can't stand your energy and sarcasm first thing on a morning. That's the last thing I want." He kissed her on the cheek all the same. "I'd rather that kiss be on your lips and not just on your cheek, Ruth Brennan." The scowl disappeared and he gave a sly wink with a mischievous glint in his eye.

"That will not be happening again, Mr Parkes," she said in a severe voice, but laughing. "I'm far too happy with life to mess it up by doing something silly."

"It wouldn't be silly for me. I couldn't think of anything better. But as I'm late, we'll talk about it another time mebbe, eh?"

"No, we will not. Let this be an end to it Dan and concentrate on your work."

"Time you lightened up, Ruth Brennan. You're becoming a right old schoolmarm since you started working with those kids in the village. Life 'll quickly pass you by if you aren't careful. I've seen many wizened old spinsters round about here," he waved his arms about dramatically before going on, "sitting in their rocking chairs, wiling away their time, just waiting for death. And all because they were not brave enough to take on young vibrant men like meself who lusted after them in their youth and would've treated 'em as if they were made of delicate china. Now, all they have are memories of what might have been. Just because they were never brave enough to grasp the nettle and show their true feelings."

Ruth scoffed. "Oh you're a right little philosopher this morning, Dan Parkes. I can't see you handling anything delicately. I also don't hear you mention the ones that did grasp the nettle and were badly stung." Ruth was indignant and with hands on hips, she carried on, "and if you're such a knowledge box on the opposite sex, how come I haven't seen any girls lining up on this doorstep to marry you. Pray tell me what experience have you to be preaching like this?"

"Huh, I have loads of experience. I just happen to be secretive about my love life. I can hardly wait to show you just how good I am. You will have no chance against my charms, Ruth Brennan. All you have to do is say the word."

"I suppose that little word would be yes, would it?" They both burst out laughing as he made a lunge for her. But Ruth was much quicker and dashed into the cottage.

Dan gave up and shouted after her. "Oh, by the way I haven't got tidied up this morning, Ruth. If you could do that and make me a couple of sandwiches for dinnertime that would be great. I have a meeting with the head keeper today."

Poking her head back out of the doorway she replied, "you see that's all men want us women for, to look after them and 'you know what else.' By the way," Ruth turned serious. "I have some grave news from Gallows Howe, Dan. Josh, Pete and Barney are all signing up to fight for their country. Had you heard?"

"No, I hadn't. But I'm not surprised. All three of 'em are searching for more than there is out here in the wilds. I'd even thought about it myself."

"Oh, come off it, Dan. Don't you clear off as well. You said yourself you love your job."

"That's true. It'd be a lot better if there was a bit more money though. But really Ruth, I'm a coward at heart. I think I'll mebbe stay here and look after all the lonely young women."

"Dan Parkes, can't you think of anything else but girls?"

Throwing his head back, he broke out laughing. "If the Lord made anything better, he kept it for himself. I'll tell you that for nothing. And with that little gem of knowledge from my good self, I shall love you and leave you until next week. Thanks for looking after things for me, Ruth." With a gun under his arm and spaniel by his side, he walked away, soon lost from her sight among the trees.

Ruth made Dan's sandwiches, covered them with a muslin cloth to keep them fresh, then tidied the kitchen.

"My goodness Dan Parkes, you certainly need a housekeeper to look after you," she whispered to herself. By the time she had everything in order, it was well turned dinnertime. Ruth just had time to check on the animals and give Dulcie, her favourite, a special hug. "I love you Dulcie but you know that, don't you?" The big horse nudged her hand for a special titbit which Ruth gave her.

Now she thought, a trickle of excitement running through her. I may just have time for a couple of hours with Jim.

Chapter 34

R uth entered the kitchen where an unusual silence reigned. Not a soul about but a fire smouldered in the grate. Ruth was surprised. She expected Martha to be in at least. Running across to the stable, she was about to check the horses when the faint rattle of cart wheels in the distance caught her ears. Her heart lifted as all three hove into view along the track, Jim driving with Martha and Albert alongside.

"Whoa, Pippen." Jim pulled the snowy white Galloway mare to a halt, immediately jumping off and lifting Martha to the ground. He swung her round as he did so as if she weighed nothing at all. Jim's laugh rang out and there was a flush to Martha's cheeks that Ruth had never witnessed before.

"Ruth, you'll never believe this," she said, her eyes sparkling. "We've just been to view the cottage we told you about in Roston, close to the church and shop. With mine work dwindling, families are moving on quicker than we thought. This one has just become empty and the couple will leave most of the furniture in. Just as it was when they moved in. That'll make it much easier for us. We know the owners and they are wanting a quick sale, if possible, so Albert thinks we should make an offer."

Jim gave Ruth a quick hug. He was not one to show emotion in front of other people, no matter how well he knew them, but the look that passed between them said more than any words.

"Oh, Mrs Styles that's great news but can you afford it?" Ruth asked. Albert came over and put his arm around her shoulders.

"Aye, we can afford it and if they do accept our offer, you two could soon be moving into your own little love nest. Your own home." Ruth studied Albert closely, only now realizing that the years of hard work, in all weathers had taken their toll. Always in good humour and forever working outdoors, Ruth had never thought of Albert as an old man. But she could see it now. The wrinkles, ploughed deep into weathered features, the greying hair, hidden under the ever-present cap, was thinning and his gait had slowed. Ruth was not even sure just how old he was, but knew from stories told that he must be well in his sixties. Jim spoke up, breaking Ruth's thoughts about Albert.

"Hey not so fast, Albert," eyes bright and dancing with laughter. "We have a lot to do before then. I mean, Ruth hasn't asked me to marry her yet. I might not accept. I have all the other girls in the valley to consider first."

"Oh, it must be something in the air this morning that's making men think we drool over them. I've just left Dan Parkes and he was full of himself. Just like you, Jim Styles. What makes you think I'll be doing the asking. Do not get too big for your boots with me or else I will have to bring you down a peg or two," wagging a finger in his direction as Martha did when she was annoyed.

Martha laughed at Ruth's accurate mimicry of her. "Come on you two, have some dinner with us and we can carry on the marriage debate. Maybe Ruth will propose this afternoon when on a full stomach." Enjoying the moment, they all wandered across to the farmhouse for dinner and a discussion on buying the cottage.

The purchasing of the cottage went through quickly as Albert predicted. Within the month the deeds were signed, sealed and completed. Martha and Albert didn't have too much furniture and belongings to pack but they were certainly kept busy for the next few weeks. Their soon-to-be-new-neighbours Robert and Esther Lawson, offered to help with removals when the time came. Robert and Esther were among the lucky few who could afford to retire early and wanted to enjoy the peace and tranquillity of the countryside, arriving just before the mining boom took hold.

Although comfortably off now, like most of the older generation who had witnessed the hard times, they had stayed quite strict and staid in their ways and were regular churchgoers. Not so their daughter, Nancy. Lively, rebellious Nancy. Approaching eighteen years old, Nancy believed she knew all there was to know about life, plus a little more. Full of confidence, especially in conversing with the opposite sex and always dressed in a slightly more provocative way than most girls her age. Having spied Jim in the village a couple of times, Nancy decided it would be a good idea to accompany her parents to help load the furniture. A good excuse for an introduction to Jim.

Come the day of the move, while the others carried the boxes out, Nancy stayed on the cart stacking everything safely for travelling. Taking the last box from Jim, she caught his eye as he wiped sweat from his brow. "More than you thought, was there?"

Jim, kept busy with the loading, rested his elbow on the side of the cart and glanced up at her. Then he looked closely, as Nancy knelt down so her face was almost level with his. The shock of shoulder length auburn hair shone like burnished copper, the strong sunlight highlighting it as it tumbled around her shoulders and the smouldering green eyes appeared to be asking a question that Jim had no idea how to answer. Embarrassed, he looked about him for a way of escape but none was forthcoming. Martha and friends were still talking in the farm house.

"Err, there was that. A lot more than I thought."

"There is quite a bit, but everything is packed safe and ready to travel."

"Hey, that was a big help for me, er... I'm sorry, I don't know your name." Jim hesitated, slightly tongue-tied in front of this beautiful girl. With her eyes fixed on him, he shot her a smile to hide his embarrassment.

"It's Nancy, Nancy Lawson. And you are Jim Styles. I've heard about you, Jim. A hero up at the mine by all accounts. I also heard about you standing up to the local bully boys as well."

Jim chuckled at this. "Ah, they didn't mean anything by it, just jumped to a conclusion, me bein' a city boy, like. But we parted friends."

Nancy was keen to talk, enjoying the chance of young male company. "Until now I'd only seen you when I was out walking. I'm pleased to say your much more handsome close up." Her lips curled into a flirtatious smile.

"I really am pleased to meet you, Jim." Nancy held a small, delicate hand out. Jim quickly swiped his down the side of his trousers and grasped it gently. A slight shiver of excitement swept through him, surprised that such an innocent form of greeting could cause such an effect. Sweat popped out on his brow again but now it was more from the warmth this young lady was generating.

Jim was saved from more embarrassment as they all emerged from the house. Martha couldn't believe the amount piled onto the carts, as she decided to leave as much as possible for Jim. It was only really the personal and sentimental pieces gathered over a lifetime together that Martha and Albert decided to take. Nancy jumped up on the first cart and scrunched tightly up against Jim on the front seat with Esther on the outside. Robert followed on horseback.

Martha, last to leave, locked the door for the final time on her and Albert's life for the last fifty years. As the carts trundled away, Martha couldn't resist a final look back and a few tears escaped to run down her cheeks. Sniffing, she grabbed a handkerchief and dried her eyes. Albert was there for her as ever, grasping her hand tightly for reassurance. "Now, don't you be getting upset, Martha or you'll have me crying. Let's not look on this as the end, let's see it as a new beginning. We've not lost the old farm, we'll still be able to come back as long as Jim's there. So come on love, cheer up. Things 'll be good, I promise you."

"Oh Albert, I'm not upset at leaving." Silence while she sniffed and rubbed her eyes again. "Well, just a little if I'm honest but I am excited as well. It's just I can't quite grasp how we've arrived at this stage of our life so quickly. It doesn't seem fair. I know we are moving to pastures new, and it will be a bit easier, but I will miss the old place."

"Aye, I know you will. Me too." He sniffed and turned away but not before Martha noticed the tell-tale crack of emotion in his voice. She knew full well that neither of them could just walk away from the home that had meant so much to them both without a few tears. So many memories. The good and the bad, the ups and downs that life throws at you along the way. It was bound to pull on the old heartstrings.

Once into the village, Jim pulled the horse to a halt under the bare, low spreading branches of the oak tree in the centre of the green close to the cottage. The Abbey Shop, directly on the left and the magnificent stone-built church stood high and proud on the right-hand side. He felt a touch of disappointment when the short journey ended. Nancy's closeness when she clutched onto him as they lurched along the rough stretches of road made him feel special. She was very attractive. Maybe slightly older than him. Definitely much more confident than he was and never appeared at a loss for words.

Jim studied the house. Steep slate roof, square frontage, four box windows and a central front door overlooking the green. Set back from the road, it allowed for a small garden at the front where Martha could add her own personal touch of colour in the summer months with flowers. The timber porch around the front door needed repair but Albert would sort that. If he could be persuaded to stay away from the farm. Jim smiled at the thought.

"Come on Jim, open up, I'm eager to see inside." He'd forgotten Nancy and her mother were standing waiting behind him.

"Sorry. Lovely place for 'em both, don't you think?" Fiddling the key into the lock, Jim opened up as the other cart drew up outside.

"I do that," said Esther. "We really are looking forward to having them as neighbours. It'll be nice to have a few more locals around the village. Don't get me wrong, the other people are nice enough, but many will be moving on again after a few years."

The front room was cosily furnished, curtains left in place, even a stack of logs by the black leaded fireplace. A small table and four chairs set at the foot of the steep staircase plus an empty bookcase placed underneath. Albert may just have to learn to read a little more if Martha fills that with books, Jim thought. On the left, a door leading through to the better end. Only sparsely furnished but the carpet added comfort to the room, along with two easy chairs either side of the fireplace.

With Esther and Nancy exploring upstairs and Martha organising, the men began to unload. Eventually, sweating and tired, everything was unloaded and Albert and Martha began to arrange things as they wanted, leaving Jim to make his way back to the farm.

Nancy came out to see him off. Head held on one side, that infectious smile flicking around the corners of her mouth once again. "You sure you're man enough to manage up there on your own, Jim Styles, or might you want some female company?"

"Oh, I'll be okay, Nancy. Ruth rides over from Gallows Howe every now and then, so I'll not be lonely." He felt slightly relieved that Nancy at least knew he had a girlfriend and she might just back off a little. "But if you're passing, call in." Jim was drawn into flirting back. He winked and beamed her a gap-toothed smile as she stood to wave him goodbye.

Chapter 35

J im couldn't resist a quick glance back over his shoulder as he turned the corner to face the climb home. Nancy had not moved and gave a final wave before disappearing into the house. The mare made easy work of the hill with the cart empty and he arrived back at a very different homestead now Albert and Martha had moved out. After a long tiring day and the sun dipping low in the sky, Jim unharnessed Pippen from the shafts and led her quietly into the stable. Albert arrived back with Farmer, so together they stabled the horses. Jim realized that Albert would need to return to Roston and help Martha put things straight in the cottage.

"You look a bit down in the dumps Jim. Anything bothering you?"

"Not really Albert…" he paused. "Well, yes there is something. I weren't going to mention it but I'm a bit worried, you know, about managing things. I know my writing is coming on a treat but there's a lot more that I'm going to struggle with." They stood between the two horses, stroking them. Albert put a reassuring hand on Jim's shoulder.

"D'you think I would have moved out of this farm if I didn't think you could cope with the spot. I would never have done that, Jim. You have a lot more going for you than you think. When I took over here after my father died, I had far less in my head than you have. Yes, I found it hard going but with help from friends and neighbours, Martha and I pulled through. In fact, that's how Martha and I met and this farm became our life. We would not be leaving it if we thought you weren't man enough to handle it."

Albert sat awhile, helping Jim through some of his worries before leaving for his new home at Roston. Jim stayed in the quiet of the stable with the two horses until the light began to fade. Rather than light a lantern, he wandered into the empty house. Immediately the claustrophobic silence closed in on him. He'd faced many hard times in his life, but he could not explain this feeling of suddenly losing something special. Emotions not felt since his orphanage days. If he could have explained his feelings to Albert, it would have helped but he possessed neither the courage or the words to express such intimate thoughts. He also realized Albert had enough on his plate at present and did not want to burden him with more.

Jim slumped into Albert's favourite chair by the fireside. It didn't feel right. He felt like an imposter, finally drawing another chair alongside. A weariness lodged in every bone in his body and Jim could not keep the tears at bay. Hanging his head, he wept. For how long, he knew not. The enormity of the task that lay ahead was just beginning to strike home and it numbed his brain.

How could he ever have harboured the thought of actually making a living here? There was a big difference between working on a farm and managing one. If it wasn't so serious, it would be laughable. A boy such as him, plucked from the back streets of a city by two strangers, Albert and Martha, who surely must have had their doubts, but for some reason, believed in him and gave him a chance. They showed him what love and caring was all about. And it was this love and belief bestowed upon him at the beginning that gave him the strength to see it through, whatever the outcome.

Jim began talking quietly to himself, trying to build a confidence that he didn't really believe in. 'Come on man, get a grip. You've endured much worse than this in your life.'

He had. He realized that but at this very moment the loneliness of his boyhood claimed him once more. His whole world had imploded. The two people who believed in him were moving on. His mind drifted back to when he arrived here with fast beating heart, unsure of what lay ahead. He vividly remembered a determination within him to find Ruth and create a better life for them both.

That seemed impossible but it happened. Was that determination or fate? Or was it just pure luck? He shook his head. Damn it, he didn't know. But now thoughts had turned to Ruth. God, how he missed her at this very moment. How he wished she was here by his side to talk things through. But even though Ruth was not with him, just the thought had lit a spark of certainty in him as he remembered her own desperate fight to break clear from the poverty and cruelty suffered in search of a better future. Surely, he should be man enough to step up to this challenge and be as strong as her.

At last, comforted by the thought that Albert would soon be about in a couple of days after settling in at Roston, his mood brightened. He smiled as he realized Albert and Martha might just possibly be experiencing similar feelings.

Darkness had clamped in totally but without bothering to light a lamp, he climbed the stairs. Strangely, he found the click of his bedside clock by the side of his bed quietly comforting.

Chapter 36

A lbert and Martha found their cottage just perfect. The shop was handy, the church just across the road and neighbours could pop in to see if their help was ever needed, or just for company.

The move hit Albert the hardest, finding a new routine difficult to adapt to and realized it could be quite a while before truly settling. The main furniture was in place but, in Albert's eyes, there appeared a tremendous amount of unpacking waiting.

Although missing Jim and the farm, he was definitely not missing the hard, manual work. Those days were over but he was looking forward to going back and helping out.

As always, Martha read his thoughts and came through from the kitchen with a cloth covering a tray of freshly baked bread. "Thought it time you had a look up to see Jim today, Albert. I put these in the oven for him. He'll think we've forsaken him, poor lad."

"No, he knows we've had a lot on our plate recently but you must have read my mind, Martha. I was just thinking of having a ride up next job."

Albert sauntered over to the small garth at the rear of the house, gave a click of the tongue and the young chestnut mare immediately raised her head and trotted over." Come on, Honey." He smiled, brushing her muzzle. "Let's get you some exercise, eh?" Honey was a beautiful, nice natured pony owned by a young girl in the village with no land or facilities to keep it. As

Albert had the field and a makeshift stable already in the corner, this worked well, Albert riding Honey when the girl was at school.

Eager to be off, he tacked up and eased the horse into a trot. The dull damp mist clung to his face and clothes as he headed towards the expanse cleared of trees. Now it was bare and with just a steady rise towards the encroaching moor above the farm house, it could easily be worked. A tremendous amount of hard physical labour had gone into the clearing but would prove well worth the effort.

Breaking clear from the clinging dampness, Albert drew Honey to a halt and turned in the saddle to gaze down into the valley and beyond. He never tired of the natural beauty of the area. Surveying Roston from above as he had done many times over his life, it appeared as if he had just ridden through, and emerged, from the clutches of a huge grey lake, the base of the valley still shrouded in a sea of mist. Just the occasional roof top showing through, or the odd chimney spiking up through the greyness, spiralling smoke into the dull sky.

Continuing his journey, Albert called at the house first. He popped the baking in through the front door, before carrying on to the top fields surrounding the farm. He guessed Jim would be busy dry walling around the recently cleared land to keep sheep out and halt the ever-encroaching bracken, now a russet brown, from clawing the land back. On arrival, Albert was surprised to see Jim had company.

"Morning, Jim. Morning, Nancy." Albert greeted both cheerfully, then turned his attention to the ongoing barrier. "Jim, you must have had a very good teacher. It's looking good." Still mounted, Albert said, "you've got on well without me, I see." He sounded slightly disheartened and admiring at the same time.

Jim gave a gap-toothed smile and said, "No, you've been greatly missed, Albert. This job is harder than it looks." Jim stepped back to study his own efforts.

"No, it is coming on well, Jim. At this rate and with a bit of help, it'll soon be done." Not wanting to close Nancy out of the conversation, Albert dismounted and turned his attention to her. Nancy, a black cape covering her shoulders was displaying the usual shock of auburn hair. "I must thank you again, Nancy, for your help when we moved. We would not have got on as well without you." Nancy came alongside to stroke the horse's neck. "Oh, that's okay Albert, it gave me something to do. Life gets a bit boring up here. It's not like there's much nightlife? Well, not much life at all when you think about it, is there?" This said with a grin.

"No, you've come to the wrong place for that. It's a bit steadier pace out here, I'm afraid," he said lightly. "In fact, I'm surprised to see you out and about on a poor morning like this, Nancy." Honey continued grazing contentedly.

"Well, I happened to be at a loose end today so I thought a breath of fresh air and a good walk would do me good. Also, I thought Jim might need some help, but I can see this is not a job for me." Brightening, Nancy said, "but as it's nearly dinnertime, I can go and make a sandwich or two for you both. I know where to find things. I was up the other day."

Jim kept his head down but Albert answered showing no concern that Nancy knew her way about, or that she was a regular visitor.

"That would be good, Nancy. I've just dropped some fresh baked bread through the door, you'll find it easy enough. We'll be there in about an hour. That okay with you, Jim?"

"'Course it is," Jim replied, as Nancy made her way across to the farm.

When Nancy was out of earshot, Albert said, "By God, I've missed the farm this last week, Jim. Didn't realize it would bother me so much. Also, I didn't want you to think I'd left you high and dry but there was a lot to do and I couldn't leave it all to Martha. Anyway, we're nearly put square now, ready for a bit easier winter."

After a short silence, he caught Jim's eye as they sorted the stone. "I thought you might be missing company up here on your own but I can see there's no need to worry on that score."

Jim knew very well what he was getting at. "Oh, Nancy, you mean. Nah, like she said, she's a bit bored. It's just somewhere to come and get her out of the house, see if I was managing okay."

"An attractive girl, isn't she?"

"Yeh, suppose she is. I hadn't noticed really," he said, bending to dress another stone to fit.

Albert laughed but his voice was stern. "Don't you try and tell me you haven't noticed, Jim. A man would have to be blind not to notice the come on she's giving you. All I'm saying is watch your step. You have a young girl at Gallows Howe who worships the ground you walk on. Do not go breaking her heart, Jim Styles."

Jim straightened. "It's not like that Albert, honest. It's ... well, she does come on a bit strong sometimes and I still remember how it feels to be rejected. I would never like to think I acted like that to anyone. I also can't stop her coming up here if she wants to."

Albert became serious. "I'm not wanting you to stop her coming to see you Jim, or to control your life. All I'm saying is do not play Ruth for a fool. She has suffered enough hurt."

"I wouldn't do that Albert and you know it."

"No, well as long as you understand how things are, that's settled then." Albert put a protective arm around the young man's shoulder, adding, "Come on, let's go and have a bite of dinner then, eh? It does feel good to be out of the house and doing something useful. Also, I have to admit, we both miss your company."

"Mmm, well, there isn't much activity up here either without you two." He grinned as he said it. "Strange thing is, when I first entered Honey Bee after you and Martha left, it's hard to explain but I felt as if my whole world had collapsed. While you were here, I had security for the first time in my entire life, but the instant you left, it felt as if I had lost everything. I wasn't sure I could carry on. After a couple of days, I got my head around things and realized once you're sorted down in Roston and can come and help out when you can, it'll be like old times."

At that very moment, a watery sun broke through the heavy cloud, shining full onto the old farm house as if to welcome them home.

Chapter 37

Castle Moor lay shrouded under a dull grey dawn as Toby swung his legs out of bed, splashed water quickly over his face and slipped into his work clothes. He had a busy morning ahead of him so a good start was essential. Running downstairs, he greeted his mother who already had the table laid for breakfast.

"Morning mam. Thanks for that. I'm in a bit of a rush. Have to be at Jacob's to get a couple o' horses ready to go out mid-morning. They asked me yesterday. I know the horses they're replacing. One's far too old for work really and the other's gone down lame."

His mother watched Toby wolfing his breakfast down. Since leaving school six month ago, she'd never seen him so happy. Although trade was slowing at Jacob's recently, Toby was finding plenty of work and hadn't a minute to spare. The war had taken many able young men away from the dales and they were gone and fighting for their country. She sighed in resigned fashion, glad that Toby had no inclination to lie about his age and go off to fight. She hoped it would all soon be over and the men return unharmed. Deep down though, she knew that was wishful thinking.

She replied, "Aye, a lot o' people are having to mek do with what they've got at present, son. Oh, by the way, don't forget, your father could do with a bit of help this afternoon if you have time."

"No, I haven't forgotten, Ma. I'll be back just after dinner all being well."

Grabbing his jacket off the peg by the back door and lacing his boots, he stepped out into a brightening morning and made his way to the stables at Gallows Howe.

Toby was a strong believer in a good start to the day, especially on a chilly morning. He swung the stable doors open and was hit by the warmth and sweet smell permeating through the building as he entered. He never felt more at home than when taking responsibility for the animals in his care. He loved them, every one of them but one stood out above all others. Pal was his favourite and he moved to him first. Leaning on its hindquarters, the horse moved over allowing him to squeeze to the front of the narrow wood stall.

"Morning Pal," he said with a grin. "Come on, move over. Help me a bit, I've come to tidy you up." Toby put his arm around the horse's neck and Pal responded by nuzzling closer to the boy. Toby continued talking as if to a friend. Well, he was a friend. Toby was there in the field when Pal first saw the light of day. He remembered it well. As Josh was busy he had asked Toby to keep a close eye on the mare as she was close to foaling. While repairing the fence, he spotted the mare sidle off to the far corner of the field and lie down beneath the cover of trees.

A few minutes passed and Toby realized she was in trouble. The pains were there but as far as he could tell, nothing was happening. Not knowing what to do, he dashed toward the houses for help where Josh heard his frantic shouting and ran back to the field with him. Toby remembered being near to tears. "What's wrong, Josh? Is she going to die?"

Josh, with more experience, took a quick look and soon became aware of the problem. "No, she'll not die, Toby. The foal has a foot back that's all. Run and fetch me some soap and water."

Toby returned out of breath and Josh lathered the soap and water up to his elbow, dropped to his knees and reached inside the mare. "You stay by her head and keep her quiet, while I get this leg in the right place." Toby did as he was bid and gently stroked the mare's neck. Suddenly a loud whinny from the horse and the foal slipped out with a bit of help from Josh. By this time Len Bailes, a retired farmer living in Castle Moor, had arrived and helped drag the foal close to the mother so she could lick him clean. The first birth Toby had ever witnessed and he'd watched in amazement. Within minutes, the new born foal had tried to stand on spindly stork-like legs that were too weak to support its body. To their amusement, it stumbled, lost balance and fell but in just a short time was prancing proudly around.

Toby and the foal became firm friends and he christened him Pal. But at just over six months old a serious attack of colic saw Pal fighting for his life. Jacob could do no more and brought the local vet in to help but after administering treatment he sadly shook his head. "I'm sorry, Toby there is nothing more I can do. Nothing more anyone can do. I'm afraid he's a goner."

Toby tried valiantly to stop the tears but was unsuccessful. Broken-hearted, he remembered saying, "Then I'll stay with him. I'll not leave him to die alone. I'll be here for him when he goes."

The vet tried to save him the suffering of watching an animal die and said, "It will break your heart, Toby. I advise you go home and let nature take its course. I'll be back first thing tomorrow morning."

Toby hadn't listened and stayed by Pal's side through the long, lonely night when everyone else had given up. When the pain was too much to bear, he placed blankets on Pal's stomach and held his head, talking all the while.

"Come on, Pal, I think you are strong enough to beat this. I'll stay with you. I'll help you every step of the way. We'll get through this, you and me. I'll never leave you." Eventually as the horse appeared to become more settled, he'd fallen into a troubled sleep, an arm draped around the animal's neck. Next morning as the sun filtered through the dusty old window, he'd felt something nuzzle close, trying to push him over onto his back.

With bleary eyes, Toby stared upward into the steady gaze of the young horse now on his feet. He continued to push Toby, then threw his head back and whinnied in triumph.

Toby had jumped up and shouted. "Pal, you've done it. You've done it. I knew you would. I just knew you could do it." Overwhelmed by the moment, tears of joy ran down his face and he hugged the animal's neck as enormous relief flooded through his body.

All the commotion had brought Ruth and Josh running to the stable. They couldn't believe Pal had made it through the night. Ruth had grabbed hold of Toby and danced around the stable before collapsing in a heap of straw. Josh had stood with Pal, who held his head on one side wondering what all the fuss was about.

Eventually, Ruth came to her senses. "Toby, I can't believe it. You stayed the night with him and pulled him through against all the odds. I always knew you would be something special where animals were concerned but I didn't ever think that this would happen."

"I'm just so happy, Ruth. To think, last night he could have been a goner and now he's back with me."

"I don't know how you did it, Toby. When Jacob told me that Pal would be dead by morning, I just cried for the both of you. Now look at him strutting around the stable."

This all seemed a lifetime ago and these memories still ran through Toby's mind as he continued brushing and admiring the smooth black sheen of the horse's coat, only one distinctive broken flash of white just above the right eye. Pal really was in tip top condition even if he said so himself.

The stable door swung open and Len entered. Len often wandered up from Castle Moor to help out with odd jobs. It got him out of the house and from under his wife's feet for a few hours. Len couldn't manage a full day's work now but he still enjoyed catching up with the younger company.

"Morning Len, glad you've come. If you have time, I could do with a hand getting those other two horses ready for Jacob's customers."

"Glad to, Toby. You must have had a good start this morning. Missus says she watched you go past while I was still having me breakfast."

"Ah, you must be getting old," Toby said with a grin.

"Yer getting to be a cheeky young pup, Toby Smith," Len said, smiling. He picked up a brush and set about grooming the other two horses. They worked quietly away, happy in each other's company, until Len tiring slightly, slipped outside for a rest.

Settling on the low wall under the low branches of the old oak tree, Len glanced up as the sound of hooves announced the arrival of fresh customers.

Or so he thought. Toby had also heard their arrival and squinting through the slightly open stable door, he was surprised to see two smartly dressed army officers. They dismounted and led their horses over to the watering trough for a drink. The shorter one, a rotund, ruddy faced man with bristling moustache and a uniform that appeared a size too small, strutted towards Len. He nodded a greeting and seemed like a man used to giving orders. "Good morning to you, sir. Can I ask who is in charge of the stables here?"

Len cast him an inquisitive glance from underneath his battered old trilby. "You can that. Who is it that wants to know, like?" he inquired cautiously. The man held out a pudgy right hand. "Major Barratt, Lord Kitchener's Army and this is Sergeant Cooper. We are here on business, as we are desperate to find more horses for the front lines." Len scowled but shook the proffered hand and answered the man.

"Aye well, the fella you want to see 'll be over at his church, the Reverend Jacob Thrall. It's just a short walk past the gallows there." He pointed into the distance.

"Thank you very much. Now, could you tell me if there is anyone who could see our horses are fed and watered? And if there was a sandwich to be had that would be very welcome before we take our leave? We would pay of course."

Toby, listening keenly behind the half-closed door, emerged from the stable shoving his cap back on his head. "Aye, I can see to 'em until you're ready to go. But we don't keep any of our own. We just stable horses here for customers." Len shot him a quick glance, but the major didn't appear to notice. "If Ruth's about," he nodded in the general direction, "she'll make sure you're well looked after and won't overcharge either."

"Thank you, young man. Right sergeant, we'll go see the man in charge and have a word with him." And they strode across to the old church to catch Jacob.

Once out of earshot and as Toby led the horses into the stable, Len said "What are you up to young 'un? Don't think o' crossing swords with these fellas, they'll cut you to ribbons."

Toby threw a furious glance in Len's direction and hissed, "You know why they're here Len, they've come to take our horses for the war effort. Well, they're not taking my pony. I've raised him from a foal, was there when he was born, helped clean him up, get him up and on his feet. Stayed through the night with him when at death's door. Broke him in, taught him obedience and everything over the years. He's come through well. Look at him now. He's not going into any damned war to be shot to pieces and die among the mud and violence and everything else war brings. Just because some high falluting men can't agree. Not for those two chaps, Lord Kitchener, or anyone else who happens to come calling."

Len was adamant. "Don't be a fool, Toby. They'll have the law on their side. You can't fight 'em, they'll tek him whatever you say or do."

Toby placed the nosebags on the officer's horses and quickly threw a blanket over the shining black coat of Pal. Toby turned to Len and said, "they'll not take him if they can't find him, Len. When they come back, promise you'll tell 'em nothing. Nothing at all, you hear me."

Unbolting the back door of the building, he led Pal out and down the rough moorland path to the base of the valley. Once out of sight, he quickly mounted and rode like the wind along a little-known winding track that followed the river before branching off for Dan Parkes cottage.

He arrived at the cottage and finding the stable empty, realized Dan must be out on the moor with Dulcie. My luck's in thought Toby, leading Pal into the stable. He tried the door to the cottage. It was open and no one about. Above the fireplace, Dan's gun hung temptingly and Toby knew the cartridges were kept in the side cupboard. Just in case they find me, he thought. I'll not let 'em take you without a fight, Pal. We'll see how brave they are, he muttered to himself and returned to the stable where he settled himself down until Dan returned.

Ruth welcomed her two visitors and seated them around the kitchen table with a plate of sandwiches. When Jacob entered, he introduced himself. "Good afternoon gentlemen. I didn't know we had visitors. I am pleased you have been made welcome. Can I be of any help?"

The major rose from his chair to shake Jacob's hand. "Very pleased to meet you Reverend Thrall. Yes, you most certainly can." Seating himself, he went on. Full of his own importance, Ruth thought as she listened from a distance.

"As you will understand, we are here on army business, Reverend. It is a very difficult job we have on our hands and that is to commandeer every horse we can from wherever we can. Of course, a generous payment will be paid for your horses as the army need more and more at the front every day. If we are to defeat the enemy, we must keep pace with the artillery and force the Germans to retreat. Our attacks must not falter." Stopping for breath, plus another bite at his sandwich, he added, "as you will know, thousands of men and animals are being killed or injured every day. We need a ready supply of men, horses and ammunition to keep the pressure on." He spoke as though they were all dispensable. Ruth, knowing Josh was among these fighting men, shuddered and walked through to the kitchen, unwilling to hear any more.

Jacob rubbed his chin, his mind also on Josh. He recalled the last letter received from him, written in a trench, unsure when the command would be given to go over the top. That was over six months ago. Nothing since then. Jacob brought his wandering thoughts back to the present.

"I understand your concern Major Barratt, but the only horses we have are the ones we use on the farm and sometimes hire out. It is our only income, the only way we have of surviving. Without the horses, we cannot make a living."

"I'm terribly sorry reverend but we must do our job and they either go with your consent or they are taken without it. How many are in the stable?"

"Four altogether but one belongs to young Toby, the farrier's son."

"Ah, he would be the one that told us they were all just customer's horses."

"Is that what he told you? Well, he is young and loves animals, so I can understand why, major."

"Right, pay the young lady, Cooper and then we'll check the stable." The major strode out, leading the way to the building. Len was busy taking the nosebags away when they entered.

"I thought you said there were four, reverend?"

"There usually is. Has Toby ridden home, Len?"

"Er, he didn't say, Jacob. Just said he had to see someone."

Jacob stared hard at Len. "Did he go on Pal?"

"I don't know, I was busy outside."

Jacob could see Len was lying and knew Toby was going to be in deep trouble when they caught up with him, which they would surely do. The major spoke first, his voice questioning.

"You know where he's gone, reverend?"

"I'm not sure, major. I know he thinks the world of Pal, having grown up with him."

"Well, there is no room for sentiment in this job." The major puffed his chest out even more. We need to know his and the horse's whereabouts, or there is serious trouble ahead for someone."

"I'll get my coat. Len, if you could get the trap out, I will try and find him." Jacob appeared weary. The war was affecting everyone. He prayed for every man fighting this useless bloody war, for all their families and particularly for Josh, to come through unscathed. By the time Jacob had his coat on, the trap was harnessed and ready to go.

"Thank you, Len."

"Where are you goin' first Jacob?" Len asked.

"I'll try home first. That's the most likely. I suppose he could have ridden to Jim's at Roston, but I will call in at Dan Parkes' cottage on the way."

Len looked worried as he answered. "Good luck, Jacob and if you do find him tell him not to do owt silly."

"I will. Follow me, major." Jacob whipped the horse forward across the moor. After an unsuccessful call at Toby's parents, he headed for Dan's cottage. An uneasy feeling that trouble was forthcoming had lodged itself in the pit of his stomach.

Toby's ears picked up at the sound of the trap wheels approaching down the track. He stayed crouched in the darkness of the inner building. Listening intently, voices reached his ears. He recognized Jacob's instantly. Toby waited nervously in the dark, he could hear muttering, then a loud knock on the cottage door. Silence. After a while Jacob's voice carried to him. "Toby, are you in there?" Then Jacob asking again, nearer this time. "Toby, answer me please, are you in the stable?"

Toby slowly pushed open the top door and peered out from the darkness of the building. "I am, Jacob and if those two men think they are taking Pal, then they better think again. You had no right bringing 'em here."

The major took charge, pushed Jacob aside and strode towards the stable. "Don't be like that, sonny. We have come to take the horse, that is all."

Toby then pushed the bottom door wide open, revealing the double-barrelled gun in his hand. "No, that isn't all, mister whoever you are. Pal is not going anywhere." The young boy's voice was cold, steady and, more importantly, controlled. No emotion. Major Barratt stopped dead in his tracks, losing some of his earlier bluster, his ruddy complexion grew pale. Not used to being addressed in such a manner, the shock showed on his face.

"Now, er, look here," he stammered, "let's not do anything silly. All we want is the horse. We'll pay well for him and let that be a finish to these heroics and I can assure you there will be no more said about this episode."

"You can talk all you like. I've told you once, Pal's not going anywhere."

The major took another step forward, calling the young man's bluff. Toby brought the gun up to his shoulder, hammers fully cocked and ready to fire. Major Barrett stopped abruptly as he stared into the steely grey double gun barrels aimed directly at his head. Sweat popped out on his brow, uncertainty and fear creeping in, unsure on how serious Toby was. His sergeant felt the same uncertainty, using the horses as an excuse to stay well out of harm's way.

Jacob tried next, talking quietly. "I understand how you feel, Toby. I know how you have cared for Pal from birth but please listen to me. We do not want any more tragedies. This war is causing enough heartache as it is. There will be no trouble if we just let them do their job and ride away."

Suddenly a clatter of hooves sounded from the rough track and Ruth galloped into view. She quickly dismounted and went straight to Jacob.

"Len told me what was happening. Can I help?"

"No, you can't help, Ruth" Toby shouted. "Stay out of the way."

She turned slowly to Toby, indignation showing on her face. "What did you say, young man? You think you can order me about, Toby Smith? What makes you think that? Just because you've got a gun in your hand." She straightened up and pushed her chin out in a defiant gesture. "Now you listen to me Toby and you better be reasonable. You want Josh to return don't you?" No answer from Toby. Ruth carried on. "Then we all have to do our bit and help where we can." Ruth was speaking from the heart now and started towards him. The gun never wavered, tight to his shoulder. "Don't do this Ruth. Don't be foolish." His voice had turned harsh.

"This isn't foolish, Toby. It makes sense. I know you think the world of Pal. He's your best friend and everyone needs a friend at some point in their lives. Jim was my best friend in my hour of need and he got me through. Pal has seen you through some difficult times. Now it is your turn to do your bit." She held her hand out toward him as she slowly walked forward but he still held the gun steady on his shoulder.

"Back off Ruth, back off, I don't want to shoot you." Remaining calm and unflinching, she continued to stare him down. "Back off," he yelled. "BACK OFF NOW!" his voice brutal in its ferocity. Ruth was only a yard away from the barrels of the gun, eyes still locked on Toby for what seemed an eternity. The gun began to tremble in his hands, the tension finally breaking Toby's nerve and he slowly lowered the gun, then fell sobbing into her outstretched arms.

Heart thumping like a hammer she tried to appear calm, taking the gun from his grasp and handing it behind her to Jacob.

"Come on, Toby, let's go inside. Let the men do their job and we'll talk it over." Placing her arm around his waist, he draped his arm over her shoulders for support as she led him inside so he would not see them lead Pal away. Sitting him down, she noticed his tear-stained face, drawn and pale, his body trembling. Toby looked at Ruth, eyes sad with the loss of his beloved Pal. He took a deep breath, trying to compose himself. "You shouldn't have come, Ruth. You took a big gamble out there with me, you know. How could you be so certain I wouldn't shoot you?" They both turned as Jacob entered the room.

"That's a very good question, Toby. That was absolute stupidity, Ruth."

This was the first time Ruth had seen Jacob really angry, his face as white as his flowing locks. He carried on. "Very brave but stupid all the same. I was so frightened I did begin to pray."

"It wasn't really brave, Jacob," Ruth said in a quiet voice, "or stupid either. I knew Toby wouldn't shoot me." They both looked questioningly at her.

"How could you be so sure?" Jacob asked.

"Well, both of you know I hate violence of any sort and when I spent time here with Dan he used to talk about his job and guns in particular. I recognised the hammer gun from above the mantelpiece straight away." She nodded over to the empty brackets. "I told Dan that shooting or killing did not solve anything. This is when he told me this particular gun was once his father's, who was also a gamekeeper. He gave it to Dan as a young boy telling him, 'hang onto this gun as one day it will be worth a lot of money. It is one of the finest guns ever made.' That's why it is kept in pride of place above the fire."

"That's all very well, but it doesn't answer my question, young lady."

Ruth could see the colour returning to Toby's cheeks and Jacob was recovering from the shock. His anger was subsiding, so she added, "well, I also said I was surprised a father would give such a dangerous weapon to one so young. And that is when Dan showed me what his father had done."

"And what was that, pray tell?" Jacob enquired mystified.

"He showed me how it worked and that the firing pins had been removed. It could never fire again unless new pins were made. So, you see, I wasn't really brave or stupid. I was just trying to save Toby from going to gaol. Do you forgive me, Toby?"

A moment's silence. "Eventually I will. Given time." He came across and hugged her.

Chapter 38

Nancy was annoyed at the timing of Albert's arrival just when she was making progress with Jim. She tried not to show her anger but quickly made her excuse to wander home once the men returned to work. Albert managed another couple of hours before reluctantly admitting that he'd had enough for the day and, if Jim didn't mind, he would leave him to it.

Jim had kept a watchful eye on the older man, noting his strength wavering, weariness setting in. No wonder. It really was back breaking work and rough on the hands, even for Jim. But as he stood back and admired the work, a feeling of self-satisfaction flowed through him at what he had achieved.

Now alone and with just his thoughts for company, his mind turned to Nancy, recalling Albert's words. Did he find her attractive? Course he did. Who wouldn't? She stirred emotions that excited him but, in truth, also made him nervous. She was up front, flirty, turning him into a flummoxed tongue-tied schoolboy in her company.

Checking the pocket watch, a cherished gift from Albert when he first arrived at the farm, Jim headed homeward and was just in time to catch Ruth dismounting. God, he was pleased to see her. At that moment it was as if a warm comforting hand reached out to grasp his heart.

He knew full well her commitments. Keeping house and horses right for Jacob at Gallows Howe; the same at Dan Parkes cottage; and now the good news that Castle Moor Primary School headmaster, Charles Haigh had asked her personally to help a little more with the children. This left little time for him and the farm but the money earned was being put aside for their future together.

She ran towards him, arms outstretched. God, I am a lucky man he thought, as he gathered her slim, supple body up in a bear hug and planted a kiss passionately on her lips before reluctantly setting her down.

"Does that show I've missed you, Ruth Brennan?" Jim's eyes just sparkled at the mere sight of her. In reply, Ruth wrapped her arms around his neck again demanding another kiss.

Finally parting, she said, "I've missed you too, Jim Styles. It seems ages since I was last here. Such big changes with Albert and Martha moving out but you must be managing okay. I have a couple of hours before I need to be back. I can go see to the horses if you like while you feed up, then I'll go do tea."

As she was about to dash away, he grabbed her hand. "I have a better idea, Ruth." Jim began to colour up but bravely carried on. "We're all alone up here now. Nobody to bother us. Why don't we, you know, go and try the bed out. It's big enough for the two of us."

Ruth pretended to look shocked. "Jim Styles, that's a very forward thing to say to an innocent young girl. I'm surprised at you thinking I would just jump into bed with you like that." She began to laugh as Jim became more and more flustered.

"Well I just thought it might...er, be a good chance to do it."

"Do what, Jim?" she said frowning as if she didn't understand what he meant, before she burst out laughing and hugged him close.

"You're making fun of me now, aren't you?" he said sullenly, his confidence blown to pieces.

As she hugged him, she whispered in his ear, "I think of making love to you every waking day Jim. Every time I see you, or know I am coming to see you. I want you so bad it hurts."

Jim's face brightened. "Well, come on, what are we waiting for. To hell with work. I'd rather be with you."

"But don't you see, Jim?" She looked deep into his dark eyes, "it is not the right time yet. We need a little more time, to be more independent, more experience of life and know that we will be right for each other."

"That could take ages." Despondently, Jim let go of Ruth's hand.

"Look at it this way, Jim. The good things in life are always worth waiting for." With a twinkle in her eye, she ran off to see to the horses.

Jim sighed knowing he had lost the argument and replied, "I s'pose so," to the disappearing figure of Ruth as she coaxed a couple of the horses into the stable.

Jim didn't mean to sound ungrateful. He was pleased with the extra help from Ruth but sometimes he needed more than her help. He realized just how much he yearned for her. Was he being impatient? There must be more to life than work.

Ruth returned to the farmhouse and on entering the still sparsely furnished kitchen, instantly noticed the sweet aroma of a woman's perfume hanging in the air, even before noting the fresh baked bread and uneaten sandwiches on the table. A knot tightened in her gut which made her feel sick. That awful gut-wrenching fear of rejection resurfacing.

Just then Jim walked in, his earlier mood of dismay gone. "You'll see Albert's been up today. Rode up this morning to help out and seeing Martha had done some baking, he brought some up so I didn't starve. It'll make an easy tea for us, don't you think?"

No response from Ruth. He turned to see an icy stare from the usually loving blue eyes.

Finally, Ruth spoke. "Since when has Albert Styles started using perfume, Jim?" Although intended to be humorous, it came out startlingly serious.

Jim sniffed the air, as if noticing it for the first time. "Ah well, that would be Nancy. You see, she happened to be out for a walk and dropped in to see if I was managing okay." He smiled, trying to break the uncomfortable atmosphere which had suddenly developed. "You know what women are like? Think us men can't manage on our own." He gave a nervous laugh and the gap tooth smile that usually did the trick. But not this time.

Haughtily, Ruth turned to the boiling kettle as if it was no concern of hers on who had called. She made the tea and placed it on the table. Eventually Jim could take the cold shoulder no longer and broke the silence.

"Aw, come on, Ruth. Nancy was only being friendly and called to see if I was okay. She was also a big help when Albert moved." More silence. "You wouldn't like rejection, would you?" Still Ruth was not forthcoming. Jim tried another ploy. "Anyway, what's so different between Nancy calling here to help out and you going to look after Dan at his cottage, eh? Are you just a little bit jealous, cos there is no need to be, you know?"

Ruth scowled. "Definitely not." But he knew he'd hit a nerve. Rising from the chair, Jim lifted her toward him. "Don't let's argue, Ruth. Time's precious for us, so let's not spoil it by arguing."

Tears pricked her eyes as he held her. "I'm sorry, Jim. Yes, I admit, I do feel jealous. A block of stone settled right here." Ruth held her heart. "That and the belief that you might possibly find someone else. I couldn't bear it if I lost you again. I never want to return to those times. Are you really telling me the truth? I want to believe you. Honestly, I do."

"You can believe me, Ruth. I've realized since I came to live here that there has to be trust in any relationship. Albert and Martha have taught me that." Jim held her tight, trying to reassure her that his love for her was strong.

"Am I forgiven?" she asked.

Jim kissed her again. "Just this once. As long as…" he paused, got to his feet then dropped to one knee, taking her hand gently in his. "As long as you promise to marry me."

Ruth's mouth fell open in shock. A moment's silence before she said, "You are serious aren't you? This isn't a joke, is it?"

"No, I've never been more serious in my life, Ruth. You mean more to me than anyone in this whole world. We can make a go of it, you and I. The farm, although small, is making a good living due to the mine and the war at present. And with your wage, I think we can scrape by quite well. What do you say?" The gap tooth smile flashed across his face.

"How could I resist a proposal like that. Yes, I'll marry you, Jim Styles. Yes, yes and yes!" Jim gathered her in his arms and swung her round the kitchen until they were both dizzy and collapsed back on the sofa, laughing.

"You have made me so happy, Jim. When do you think we should tie the knot?"

"As soon as possible. We have a ready-made home. The only thing is you would have more riding to do to get to work."

"But I already ride up here to see you and help out. It won't be a lot different. Oh, Jim, we have so many plans to make now."

Then Ruth's face turned serious. "There is one thing though, Jim. I would like to wait until Josh returns from the fighting. Or," she hesitated, serious, "we hear otherwise." She could not bring herself to utter the dreaded words, lost in action.

Ruth went on to tell how the army had called and requisitioned a couple of horses from Gallows Howe. One of them Toby's favourite, Pal.

"Hell, he'll be heartbroken, is he? He thinks the world of that horse."

"So heartbroken I thought it was going to end in a shooting." She did not tell him it was her who faced the gun.

"Wow, you get all the excitement at that place. There's nothing happens up here apart from hard work." After catching up on news and gossip Ruth was back to her earlier happy self and finally extricating herself from Jim's exploring hands she placed a farewell kiss on his lips, before setting out for her ride home.

Chapter 39

The familiar surroundings of Gallows Howe felt a million miles away for Joshua Thrall, as he sat hunched in a foetal position at the base of the trench. Once again, he would face the enemy in another crucial battle of this never-ending war. White knuckled hands clutched the butt of his rifle, like a small child clasping a comfort blanket for security. The mud and slime had risen far above the duck boards at the base of the trench, almost up to his knees now and was continuing to rise with the constant, persistent rain. Would it ever stop? The cold, sodden conditions had sucked the last vestige of feeling from his feet. He was afraid to remove his boots to inspect. The last time he peeled away the sodden material that were once socks, patchy black skin was creeping up to affect his lower limbs and his toenails lifted clear of the flesh with the material. Trench foot. Maybe? He'd seen many others suffering the same.

The cold continued to penetrate every pore of his body. So much so that he experienced no pain, just a numbness in every limb. God knows how he would bring himself to move when the time came.

The violent crash and whine of the British bombardment hammering the German front line, rang incessantly through his head. The Germans retaliated with their own heavy guns, shuddering the ground and showering clods of earth and rubble around them. How much longer before they hear the shrill blast of the whistle to send them over the top? Please God, make it soon. He knew full well what awaited. Had already pictured it many times in his mind's eye, blundering over unknown territory, across no man's land towards an early death. But surely that would be a blessing rather than dying like a rat, buried underground. These horrendous conditions were taking their toll as much as the fighting.

His close friend, Pete Eccles had taken a shot to the stomach months before and Josh was sure the incessant bombing had affected his mind. Josh could only watch as the stretcher bearers carried him away, uncertain of his survival. Trying to be optimistic, maybe Pete had already been shipped back home to convalesce. Josh prayed that was the case. Barney Stopes was still here with him though, somewhere along this twisting, wretched dug out, which Josh realized could be their final resting place.

The repetitive crunch of bombs continued to obliterate everything else, to hammer at his brain, as if battering him into submission. He cocooned himself in his own little world. The putrid smell of rotting horse carcasses, bodies of comrades lost to the clinging mud, never to be found, hung in the air and cloyed the back of his throat. Only when scenes of home filtered into his mind did he feel relief as instead of the stench of death in his nostrils, with a strong imagination, he could smell the clear fresh moorland air of his birth.

God, what a time to be homesick. How he yearned for the simplistic life and the family and friends that he left behind. If he was lucky enough to survive this damned war, he knew he would be a changed man after facing such atrocities.

Although circumstances at home had forced his hand to sign up to fight, he would never forget Freda but she would now have the space and time to rebuild her life without him. The dreadful scene back home became more distant with each passing day. It had not gone smoothly but the parting was amicable. Ruth had taken it the hardest, hugging him close, fearing it could be the last time she would ever see him but, reassuring her the war would soon be over, she accepted his decision. Poverty had also played its part in his decision, Josh realizing the stables were never going to earn enough for Jacob to pay him a reasonable wage to live on.

Pushing these thoughts aside, he returned to his world, the real world of discomfiture, slaughter and death. Joshua hoped to God his luck held out when the order came to attack. He knew he possessed a hard-enough streak to kill, or be killed but he was not sure about Barney. How would he react if suddenly faced with a life and death decision?

Josh managed a smile at his situation. For the first time in his life, he had money in his pocket and here he was, cooped up at the bottom of a stinking trench up to his knees in mud, surrounded by death and nowhere to spend it.

He'd assumed leadership at the very beginning, striding into the office ahead of his friends. All so easy. Each rubber-stamped fit for duty, sent to Ripon barracks for a month's hard training and bayonet practice on sacks of swinging straw. He'd found it hard to take seriously, screaming and stabbing a useless bag hanging from a frame. It wasn't as if it could fight back, could it?

The shooting drill was different. He enjoyed it immensely, proving to be an excellent shot. He had Dan Parkes to thank for teaching him the art of remaining calm. But the playground acting had soon drawn to a close and a far more sinister threat confronted the three of them now as they laughed and joked their way toward the front line and the enemy to defend King and Country.

Sitting in the squalor the first few weeks, the stench had made him wretch violently. Now, his mind and body had adapted to it somehow.

Josh was jolted back to reality by the overwhelming, fearful silence that hung in the morning air. Had he slept while reminiscing? He could not recall the bombing stopping. Not a word spoken amongst the men. Silence reigned as the unknown beckoned. A few whispered prayers filtered along the trench. Every long minute twitching already taut nerves even tighter.

General Stead strode through the slime, quietly giving the order to fix bayonets ready for the whistle. The frightening silence dragged on and on, everyone lost in their own thoughts.

A shrill blast from the whistle rung out along the miles of trenches. Somehow the men forced their cold, numb, aching bodies into action and began a mad clamber up the makeshift ladders to face the threat of no man's land and a hail of bullets from the German forces, unless the bombardment had done its job.

From the silence of a second ago, a crescendo of noise threatened to split Josh's eardrums as a barrage of rifle fire and big guns opened up. Now, up and out of shelter, bodies suddenly crumpled to his right and left. Crouching low, he forced reluctant limbs to keep him upright and move forward, walking headlong into a suicidal swathe of lead and death from the German front line. Soon they would face the dreaded wire, liable to rip a body to shreds, or capture you to die a slow and painful end hanging from its razor-sharp barbs.

General Stead was at his elbow shouting, urging his men forward. Barney was on his other side eager for combat, smiling, eyes bright with excitement. Adrenalin pumped through Josh's veins and the heat of battle spurred him into action, even though men continued to drop like puppets cut from their strings. Bombs everywhere, spraying up huge mounds of earth and debris that rained back down threatening to bury them all. Suddenly the blast and whump of a bomb to Josh's left lifted him clear off his feet, catapulting him high in the air to land yards away. And then nothing.

Chapter 40

⟨ornament⟩

On opening his eyes, Josh stared hard at the blue-black sky. He lay on his back in the mud, body rigid with the paralysis of fear. But he was alive. His scrabbled senses slowly began to clear and the vulnerability of his position spurred him into action and he crawled forward on his belly to find shelter behind the prone form of a dead comrade.

Complete silence again. The guns had ceased their hail of lead. His eyes searched the surrounding gloom only to see men, mouths open, eyes staring terrified, still dying from the hail of bullets, but he heard nothing. Total silence. Pressing his hands over his ears, he rubbed hard. Blood dripped from his fingers. Damn it, the blast must have damaged his hearing. He was completely deaf. Frightened, but thankful he was still alive, Josh glanced across and saw Barney gathering himself up and begin crawling toward a break in the wire. He turned his head and shouted at Josh.

Josh could only guess at the frantic message. He screamed back. "No Barney, no. They'll have it covered." But Barney did not listen or, like Josh, was also deafened by the recent blast. Josh could only watch in horror as his friend, caught in a hail of lead, sank to the ground clutching his leg, a look of shock, then fear, spreading across his mud smeared features. Josh ran and pulled Barney upright as bullets tore at his clothing. Strong as an ox, he half carried, half dragged his friend to a bomb crater and plunged quickly down and out of the line of fire.

Safe. For now. Stead was nowhere to be seen. Had he been cut down? The attack finally began to falter as more and more men fell, wounded or dead, in this futile push forward to gain the German front line.

Josh tried to reason out what to do, the constant ringing in his head scrambling his brain. He couldn't think straight. God, such a pounding in his skull and his ears hurt like hell. But at least they were ringing, so maybe no severe damage done. He took a quick look at Barney's injury. Good God, he'd been lucky, just the one bullet wound to his leg. He could have been cut to ribbons. The bullet had entered the front of the shin and torn the flesh badly as it exited through the calf muscle.

Working feverishly, Josh cut part of his rifle strap up to use as a makeshift tourniquet, then from his field medical kit, bandaged the ripped flesh tightly together. "Okay Barney, you might limp a bit, but this'll keep you alive until we find some of our own lads, or the Germans find us first." Poking his head above the crater, Josh could not believe the carnage. Bomb craters deeper than houses, bodies littering the ground and hanging in the cruel barbs of the wire. Broken, human scarecrows. Men still alive, guts hanging out, blood running through hands that were vainly trying to push intestines back inside their stomachs. Others with faces blown away and limbs torn off, ragged flesh showing broken bone and tendons. This was Hell on earth.

As the urgency of the attack faded, Josh's hearing began to clear as he could hear the noise of the bombing abating and only a sporadic crackle of gunfire every few minutes from the German front line. Nothing from our lads, thought Josh. Where was everyone? Was anyone left alive? How long had it lasted? A couple of hours? All day? He had no idea.

The murky, dull redness of dawn began to split the sky on the far horizon. Full trees, blown to just broken stumps, stood silhouetted starkly against the lightening sky, across what was now a pitiful barren wasteland of death. The attack must have lasted all night. Way over to his left, shelling and gunfire could still be heard but nothing in front or to his right.

What the devil do we do? Retreat or push on? There were no commanding officers shouting orders, either to fall back or attack. Josh was beginning to tire with the effort of carrying and dragging Barney. Forcing his brain to function, he decided to wait and see if any officers or men from his battalion showed up.

Silence again, heavy, frightening. Not even gunshots from the enemy. Taking a deep breath, Josh plucked up courage and poked his head above the barrier of protective soil. Not a living soul, only the odd pitiful cry of wounded, dying men begging for help. Josh couldn't help them. He broke down in tears of frustration. Also, the fear and uncertainty of what to do next terrified him. Wiping the tears away, he sat and began to list their options. They were limited.

First off, he could spot no sign of the enemy as he peered over the mound in front of him.

"Where is everyone? Surely they can't all be dead." Josh muttered.

Barney finally roused from his unconscious state. "What the devil happened, Josh?" His muddy face was pale from blood loss, pain and fear. "God, Josh, the throbbing in my leg hurts. Hurts like hell. Is it going to be okay, d'you think?" He grimaced in pain.

Josh dropped to his side. "Yeah, your leg'll be okay, Barney. Just a scratch really. I've stopped the bleeding." Josh put his arm around him. "Come on, Barney old mate. No time to whinge about a bit of a bullet hole."

"I'm not whinging, Josh. Honest, I aren't. I'm just letting you know it's bloody painful." Barney tried to smile. It didn't work.

Fancying his chances due to the still dim light, Josh crawled slowly out of the bomb hole on his belly. Hauling Barney up alongside him with his one free hand and keeping low, they began to slither forward. The progress was slow and the threat of the enemy always there. Barney was doing good work, helping himself with his sound leg through the clinging mud. Josh had only one thought in mind and that was to somehow make it through the abandoned enemy front line without being spotted, then he may have a chance of receiving help for Barney. He was unsure how but if they could reach safe ground and find some old buildings or a wooded area, he could work out what to do.

Silhouetted on the skyline there appeared to be a higher mound, whether from a bomb crater or a machine gun post, Josh couldn't be sure. Keeping as low as possible they continued to gain ground.

Turning to Barney, Josh whispered, "What do you think, Barney boy? Do we throw a grenade in first and alert any Germans in the area? Or do we take the risk on it being empty?"

"I think we take the risk, Josh. It's been quiet far too long for anyone to be still there."

"I agree. Come on." He grabbed Barney's coat and began the long haul. A deathly silence all around, only the squelch of mud beneath them sounding loud to their ears in the morning air. With rifle at the ready, Josh closed in on the trench while Barney squirmed to the other side. Carefully Josh peered into the darkness of the dug-out.

A loud crack and a flash from the depth of the trench and a bullet tore through Josh's upper arm. Blinded and acting purely on instinct, he fired towards the flash. A scream followed and Josh quickly slid to the bottom of the trench, bayonet fixed. There was no need to use it. A wounded German soldier, left by his army in their retreat sat upright against the back wall, blood pumping out of the gaping hole in his neck. He was still alive but not a danger anymore. Josh guessed he was near death and knelt by his side. The man's face, even in the dull light of the dugout, was as white as marble, the gut-churning fear of the unknown clear in his eyes.

"Dis wasser, bitte." His eyes flickered, trying hard to focus and with great effort pointed to his open mouth. Josh understood and raised his canteen to the man's lips, allowing him to sip slowly. The man's head dropped and his helmet fell to the ground by his side as he uttered his last word, "Dankeschoon." Josh slowly closed the man's staring eyes and went outside for Barney.

As they sat in the confines of this enemy dug-out, Josh rebandaged Barney's leg. "You were lucky there, Josh. He could have blown your head clean off."

"Thanks for that gem of information, Barney. I do realize it was bloody close." He poked a finger through the hole in his coat sleeve and smiled at his luck. His arm ached but it was still usable. Then he stared at the dead German body. There but for the grace of God, go I.

Suddenly all the fear, the killing and suffering witnessed over these last few years engulfed him. His emotions took hold and hanging his head, Josh cried.

Barney limped over, put an arm around his shoulders and tried his best to console his friend. "Come on, Josh old mate. Don't feel bad about shooting the enemy. It was either him or you. You did what you had to do."

Wiping his tears away, Josh replied. "I'm not crying over the killing, Barney. I'm crying because I realize just how lucky we've both been so far in this rotten, evil war." Their eyes met and they sat down and somehow through all this meaningless slaughter of human life, they managed a smile.

"Do you think Barney that if there was a God up there, that he would allow such atrocities as we've witnessed happen." Barney did not answer. He just gave a shake of his head.

Gathering his senses, Josh rummaged through the discarded boxes, finding rations of sausages, cheese and some bread. Happy with this find, Josh asked, "How's the leg feel now, Barney?"

"You've done a good job, Nurse Thrall." They both broke out laughing. "No seriously Josh, the pain isn't too bad. I can go on when ready."

"See, I told you it was just a scratch." Hoping Barney was reassured, he added. "Now it's decision time. Like which way do we go from here? I haven't a clue where we are." He hesitated as he thought. "My thinking is this. The sensible thing to do is get back to the trenches somehow. We can't have travelled that far. Stretcher bearers will be out gathering the wounded now the shelling has ceased. That way you will get treatment. If we continue, we do not know what lies ahead of us, or how far the enemy have retreated. Worse still Barney, we could possibly be classified as deserters. What are your thoughts on it, old mate?"

Using his rifle as a crutch, Barney had climbed a ladder to the top of the trench to survey the devastation. "Right, the way I see it Josh is this. Yes, we could be seen as deserting but there are two of us to relate our story. Yes, we could both do with some treatment as soon as possible. But what do you think of heading for that old farm house? Amazingly it's still standing, with a range of buildings surrounded by trees." He turned to find Josh staring over his shoulder as the sun began its slow ascendency into a clearing sky.

219

"I agree, Barney. It's not far. Come on, what are we waiting for." There was more optimism in the pair of them now and taking Barney by the arm stealthily made their way across the remaining waste land. Reaching the buildings safely, Josh hauled the rickety wooden door open and they fell into the shelter of a cowshed. A couple of black and white cows turned their heads and stared balefully with apparent indifference in their direction, while still contentedly chewing their cud.

"What a piece of luck, Barney. You're good at milking cows. We'll not go thirsty, eh?" He broke into a laugh and flopped into a pile of hay at the end of the stalls. "The only thing we have to worry about now is when, not if, someone comes to feed up."

Barney eased down into the hay alongside his friend and after surviving the battle with the enemy, plus stumbling on this place of relative safety, a feeling of relief swept over the pair. With efforts and energy spent, they slept.

The cowshed door opening brought Josh awake. He nudged Barney in the ribs, holding a hand over his friend's mouth. Entering the byre was a tall, slim dark-haired girl dressed in a blue pinafore dress and white bonnet, carrying a bucket and stool.

Josh raised a finger to his lips. "Shh, be quiet please. We are not here to hurt you."

Her hand shot to her mouth in shock. She was about to turn and flee when she noticed their uniforms. "You are English?" she whispered.

"We are. Do you speak English?"

"Yes, a little only."

"Thank God for that." Josh was relieved. Explanation would be easier now. "My friend is injured and needs somewhere safe to stay until I can get back to my unit and have him picked up. Would it be okay for him to stay here?"

"Yes, I think so but I must ask my grandparents first. The Germans have gone. They will not be back. All that bombing. I am very frightened." She held both hands to her ears, as if the deafening noise still pounded inside her head.

"Thank you so much. What is your name?"

"Maria." She smiled and the dark eyes, although frightened, were bright and sparkled with friendliness. "You are, how you say in English, a mess, okay?"

"I'm afraid we are." Josh looked down at his mud-caked coat and blood-stained uniform and then at Barney's. He smiled back at her. "But remarkably we are still alive. My name is Joshua and this is my friend, Barney. He is badly injured and shouldn't be moved. Would you please ask your elders if he can stay until the stretcher bearers come for him?"

"I will. Right now, Mr Joshua." With that she dashed out. Josh began to gather his rifle and bags up and when she returned, it was with a stooping, elderly grey-haired couple. Josh explained their predicament. Speaking fluent English, they were in full agreement.

"How is it that you and Maria speak English so well?" Josh asked

"It is a long story and if we ever meet up again, I will tell you all about it. Now go and bring help for your friend as he is in pain. The sooner he receives treatment the better. We will do what we can."

Josh bent close to Barney. "These people will look after you, Barney. I'll go get help. It shouldn't be too long in coming. Our lads must realize this part of the German line has retreated. How far, no one knows. Stiff upper lip, Barney." Josh thanked the elderly couple again and left to try and make contact with his own battalion and get help for Barney.

Chapter 41

R etracing his steps as best he could remember, Josh made as much haste as was humanly possible. The sinking mire threatened to pull his hip joints clear out of their sockets at every step. Breathing hard and tiring fast, in the distance he spotted stretcher bearers heaving bodies clear of the deep, clogging slime and checking for any sign of life. If so, they were hoisted onto the stretcher and carried back to the treatment tents. If not, they were dropped where they lay and the mud fields of this forsaken piece of land would be their last resting place.

Exhausted, Josh eventually reached the trench and fell gratefully into it. A few minutes later he began to realize the full extent of this horrific confrontation with the enemy. Before the whistle sounded, the trench was crowded with men. Frightened, yes but also expectant and excited. The time for battle had arrived. Josh studied the few faces of the survivors. Terrified, mesmerised, injured, caked with the dirt and blood of war, some bandaged, some shaking uncontrollably. Josh's eyes filled with tears as he saw what the violence had done to these brave men. His friends. He looked to the heavens as if for an explanation from above. None was forthcoming.

Josh realized that a man stood before him. A senior officer stared directly into his eyes. A tall figure of a man, firm jaw, pencil moustache. Josh's first thought was, how has this man kept clear of the mud that was caked on everyone else in the trench? The man's gaze hardened. Josh jumped to attention and saluted.

The man shook his head as if to say, no need for that at present. "What's your name, soldier?"

"Joshua Thrall, sir. I went over in the first wave. Has General Stead returned?"

"Not as yet, private. The bearers are still bringing bodies back. It doesn't look good. We have lost a tremendous amount of our men."

"I need to speak to the bearers." Josh looked wildly around before making a dash for one of the ladders.

The general hauled him back. "They are all busy doing a job, private. They'll find whoever is missing."

No, they won't, sir." Josh went on to explain what happened and where Barney was.

"The Germans on the south side have retreated, abandoned their posts. The way forward is open but all our men were cut down. There was no one to follow us. The generals, everybody. We didn't know what to do."

The general eyed him with suspicion. "How do you know this?"

"Because that's how I got Barney to safety. We pushed through their front line and eventually reached some farm buildings."

"All communications are down at present but I'll see they get the message. Now can you walk or are you too badly injured?"

"No, I'm not injured. It's Barney."

The general rubbed the blood still seeping down the side of Josh's face."

"Whatever you are inclined to think private, you are injured. If you can make it back to the tents under your own steam it might be quicker than waiting for a stretcher."

"Yes, sir." They both saluted. "But please, promise me you'll find Barney and pick him up, or else I don't go anywhere. He's in the old farm outbuildings next to the wood. He's badly injured and needs treatment fast."

"I promise I shall make sure your friend is picked up and thank you for the information. We can now act upon this."

With reluctance, Josh turned and followed the bearers in the direction of the tents where medical treatment was being administered.

Chapter 42

⌒⬦⬦⬦⌒

Chaos reigned at the treatment camp. Haphazard lines of cobbled-up tents with makeshift beds were crunched tightly together. Heavily bandaged and wounded men, some screaming in agony, others laid prostrate, were being attended to by frantic, desperately over-worked doctors and nurses. They were doing their utmost to administer injections to the most serious who needed immediate amputations. Bottles, pills, bandages and splints were for the lucky ones.

"Come here, son." A doctor collared him by the arm, sat him in a chair and began to wash the congealed blood away from his face and ears.

"Can you hear me okay, soldier?" he asked as he checked each ear with an instrument.

"Yeah, a bit quiet but quite clear."

"Do not move your head, just follow my fingers with your eyes." The doctor removed his blood-stained gloves and held three fingers in front of Josh, moving left and right.

"No problem there, son. You'll live to fight another day. You'll also be able to hear properly, eventually. No damage done. Right, a nurse will be along shortly with fresh bandages. Keep them on until she comes around to examine you again. Don't worry, young man, you'll soon be back in the front line," The medic found him a bed before dashing off to the next patient.

Josh smiled, not sure if the doctor was joking, or serious. He hoped to

God his injuries would keep him from returning to the front line for ever.

The comfort of hospital, even though just a tent, felt unreal. Clean white sheets and a soft pillow were like heaven to Josh. How long had he suffered in that wretched trench? How long had he been fighting? For the life of him he couldn't remember. He didn't even know what day it was. One good thing, he did get the message back about Barney and the break in the German line. Barney might even be somewhere among this lot and being taken care of.

Recuperation took longer than anticipated but Josh was not complaining. Food was good, the nurses attractive and friendly but always rushed off their feet. A week passed and a nurse that Josh didn't recognise began handing parcels and letters out to some of the beds.

She halted at the head of Josh's bed, read his name and asked, "Are you Private Joshua Thrall?"

"I certainly am, nurse."

"This is for you then. Enjoy your read." The dazzling smile she gave him before she left lifted his spirits. Josh shouted after her but it was too late. It didn't matter, he knew this must be from home. Hoping for good news, he slit the envelope open and drew the letter out. His heart leapt. It was from Ruth. He held it close to his chest before reading.

> *Ruth Brennan*
> *The Stables*
> *Gallows Howe*
> *February 10th 1916*

Hope you receive this, Josh.

First thing to ask is, are you safe and well? We keep hearing the dreadful news of the many deaths and we have had no letters from any of you. The generals have been and commandeered the horses from here including Pal, Toby's favourite. He is heartbroken. Jacob's faith in God is keeping him going and Jim is making rapid changes to their farming methods at Honey Bee.

Albert and Martha have retired but Albert is still spending a lot of time at the farm as Jim is growing more and more barley, corn and root crops to help feed the Nation. In the busy times, they even employ a couple of lads from the mine who are short of work. They are really good workers.

Can you believe it Josh, Jim has asked me to marry him but we haven't set a date yet as we await your safe return. Martha and Albert have bought a house in Roston.

I understand the difficulty in writing, so I will keep writing and hope that you come through this conflict along with Barney. I did hear news that Pete is alive and expected home. It cannot go on forever.

Much love from all of us here and our thoughts are with you. Please write if possible.

Ruth.

Josh held the letter away from him so his tears did not smudge the writing. Drying his eyes, he slipped the letter into the top pocket of his uniform hung by the bed. Never before had he felt such loneliness. In a foreign land, far from home and fighting a bloody, senseless war that he may not survive and totally helpless to do anything about it.

With all his writing material ruined, he raised himself from the bed, slung his jacket over his shoulders and limped over to the dimly lit desk in the corner, asking the young girl if she had envelope and paper so he could write home.

"Have you the money to pay for them, private?"

"Yes. That isn't a problem but could I leave it with you to post? I'm not sure if I'm allowed out."

"Drop it on my desk, I'll see to it for you. Better do it next job. Never know when you'll be requested to move."

"Thank you. While I'm here, could you tell me what day it is?"

"Friday, July 17th."

"And the year?" She shot an inquiring look at him. He replied quickly. "I'm not usually as thick as this. I think the bomb blast must have rattled my brain, sister." He tried a smile but she still looked worried.

"1917. You are one of the lucky ones. By what I've heard, this has been one of the bloodiest confrontations in the war. More lives lost than any other battle. Up to now, that is," she added with a frown.

Josh returned to his bed and eagerly began to write, informing them he was safe and well. He missed out the bad bits and added that he hoped Barney would be found.

Sealing the envelope, he dropped it on the now empty desk, assuming the girl would be as good as her word.

A week later, Josh was on the march. Much fitter, with a clear head, clean uniform and, although his feet were bandaged, they were much more comfortable again. He felt like a new man. Thank God he was clear of the mud. He still suffered nightmares of sinking into the mire until it reached his mouth and would then wake up shaking, drenched in sweat.

A beautiful clear morning, the air fresh and the rain had ceased. Only the thud of marching feet could be heard. But they were sadly depleted. Many of his friends missing. The men marched in silence along country roads, sheltered by overhanging trees, each lost in their own thoughts. The soldier to Josh's right spoke out of the side of his mouth. "I've heard we've got a hell of a march ahead of us today. Supposedly trying to achieve another breakthrough, keep the enemy on the run now we've broken through their front line." Josh gave the man a quick glance. A much older man, in his forties, with a face like leather. The man took the hint. "Ben. Ben Lindley. And yours?"

"Josh Thrall. Rawlinson's fourth regiment."

Ben told Josh he had joined up with the Bradford Pals regiment early on in the war. "You up for it, sonny?" he asked. "The march, I mean."

"I'm a hell of a lot better than last week, Ben. I've had a good clean up. Lovely nurses looking after me and decent grub for a change. Yes, I'm up for it now, mate. I feel as if I could fight the whole damned army. The rest has done me a power of good." He didn't mention the letter that was in his top breast pocket that had also given him a much-needed boost.

"Just as well. We have a long slog today, we're heading for Amiens. They're saying this could be the last big one. I've heard the tanks 'll be backing us. We'll be home before long, young 'un. You'll see."

"God. I wish I could believe that, Ben. We just need our luck to hold out a bit longer, eh?"

"You know what Josh, my mother always told me everyone is born with a jar full of luck alongside them and every so often, as we pass through life, we have to take a dip into that lucky jar. Let's just hope we still have a little bit left in ours, eh?"

They marched on in silence passing through a devastated, soul destroying landscape. Villages decimated; blown to pieces; rubble littering the road. Carts with stinking horse carcasses hanging from their harness in the shafts, just left to rot. Personal belongings scattered wildly across the pot holed roads. And still they marched on. Only one destination in their mind. Amiens.

Chapter 43

W hat was left of the fighting men sat amongst the ruins of shattered buildings to eat their meagre rations. There was a definite buzz of enthusiasm circulating and all talk centred around the news that this could be last big battle. The Germans were on the run and the end of the war was in sight. Or so they were led to believe.

Ben studied the man in front of him and said, "How many times have we heard that, sergeant?"

"I know it takes some believing soldier but the news from the top is that we are winning on all fronts. The enemy are on the verge of collapse. We have got to believe this to be true, men." He was a commanding figure at any time but with victory in sight, his enthusiasm was infectious, firing these courageous battle-weary troops up for one last onslaught. "The time for optimism in this long miserable war is right now. I know we still possess the strength and the guts to finish it off. Then we can all go home."

Josh looked at the tired, haggard faces. Surprisingly he felt fresh, even after a ten-mile route march. This was luxury to him after suffering trench warfare for so long. He knew there could be more to come but if his luck held out, he was beginning to think he may just see home again.

"Up and at 'em, lads." The sergeant was back. He gave them all of a minute to be on their feet, then, "Quick march, left, right, left, right," their boots quickly falling into a rhythmical beat. The company finally arrived at a wide, desolate landscape. Miles of winding trenches had already been prepared and this, thought Josh, was his refuge for the foreseeable future. Soon they were cocooned in darkness as night drew in quickly and most of the troop were glad of a rest. As Josh slithered down into the trench alongside Ben, he noticed these were dug from a more, chalky white soil and rock.

"Apparently, we have tank and airplane back up on this one, sonny." Ben opened a pack of battered cigarettes, offering the pack to Josh.

"No thanks Ben. I don't smoke. Really bad for your health, the doctors tell me." They fell about laughing. Others did not join in.

"Go on, take one. I bet it makes you cough. It did me when I first tried 'em."

"Okay." Josh drew one out. Capstan Full Strength it said on the packet. Ben struck a match and lit it for him, watching intently. Josh inhaled a lungful of smoke. A second later he caught his breath and held his throat. With eyes bulging and watering, he coughed for a full minute as Ben and everyone watching thought it a big joke. Josh roughly shoved the cigarette back at Ben and when able to breathe properly and still wiping his eyes, he spluttered out, "not for me, Ben. You can keep 'em."

An order went down the trench for silence. The attack was on for 4.30. a.m. Just before first light.

"Get a good night's sleep, men. You could be in for long day tomorrow."

"These dug outs are plush to the ones I was used to," Josh said as he settled into the chalk-like hole big enough for four men.

"Well, don't get too comfortable," a gruff voice called out, "'cos if you snore, you'll get a rifle butt in your belly." They were all apprehensive but after the long march and the silence of night upon them, sleep came easily.

A sudden kick from the sergeant in the middle of the night broke their slumber. "Shhh. Get ready quietly lads. We go in half an hour." He disappeared into the darkness, rousing each as he went.

Nerves immediately tightened, the familiar tension of danger building again. Josh remembered his last terrifying battle with the enemy. Would he be lucky again? He thought about his luck jar. How much had he used up? God only knew.

4.30 a.m. The blast of the whistle had the men scurrying up the ladders. Josh was in the second wave and they ran for their lives, keeping low, ducking, weaving and making themselves as difficult a target as possible. Gaining good ground, they dropped on their bellies as a barrage of bullets almost obliterated the front line. Ben was to his left, breathing hard. Josh spotted the machine gun post chattering and strafing the ground from right to left, the white chalk puffing up little clouds of dust as men fell in droves. Josh, on his belly, slowed everything down. A calmness swept over him. Controlling his breathing and keeping the sights of his gun steadily fixed on the target, he eased his finger on the trigger. A resounding crack, a strong kick on his shoulder and the machine gun suddenly stopped its menacing tic-tac rattle of death. A whoop of joy from Ben. "Well, you mebbe can't take a cigarette, sonny but you're one hell of a shot. Come on, let's go."

Back on their feet they made a dash toward the German front line, then Josh's luck ran out. The next few minutes played out in slow motion. A final group of defiant Germans rose swiftly and menacingly from the depth of their dug out, grimly deciding to give everything for their country. Determined not to be captured, a hail of lead sprayed through Josh's battalion. A searing, white hot pain shot through his skull, slicing the side of his face open, helmet spinning away to his right. Josh, like a punch-drunk boxer, spread his arms out in a futile attempt to catch it. Another bullet slammed into his upper thigh tearing the flesh open to the bone. Then he dropped like a stone.

Chapter 44

The early grey mist of dawn cast an eerie stillness around York city's gaol, the dour depressing building slowly emerging from the bowels of the city like a shipwreck from the deep into the heavy smoke laden gloom. The dull light began to edge its way up the solid stone walls, until reaching the small barred windows where Patrick Brennan perched uneasily on the edge of his bunk. He watched disinterestedly as it gradually forced the oppressive darkness from his lonely claustrophobic cell.

Patrick had more on his mind at present. Head held slightly to one side he waited patiently for the expectant thud of heavy boots along the long stone flagged corridor that would herald the arrival of the prison guard.

The years inside, caged like some animal, in this wretched unforgiving shell of a building had not only aged him, it had also broken his will and self-esteem. Everything. The once handsome face was now creased deep with lines, the hard chiselled features of his former years gone forever. The sharp black eyes, once full of humour, now carried despair and loneliness behind them and the shock of black hair, struck through with more than just a silvering-grey thread at the temples was testament to the hardships suffered. The one thing he had worked hard on was regaining some of the lean suppleness to his body after the self-destructive years of his alcohol fuelled past.

But the time was almost upon him, the agony of waiting would soon be at an end. For God's sake. Patrick, do not look back whatever you do. He muttered this quietly under his breath. You have survived, be thankful for that. Think of freedom and the future. Grimacing, he shut his eyes tight. What future? A nervous tremor rippled through his limbs. He was actually shaking with fear. Of what? Tomorrow? The outside world? Slowly raising his hand in front of him, the shake was unmistakable. Come on Patrick, concentrate, gather yourself for this meeting. You have faced far worse than this.

Too late, the familiar thud of footsteps sounded. Heart beating fast, he took several deep breaths in a last ditch bid to control the nervousness rising with every passing second. What if they wouldn't allow his release? Had they the power to do that? He'd witnessed far stronger men than himself return to their lonely cells, utterly destroyed by the verdict of the men in power. He'd witnessed one man who had cracked under the prison regime. Patrick was first to find him, lying in a pool of blood, wrists torn open using a piece of jagged metal broken from his bunk. How desperate must you be to end your life in that way?

Patrick looked to the heavens. If he expected help from above, he would be disappointed. God, what a soul-destroying place this was. He hoped he would be strong enough to see it through and pinned his faith upon the years of impeccable behaviour. Never a role model for other prisoners but at least never causing trouble.

The loud click of the key turning in the lock broke the heavy silence of the morning. Think positively he told himself. The door swung open, clanging hard against the edge of the iron framed bed and in strode the guard. Guthrie. Big, bluff and barrel-chested. His voice was gravelly, like sandpaper, grating on Patrick's already taut nerves. "Come on, Brennan. Get a move on, the governor waits for no one, you know that."

Patrick answered quietly, "I'm all ready to go." He tried to sound confident but his unsteady voice clearly betrayed him.

"Big day for you, eh? the guard sneered. "Think you might be leaving us in a day or two, do you? Well just remember this, all old lags like you who can't wait to get out of here finish up on their knees at the gate, begging to come back in." He paused, his eyes challenging Patrick, tempting a reaction. Patrick held his tongue and remained silent. With no response, the guard tried again. "Can't manage on their own, see. No work, no money, nowhere to stay. Bitter cold nights out there if you haven't got a roof over your head. Most of you misfits have no family and even if you have some sort o' kin, most of 'em don't want you back again. Glad to see the back of you, I expect." He was silent for a minute while he checked every nook and cranny in the cell, dragging the ordeal out. Patrick thought the verbal assault was finished. It wasn't. "You see, we look after you too well in this establishment. Tell you when its meal times, tell you when to eat, tell you everything. Like nursemaids, we are. Spoil you rotten, like mothers with little babies."

Patrick ignored the goading but the family one hit home, like a stab to the heart. 'Families don't want 'em.' Close to breaking, Patrick held his rising temper in check. He only had to keep it together for these final few moments. If he rose to the bait his chance of freedom could be destroyed. But the cruel words cut deep, refuelling memories. A daughter lost to him. She would be in her teens now. Grown up. Without him. Without her mother, Sarah. Patrick forced the nightmare thoughts of the past from his mind again. For now.

Time to go. Guiding Patrick from his cell, Guthrie finally lapsed into silence and led the way to the governor's office and knocked on the door. A shout of enter reached their ears and Guthrie ushered Patrick in front of Mr Ashton's desk before departing. Ashton didn't look up from his writing, never acknowledged their entrance to his office. Patrick quickly took note of his surroundings. Sparse furnishings, just the one single light hung centrally in the room, décor a dull grey. Very little comfort, a small window overlooking the exercise yard and only the one chair which Ashton occupied behind the large desk. A few books were scattered untidily on top, plus a tray for correspondence. A plain oak photo frame stood at an angle and Patrick noted the two young boys, possibly mid-teens, with the unmistakable figure of Mr Ashton standing between them, arms draped around their shoulders in a fatherly gesture. All smiles. A happy, family photograph. Something Patrick would never again experience.

Mr Ashton finally raised his head and Patrick returned to reality. "Good morning. Patrick Brennan isn't it?" He threw him a questioning look.

"It is that, sir," Patrick replied nervously.

"Well, the time has finally arrived for your release." While Mr Ashton studied his files, Patrick studied him. No more than forty years old at a guess. Smartly dressed in dark suit and matching waistcoat, a small, neat gold chain disappearing into one of the pockets. Of medium build but with an air of authority about him. A trim moustache and cold searching eyes that held Patrick's gaze. Not a person to be messed with, thought Patrick.

"Yes sir." he replied after a short pause.

"It appears that you have been a model prisoner. You have shown remorse for your wife's death and taken a long time to recover from it. Once you accepted the punishment, you dealt with it admirably." He paused before adding enquiringly, "what have you waiting outside these walls, Patrick. Any idea?" Patrick was taken aback by the concern on Ashton's face.

"I have never thought about release, sir. I dare not think about it, in case it didn't happen. I had heard that some prisoners were kept in well past their release dates, so I have no plans made, no one to turn to. At one time I thought I may try and find my daughter but I am not sure I could stand the rejection if she turned me away, which I could understand if she did. Another thing is, I would have no idea where to start looking."

"I understand," Mr Ashton said. "Well, to put your mind at rest before your imminent release," Patrick's hopes soared at these words, "under the former governor, certain prisoners who breached or broke rules, it was his decision to punish them further. I am the new man here and I run this prison my way. Does that answer your first question?"

"Yes, sir."

Now, back to the subject of coping with the outside world and finding your daughter. Would it help if I had the parson come and have a word with you? I see you attend services every Sunday."

"Only because it's compulsory. I am not a religious man, Mr Ashton."

"I see." Ashton studied him for a while. "Well, I am going to give you an address that will make sure you have a roof over your head for a while and a square meal every day. It is run by the church, so you may have to curb your views on religion for the next few months." A hint of a smile on Ashton's face eased the tension in Patrick, a deep sigh escaping his lips as he knew for definite his release was going ahead. Ashton came from behind his desk and grasped Patrick's hand in a firm handshake.

"The best of luck then, Patrick. Here is the address and Guthrie will see you have all your belongings. I was going to add may God go with you but in this case, I think that would be inappropriate."

"Maybe," Patrick answered with a wry smile, "but I do realize I will need all the support I can get. So, once I've gone, if you think it might help, whisper it quietly and if He is listening then, who knows? I may even find a daughter!" On leaving the office, Guthrie was there, waiting in the corridor, not a glimmer of emotion on his face.

"Follow me." It was an order and Patrick followed Guthrie back to his cell to gather his belongings.

There wasn't much to collect. He came in with nothing. He would leave with nothing, just a few scraggy paperbacks swopped for cigarettes; an assortment of drawing materials; a couple of pencils; a sketchpad and a change of underwear packed into his small case, plus the clothes on his back. He did have a small amount of money, three pounds to be precise. Patrick realized it would not go far and, unbelievably, the fear of release almost struck a paralysis within him as he walked hesitantly across the exercise yard in the strong sunlight. A guard stood at the side door to the main gates, ready to unlock the gateway to a terrifying new world.

Chapter 45

Patrick flinched at the sound of the heavy metal door clattering shut behind him, followed by the dull click of the lock. His legs felt unsteady beneath him. The sensation of the unknown gnawed like a cancer in his gut. Was he about to throw up? Suffering from a sense of foreboding, he stood motionless for a while. He stared at the outside world, uncertainty clouding his mind on what his next step should be, or which way to turn. For the last decade of his life, he had been manipulated by the prison system. Told when to rise; when to go to bed; when to exercise and when to eat. Ordered and precise. Every day. This clockwork regime had continued to erode any independent qualities that he'd ever possessed.

Surely there should be a feeling of joy and elation at this freedom after so long incarcerated. But there wasn't. He was terrified, no doubt about that. But if Guthrie's words were not to become a reality he must be positive and try to pick up the delicate gossamer threads of a life outside the prison and learn to live in the real world.

He glanced up and down the quiet street. It was mid-morning, the sun still in its ascendency, casting a warmth down on the street, despite the time of year. There were few people about and Patrick had expected it to be busier. Gathering his thoughts, he fished for the scrap of paper in his pocket and studied the address that the governor had scribbled out for him on leaving his office. *Reverend Simmons, St Catherine's Church, Eden Close, York.*

Mr Ashton had given explicit instructions on finding the church and Patrick had a vague idea where it was but such was his state of mind the directions had not registered. He knew if he got in the right area, then it would become clear.

Lifting his head from the scrap of paper, he noticed a man loitering across the other side of the street, studying him. Uncomfortable, Patrick began to walk towards the city centre and sensed the man following. Turning a corner, Patrick slipped through an open gate and waited in the shelter of a small brick outhouse. A few seconds later, the stranger walked past the entrance.

Patrick stepped out, aggressive in his manner and clutched the man's arm. "Why are you following me?" he asked.

The man spun round, caught off guard by this unexpected reversal of roles. Slowly, a smile creased his face. "It is Patrick Brennan, isn't it? The years inside have not been kind but I recognize you now that I'm closer."

"Jack? Jack Devlin?" The years had also aged Jack. Crow's feet around the eyes and the dark hair well peppered with silver. Patrick threw his arms around Jack's shoulders and hugged him close before stepping back and shaking his saviour's hand. "I'm sorry Jack, I'm not really thinking straight at present. I really am pleased to see you, to be sure I am, but you were the last person I expected to bump into on my first day of freedom."

"It's good to see you, Patrick and also that you did survive. Not all come through as good as you have." His handsome features creased into a good-natured grin again. "But I am not here just by chance. I had asked the former governor to give me a nod on your release date and I am pleased to say the new man, John Ashton, carried it out. So here I am. Right, first things first, I'll treat you to a pot of tea and discuss what happens from here on in."

Once over the shock of meeting up, Patrick felt more comfortable. With Jack taking the initiative, for which Patrick was very thankful, they nipped down one of the side streets and soon settled themselves at a corner table in a small café. Patrick savoured the taste of his first decent cup of tea in more than a decade.

"Anything to eat, Patrick?" he asked. Patrick shook his head. Once the waiter was out of earshot, Jack got down to business.

"Right, I suppose you are wondering what on earth I'm doing here the very minute you walk free from prison."

"Yes, I am. But, by God, I'm pleased to see you."

"Well, let me explain. This is a crucial time when the judicial system lets itself down. Prisoners locked away for any length of time soon become used to the security of being told what to do, when and how. This is followed by loss of identity and independence, among other things. Once free, they are expected to pick up the pieces of a life, often totally destroyed. They either roam the streets and sleep rough, as work is almost impossible to find. Or they revert to the criminal way of life which leads straight back inside. A vicious circle."

Patrick poured another cup of tea to help spin out more time with Jack. Guthrie's words came back to Patrick. "Yep, one of the guards warned me that I would be thankful to return to the security of prison if I wasn't careful. I can see the truth in that. I'm not sure I am strong enough to handle this at all, Jack."

"What have you in mind? Have you any contacts outside at all? Any relatives, or friends that could offer shelter for a few nights?" Jack questioned.

Patrick shook his head. "There was a next-door neighbour where Sarah and I lived but those houses were due to be pulled down. I sent a letter asking if she had any news about Ruth, my daughter, but I didn't receive a reply." Patrick fell silent and wiped his eyes.

Jack took over, careful not to push him over the edge. "How serious are you about contacting your daughter, Patrick?" he asked.

Patrick considered this question for a while before answering. "Through the hard times, it was the one thing that kept me sane. Now it's a possibility, I'm not certain I'm brave enough, Jack. If she did reject me…" He didn't finish, just shrugged his shoulders.

"Whichever way you decide, let me know at our next meeting." Jack left it there. Then Patrick suddenly remembered the note. "Ah, I almost forgot. Mr Ashton gave me this address." He fumbled in his pocket for the note and showed Jack the name.

"Yes, I know him. Just taken over as rector at St Catherine's and opened a canteen next to the church. He also knows of cheap accommodation for anyone who is homeless and I think at present, Patrick, you come into that category. Do you know your way there?"

"Mr Ashton did tell me but with everything that's happened, I can't remember, Jack, I'm sorry." Patrick lowered his gaze, ashamed at his memory letting him down.

"Don't be, it is understandable. We are not far away. I'll walk with you and make the introductions if it will help."

"To be sure, Jack. If you have the time, I would appreciate it."

"Come on then, let's go."

When Jack returned from paying the bill, Patrick said, "I have some money to pay my way Jack. How much was it?"

"No not this time, Patrick. Next time we meet you may be in a better position to buy me a cup. Let's hope so, eh?" and they walked out onto the street towards what hopefully would be a new beginning for Patrick.

Chapter 46

J osh heard talking to his left. He opened his eyes as though from a long sleep. Objects appeared blurred. The side of his head and his right leg felt numb. Firstly, his good arm felt for his right leg. It was still there, they hadn't amputated. He gave a sigh of relief.

Lifting his hand, he touched the blood caked bandages wrapped tightly around his head. Where the hell am I, he wondered? He didn't recognise the surroundings, or the ramshackle old buildings. There appeared to be a lot of activity, people rushing about, laughter and shouting all around.

"Doc, this one's coming back to life." Josh recognised the voice.

"Ben. Is that you, Ben?" he asked in a voice no more than a whisper.

"'Course it is. Who did you expect, God? Or were you afraid it might be old Beelzebub himself?" Typical Ben. He went on. "Thought you were a goner, sonny but you must have had a little bit left in that jar of yours, eh? Grazed your head and smashed through your upper leg but the medic reckons you'll live."

"Where are we, Ben?" Josh's voice was weak. Ben bent in close to hear him.

"Well, I'm not really sure, Josh but they've christened it the return centre. As far as I can see it's just a load of old farm buildings that have escaped damage. The good news is there'll be no more fighting for us lads. The war is over and we've survived. We are on our way home as soon as we receive the all-clear health wise." Ben looked to his right. "Talk o' the devil and he shall appear. Here comes the medicine man. Will see you later, sonny."

The medic was an elderly man, rushed off his feet and harassed but still very efficient in the circumstances.

"Okay, Private Thrall, is it? What a lucky man you are. If that bullet had hit half an inch to the right, it would have been goodbye world. Not sure about the sight in that eye but the leg should heal sufficiently, if we can keep it clear of infection. You might suffer a slight limp, that's all." He administered an injection. "For the pain," he informed him.

Josh drifted back into oblivion. For how long he knew not. On awakening the pain was minimal and his sight much clearer. Instead of slightly fuzzy images, he could see the injured men lounging about. Some were sitting, some lay on makeshift beds. The ones with missing limbs were propped up on crutches.

Josh's fighting streak and stubborn spirit came to the fore and he continued to make good progress. Within a week he was hobbling about on a home-made stick. Ben kept a watchful eye on him. Having come through so much fighting and bloodshed together, they had become good friends.

Boredom was now the soul destroyer as they fought to regain fitness and Ben, always on the go, or keen to be doing something, called for a game of cards to pass the time. His arm was healing quickly from the bullet wound and he'd brought a couple of his regiment to Josh's table for a game. "You don't mind if my mates join us for a game, Josh, d'you? It's just I would feel guilty taking your money off you all the time, seeing as you're just a country boy, like."

"By, he's a cocky sod, isn't he? Josh said to the new men, his face creasing into a grin and nodding in Ben's direction.

One of Ben's mates replied "Aw, don't worry about him, matey. He's always like this. You get used to him after a couple of years," and their laughter rang around the old buildings. The mood around the camp was mostly light-hearted, the weather was reasonable and they were sure in the knowledge that they would never have to face the terror of the German guns again, which brought a huge sense of relief.

Drawing their seats up around a rickety old table placed outside and throwing a few pennies into the kitty, they were just about to settle into the game when they were interrupted by the arrival of a major. He appeared very much out of place amongst this dishevelled group of injured fighting men.

He was a solid, rotund looking figure with an immaculate uniform. His boots, brass and medals so highly polished they gleamed, even in the dim light. He held his swagger stick under his arm. With no introduction, he went round to each group of wounded men to give them a morale boosting talk. When he began to address the group close to Josh's, Ben said, "It's a bit late for that." His voice carried across to where the major stood with his horse. He turned his head in Ben's direction. "What was that, private?" His voice loud and loaded with authority. Ben had gained his full attention and he strutted over, leading his horse by the reins.

"I said it's a bit late for a pep talk for us lads, major." Ben looked the major straight in the eye but never once stopped shuffling the cards. "We're on our way home." Ben did not appear at all perturbed about upsetting the top brass.

"What's your name, private and what regiment are you in?" The brusque, demanding manner was beginning to rattle Ben. He could do without this sort of pomposity now.

"Private Ben Neil, Bradford Pals regiment, sir." The major's horse lifted its head sharply and whinnied.

"And yours," he nodded to Josh in an off-hand way.

Private Joshua Thrall. Rawlinson's Fourth Army, sir."

The major nodded to the next.

"Private John Denley, a Bradford Pal, sir."

Again, the horse suddenly lifted its head, becoming more excited, a shrill whinny this time. The major gave a sharp tug on the reins.

"And you, young man?"

"Private Daniel Dale, another Bradford Pal, sir."

The major's horse became more restless, whinnied again and pushed forward. The major held tight onto the reins. "Steady, steady there," he said trying to calm the animal down.

Josh rose from his chair and began to take an interest in the horse and ran his hand over the jet-black coat, glossy and silken under his light touch.

It would never have entered his mind about the horse if he hadn't received Ruth's letter. There was one thing causing him doubt though. Where was the broken white mark on the head? Trying to quell his rising excitement, he continued to limp around the animal and when shielded from view, took a rag from his pocket and quickly brushed it over the horse's forehead. A black smudge appeared on the rag. Josh almost fainted.

The major had suddenly lost interest in Ben. "What do you think you are doing, private?"

"As a matter of fact, I was admiring this animal of yours, major." Josh replied.

"Well, there is no need to show any further interest. The horse is not for sale." The major turned to walk away.

Josh barred his way. "Before you go, major. May I ask you a question?"

"Of course, but it will have to be quick. As you can see, I do not have very much time. I'm a busy man." He glanced at his watch as if to prove it.

"I understand." Josh's voice, although quiet, carried a certain menace with it. "Could I ask if you are the rightful owner of this horse, sir? And if so, how long have you owned him?"

The men around the table quietened, sensing a confrontation. As had others. Heads turned. It had become contagious. Word quickly spread and more men gathered round.

"Well, I do not see this as any of your business but I shall tell you anyway. I've had this animal from the beginning of the war."

"I hate to contradict you, sir. I believe this horse belongs to an acquaintance of mine back in England."

The major became flustered and his cheeks took on more of a ruddy glow. "Are you calling me a liar, private?"

"No, but what I am saying is, this horse belongs to Toby Smith. I believe, once cleaned there will be a broken white mark above the eye on its forehead. It is one of the more distinctive markings that make it recognisable. Toby and I were there when the mare gave birth to this horse. Later on, Toby stayed with it through the night when it almost died."

"Rubbish. As for markings, there are hundreds of horses with similar markings. Now, let me be on my way."

With his heart beating madly against his rib cage, Josh remained defiant. "No, sir, I won't let you on your way. If you won't take that for proof, I shall prove it another way. If you don't believe me after this then I shall apologise and walk away."

Josh was almost sure this was Pal. He was now hoping against hope that he could pull this off, not only for his own sake but for Toby's as well.

"Please let go of the reins, sir."

"I shall do no such thing." He tried to push through the enclosed crowd and move on.

"I wouldn't do that major if I were you. Let the boy have his say." It was Colonel Rawlinson, Commander of the Fourth Battalion. Still mounted, stiff backed, authoritative, he had eased his horse gently forward to the outer circle of interested spectators.

The major looked up in shock, face reddening by the second. Without uttering a word, he eventually let the reins drop.

"Thank you, major." Josh said. "Now, if you would all stand back." Every able man was now craning his neck to watch this confrontation between Josh and the major. The circle widened, pushing back until Josh and the horse stood centre stage. Josh hoped to God Pal remembered the trick Toby had taught him all those years ago. How good was a horse's memory? He had no idea but he was about to find out. Too late to back out now.

Walking steadily forward, he patted Pal on the head. "Hello, Pal." Pal threw his head back then brought it down to snuffle against Josh's pocket. "Pass me a sweet someone, please?" A sweet was passed and Josh held it in his open hand as he had seen Toby do many a time. The horse took it gently out of his hand. Taking a couple of backward steps away from Pal, Josh continued to keep eye contact with the animal all the while. Leaning heavily on his stick with his injured leg pushed forward, Josh bent low at the waist in an exaggerated bow. Pal put his head on one side, seemingly uninterested, content to study the crowd of people. Josh was pleading inside for him to understand. The tension built. Spellbound, a hush had fallen over the onlookers. Everything depended on the next few minutes.

Josh repeated the procedure. No response. Josh was just about to give it one more try when Pal raised his head, snorted, then slowly, ever so slowly began to ease a leg forward. He bent the other leg until his nostrils brushed the ground in front of a very relieved Josh. After a few seconds, Josh ordered, "Up, Pal, up." The horse stood with its head held high and gave a shrill whinny. He then stood stock still, as if to attention. Josh, tears of relief in his eyes, handed Pal another sweet. He deserved one.

The clapping began slowly, building into a crescendo, then cheering. These fighting men knew they had just witnessed something special, a bond of true friendship between horse and human spreading across the heart-breaking years of war. When handshaking and cheering died down, Colonel Rawlinson spoke. "I think Private Thrall has made his point very clear, major. I do hope this will be the end of the matter. By the way, if you have the time, I would like a formal word with you before you leave."

Flustered, he answered, "Of course, colonel." He gave a hasty salute and left, pushing his way through the throng waiting to shake Josh by the hand. The humiliation of an officer was not often witnessed.

Chapter 47

J im and Ruth had set their wedding date for 10th December, as late in the year as possible and as word spread that the war was finally over, so did the euphoria. Victory celebrations swept across the whole nation. Everyone was thankful to see the end but the aftermath would leave its mark on many.

In the Thrall household, although trying to keep their hopes up for Josh's homecoming, there was also the underlying fear that Josh may not return. There had been no communication from him for more than two years. On the positive side, they had not received a dreaded telegram either, informing them of his death or missing in action. Also, Barney Stopes had lifted everyone's spirits with good news on his recent return, relating the story of Josh's heroic effort in dragging him to safety when shot in the leg. Josh had definitely saved his life. Barney couldn't be certain but he was pretty sure Josh would have survived this particular bloody battle, so there was still a chance he could make it home.

Pete, a shadow of his former self, had returned to his family much earlier, having survived the atrocities but the young man was still a casualty of the war. His youth, good humour and outgoing personality he possessed were blown to pieces, left strewn somewhere on the bloody battlefields of France. The effects of the stomach wound and the shelling had taken his youth and destroyed him, leaving him a broken man.

Late one evening, Jacob and Ruth were sitting quietly reading in front of the dwindling fire at home, when Jacob broke the silence. "You realize this will be the last service at the old church up on the moor here, Ruth?" Jacob sounded quite melancholy. His church, he always thought of it as his church, would be demolished in the near future. Hopefully some of the items would be reused in the new construction at Castle Moor.

Ruth studied the deep furrowed face, the arthritic hands, eyes that had lost their bite, their brightness and vitality. "I do, Jacob. It will be a sad day for many, you included. I will certainly miss the old place, as it has played a big part in my life. But I understand, it is different for me as I move toward a future that I could never ever have imagined just a few short years ago."

"Yes, a sad day but a happy one also." He managed a smile. "Who will be giving you away on your big day, may I ask?"

"Well, I would love it to be you if that's possible?" Ruth looked at him hopefully. "If you can manage both jobs. Giving me away and the marriage service."

"With pleasure, my dear. And Jim's best man?"

"This is slightly more difficult as Jim's first thought was for Josh but that is unlikely to happen. So, the other day, Jim asked Pete if he would mind stepping in. He said he would be glad to, as long as we don't expect him to make a speech."

"That sounds a good plan. And hymns?"

"Well, I better not pick 'Fight the Good Fight,' had I?" she said grinning. "Seriously, Jacob, I would like two of my mother's favourites, 'Love Divine,' and 'In Heaven Love Abiding.' Do you think Isobel Peters will play the organ for us?"

"I think Isobel would be delighted if asked to play on such a special day, Ruth. You know, she almost treats that organ like part of her family." He smiled as the thought of Isobel's love for the organ came to mind. "Have you a particular dress to wear, Ruth? You don't have to have, you know. There are no special rules on dress."

"Oh, I have, Jacob. Very special. It is the very one Martha wore when marrying Albert all those years ago. Martha lifted the box down from the top of the wardrobe and unwrapped it for me just a few weeks ago. I tried it on and, would you believe it fits perfectly. Isn't that marvellous?"

"It surely is, Ruth. I am looking forward to a very special day." Jacob glanced at the clock. "Now, if you'll forgive me, I shall retire to bed. I do seem to tire easily nowadays. Goodnight, my dear."

"Goodnight, Jacob."

Ruth sat on, enjoying the comfort and solitude of the late evening until the fire died and the chill of the night crept into the room, then retired upstairs. Slinking under the covers, Ruth realized her life was about to change dramatically in the next couple of weeks.

Chapter 48

A fortnight passed and Josh was deemed fit to leave for home. Colonel Rawlinson gave all the injured men a sobering and heartfelt leaving speech, it even touched the hardest of men. Some hung their heads, sobbing quietly in remembrance of lost friends and what had been achieved over the past gruelling years. He finished with. "We are victorious because of the courage of all you men and those no longer with us. The country will never be able to thank you enough for the sacrifices made. Now, please return home to your loved ones, resume your lives and leave behind, if you can, the horrors of this conflict. Thank you." He turned and Josh watched him ride into the distance through red-rimmed eyes.

Before him stretched the long trek home. Josh and Ben were put in charge of a dozen horses, Pal being one of them. They boarded the ship with many others and shared the same emotion. Relief.

Once the horses were loaded below deck, the ship set sail for England and their landing point, Hull. Josh stood on the deck alone with his thoughts. He didn't know whether to thank God, thank Ben for dragging him to safety in the last onslaught, or thank his luck jar for having a little bit left in it.

The morning air was cold as the vessel heaved and swayed its way across the rising dancing tips of the waves. Foam sprayed into his face and he relished the stinging coldness on his skin. Will Barney and Pete have made it home before him? Had they survived? It was a sobering question and Josh became emotional, so turned his attention to more positive thoughts. How was Freda? Would Ruth and Jim be married? How would Toby react when reunited with Pal?

A smile spread across Josh's face. Not long before he found answers to these questions that occupied his mind. As he screwed his eyes tight against the spray, Josh thought he could see a slight smudge on the horizon. His heart leapt. Men began streaming up alongside him, all urging the ship to go faster. Land in the distance. Their land. The land they had fought for. And many had given their lives for. Almost home.

Ben sidled quietly up alongside, his usual light banter cast aside and replaced with a more serious tone. "Can you believe it, Josh? We've actually come out the other side of this bloody awful war." There was a sadness hidden in these words as well. He went on. "Not unscathed, I admit, but we are heading home." Slinging his arm over Josh's shoulder, he looked him in the eye. "Yep, we made it through, sonny. We're among the lucky ones." Ben studied the nearing coastline before adding thoughtfully, "I've fought alongside you for many a month now Josh Thrall and we've always kept our talk light-hearted, maybe in the hope of keeping our spirits up. It's only now I realize I don't know the real Josh Thrall."

Josh contemplated these words for a few seconds then threw his head back and laughed, a surge of happiness overwhelming him. An emotion that had rarely been brought to the surface these last few years. He had experienced tears of sadness, pain and relief. Yes, all these emotions but never tears of happiness. He was experiencing them now

Josh answered. "Ben, there is very little to know about the real Josh Thrall. What I will tell you is that I regard you as one of my closest friends. We've been through hell together and come through it. You took the ultimate risk and laid your life on the line to save mine. No one can ask for more from a person. I will never be able to thank you enough and will always be in your debt."

"You've been there, sonny. Went through it with your mate, Barney. Heat of the battle, adrenalin flowing and all that, you know." Ben looked embarrassed and changed the subject. "Have you got a wife or a bonny young girl waiting to greet you? Or are you like me, a lonely man but for his thoughts. No brothers or sisters. I only had my mother who died a few years back. One of the reasons I joined up. I did my best to look after her as I couldn't bear her going in a home."

Josh sympathised. "I'm sorry, Ben. That must have been difficult for you."

"It was. We were pretty close. The chance of marriage never seemed to come along somehow, so as you can imagine, it will be a totally different home that I will return to.

"It will be to start with but life eventually changes, Ben. In my case, there was someone before I left but it didn't work out. I do have family though," he added, "who I do miss tremendously."

"Nothing like distance to lend enchantment."

Josh laughed. Ben always had a saying for everything. "In case we don't meet up again, or get lost in the crowd," Josh scribbled his address down. "On the off chance that you might visit 'the lad from the sticks' for a game of cards." Laughing, they turned away from the rail as land approached. With a throng of cheering people lining the quayside, they headed below deck toward the horses. One last shake of hands from the pair, both knowing they may never see each other again. Just comrades in arms, silently sharing feelings that needed no explanation.

Gang planks clattered noisily onto the dock and army officers were waiting to take the few surviving horses to stables to wait collection. One reached up to take charge of Pal. "Sorry, officer this one is mine," and Josh held firm on the reins.

"I cannot allow you to keep the horse, private. I have my orders to take all stock to the stables for them to be requisitioned to their rightful owners."

"I am the rightful owner, officer."

"By whose authority."

"Colonel Rawlinson. Commander of the Fourth Army."

The officer did not believe him. "Wait here, private while I go check. Name please."

"Josh Thrall. Thank you." Josh leant against the shoulder of Pal, the warmth of the animal spreading through his body while he rested his aching

253

limb.

Ten minutes passed before the officer arrived back.

"Confirmed," he said, sheepishly. "On your way, private."

Slinging his kit bag over his shoulder, Josh pushed his way through the throng of clamouring people hugging, kissing and crying. Nothing held back. Once clear of the quayside, Josh mounted, with difficulty, and looked back to see if he could see any sign of Ben. Not a chance in all that crowd. With a smile on his face, he began the long ride home.

Asking instructions, he was told to stick to the coastal route as it would offer more shelter if the weather turned quickly, as it could at this time of year. Sticking to this plan, they made good time and were soon teetering high above the North Sea, the high craggy cliffs of the coastline keeping the surging waves at bay. Staring inland, flat, featureless squares of bare brown stubble greeted his gaze, as a few stray sheep cropped the last bit of colour from the land and eyed him warily as he rode onward. The people he encountered along the way all cheered and waved, wishing him well on his journey.

Josh really did begin to feel like a returning hero, a wide smile on his face as he waved back. The overriding thought driving him on was Ruth's marriage. He had no idea if they had set a date or not. He realized it could be imminent as Albert and Martha were moving. Selfishly, he was hoping nothing had gone ahead as yet. They might even leave it until the new year.

The pain in his leg was becoming unbearable and he knew Pal would need feeding and a drink before long. A headwind of breath-taking severity, caught them full on, buffeting and sapping energy from the pair of them as they made their way up through a small coastal village and this finally decided Josh to call a halt for the night. In the distance, lights from what appeared to be a wayside inn with outbuildings beckoned, so a good chance of stabling for Pal. All was quiet at this time of day as Josh rapped on the front door. A young girl of school age with large blue eyes answered his knock.

"Yes, sir. Can I help?"

"Hello there. My name is Josh Thrall. I am trying to find shelter for me and my horse for the night. Would that be possible, do you think?"

"I'm sure it would. I'll just ask grandad." She rushed off and a minute later returned. "Grandad said yes. If you come with me, I'll show you the stable." Josh duly followed, smiling at the confidence of this young girl. Noticing his unsteady walk, she asked. "Were you injured in the war, Mr Thrall?"

Quite taken aback, Josh replied. "Yes, I was but I am one of the few lucky ones returning home."

"I think you are a very brave man."

"Thank you very much. But it wasn't so much bravery, dear girl, as none of us soldiers had any other option but to fight."

"Well, I still think you were all very brave. Now, after you have seen to your horse, please come in and we will find a room for you." She quickly ran off.

"Thank you," Josh shouted after the fast disappearing figure. He untacked and bedded Pal down, then picked up his kit bag and followed the girl inside.

A fire was already burning, taking the chill off the night air and an elderly gentleman came over and introduced himself to Josh. Heavily built, with grizzled features that were partly hidden under a battered old trilby hat. He lifted it slightly and his twinkling eyes met Josh's.

"Very honoured to meet you, young man. My name is Gerald and my granddaughter you just met is called Daisy. Now, how about a sandwich?"

Josh took his hand. "Josh. Josh Thrall. This is very good of you, Gerald. That would be good before I retire as I'm ready for my bed. It's been a long day."

Gerald shuffled behind the bar, pulled a pint and set it before Josh. Josh reached into his pocket to pay. Gerald lifted his hand. "This one is on the house, Josh. We are so pleased to see some of you lads returning. We owe you not only our freedom but freedom for the generations to follow. This country can never thank you enough." There were tears in the old man's eyes.

"Thank you, Gerald. I appreciate this." A pint of beer had never tasted as good as this one.

Next morning a leaden sky and a sharp north wind greeted him and after a good breakfast prepared and served by Daisy, Josh paid his bill and waved goodbye. Josh calculated he may need one more stop along the way, not only for food and drink for Pal but also for himself. Gerald thought his best route would be to carry on along the coast then take off across the moor road before Whitby.

Both horse and rider were tired and weary as they toiled up the long steep climb from the coast to head inland and Josh called a halt. Pulling up at the side of the road, a stout, grey haired lady, outside shutting the hens up for the night, spotted him at the farm gate. "Can I help you, honey?" she shouted in his direction.

"We are looking for a place to rest for a while and maybe something to eat and drink for the horse. I have the money to pay."

The lady opened the creaking old gate and ushered the pair of them through into the yard. Pal spotted a trough and trotted across to it.

"He doesn't wait to be asked this one," Josh said grinning. "We've had a long ride from Hull. I'm Josh Thrall."

Bless you, dear boy," she said, shaking his hand. "Once he's slaked his thirst, you wander over to the mounting steps where it's easier to dismount," eyeing his bad leg, "while I pop inside and find a bite to eat for you."

"Thank you."

Once inside, Josh seated himself at the table and glanced at the clock on the mantlepiece. He realized darkness would soon be falling and gratefully sank his teeth into the sandwich.

"Where are you headed, Mr Thrall?" the lady asked. "Have you far to go as it will soon be dark? Comes in black as pitch this time of year, you know."

"Well, I was trying to make Gallows Howe, just above Castle Moor before nightfall. Do you know it?"

"I know it well. My husband takes me cheeses there, on market day. Where are you going to stay tonight because you'll not make it to Castle Moor?"

"Oh, Pal and I can just pull off onto the moor and sleep under the stars for one night. It will be a lot more comfortable than the trenches."

"No, I'll not allow that, young man. There's a spare bed already made upstairs." Josh was about to say there is no need, when she added sternly, "and I won't take no for an answer."

"Well, thank you very much. It is appreciated." After more talk on the war, Josh stabled Pal up, fed him and returned inside, glad of a comfortable bed for the night.

After a hearty breakfast and another sandwich packed in his kit bag, "just in case you get hungry on the last leg of your journey," Josh set out early. A cold morning but clear skies with just the odd cotton wool cloud floating slowly by and he soon hit the road cutting across the open moor, knowing it shortened his journey by many miles.

Josh's mind was muddled. Somehow, he could not keep track of days and dates. He should have asked at the farm but he forgot. He felt much happier now he was in country that he recognised and stared into the wide, sweeping dales spread before him. His ride home to see the ones he loved was almost at an end and as he rode, he wept. But they were tears of relief and happiness. He was almost home.

Chapter 49

E xcitement reigned at the farm when Martha and Albert arrived to make sure Jim was ready. He was ahead of them, dressed in dark suit, shirt and tie and shoes polished. Martha was wearing her best navy-blue dress and a look of admiration spread across her face when she saw Jim. "Never seen you looking so smart, Jim. Have we, Albert?"

"Never in my life. Are you nervous, Jim?" he asked

"A bit, but only about the speech really. Otherwise, I couldn't be happier."

It was a beautiful day for a wedding Martha thought, her gaze scanning the moor top. A clear blue sky, only a few wispy clouds flitting close to the horizon.

"Not bad for the time of year, though," Albert remarked as he lifted Martha onto the front seat then settling next to her. Jim took the reins and they were on their way to the biggest day of his life. A cold north wind bit into their faces on the high moor but on nearing the church, they soon found it sheltered.

Pony and traps lined the moorland tracks close by and horses were tied up alongside the stone watering troughs by the side of the stables. Jim's heart began to beat just a little faster.

Drawing to a halt in front of the church, Jim jumped off. He helped Martha down and Albert held her hand as Jim led the way along the old stone trod. On opening the doors and pushing aside the velvet curtains, his stomach suddenly lurched inside him. If he hadn't felt nerves before, he certainly did now. Never a regular church goer he had no idea what to expect.

The dozens of candles cast a welcome, flickering light at the front and small bunches of flowers adorned each side of the aisle and Isobel, seated at the organ, played softly in the background. Jim had never expected so many people to be there. Quickly scanning his eyes over the guests, he spotted John Durville and Edith and smiled. Len Bailes and family, Dan Parkes, the McClouds, Toby and his parents. Freda and Doctor Rourke. After that it was just a blur. All the village and beyond appeared to have turned out.

Jim took his place at the front. Pete was already there, alongside, his nervousness showing as he constantly checked his pockets for the rings.

"Thanks for doing this for us, Pete," Jim said. "We both appreciate it."

"I'm pleased to be able to do it, Jim. Glad you let me off the speech, though." Jim slung an arm around him in reassurance. Jacob stood solemnly behind the lectern, checked his pocket watch then walked slowly to the rear of the church.

Jim's expectancy grew, knowing it must be time for Ruth's arrival. Pete nudged him in the ribs. "Not having second thoughts, are you Jim?"

"Not likely, Pete. Although, I'm feeling a bit nervous now." His face broke into the trade-mark grin but it could not hide the tension within him.

The organ stopped. Silence for a minute. Then Isobel, in her element, began playing the Wedding March and the guests rose to their feet as one. Jim was sorely tempted to turn and watch Ruth but Martha had strictly forbidden it. It brought bad luck, she told him. He would not dare go against her wishes.

Gasps of admiration reached Jim's ears as Ruth made her steady walk up the aisle, Jacob gently holding her arm. Attired in Martha's all white wedding dress, Ruth was a vision of pure beauty. A fine veil covered her face and her long blond hair fell about her shoulders. A small simple posy of wild flowers she held in front of her.

On reaching the alter, Jacob placed her hand in Jim's, then turned to face them, the expectancy growing. Jim swallowed hard in a futile effort to stay calm and finally decided to steal a glance sideways at his bride to be. Even on first sight at the orphanage, Jim had known this girl would somehow be special to him. Now he knew it for real. Never had he witnessed such a beautiful woman. Slowly, Ruth lifted her gaze, their eyes met and she smiled at him. The nerves vanished.

Jacob was on the verge of speaking when his practiced ear picked up on the sound of the outer door clicking open. Raising his head, he waited a few seconds before beginning on the marriage vows. He did not want an interruption if it could be avoided. The inner curtain slid quietly to one side and there stood a dishevelled figure dressed in army uniform.

Jacob stared, waiting for the man to come forward. He did not recognize the figure and he was sure the man would speak and explain himself but nothing was forthcoming. Then slowly, the realization began to dawn on him. Yes, this man was thinner, older, the head of blond hair much shorter and this stranger had a rough stubbly beard. But the stance was unmistakable. His son Josh had finally returned home.

Jacob's expression crumpled. Tears he could no longer contain trickled unashamedly down his pale cheeks. Following Jacob's gaze, heads turned to the rear of the building, inquisitive as to who this late comer could be. Josh stood for a second, surveying the crowded church before beginning his slow stilted walk up the aisle. Jim, Ruth and Pete were staring worriedly at Jacob, before turning as one to watch the determined figure of Josh limping purposefully to the head of the church.

Reaching the front, Josh asked in a quiet voice, "Pete, old friend, do you mind if I take over. I'm sorry if my timing is a bit out but I got delayed with the war."

First, he hugged Ruth close, then Jacob. "I told you all I would be back to see you and Jim wed, didn't I? Surely, you didn't think I would miss out on a family gathering and a wedding feast, did you?"

Ruth sobbed into his arms, unable to speak for several minutes then said, "Josh we are all so glad you're safe. We never had any news. We just lived in hope."

The atmosphere had become so emotionally charged that noses were blown and eyes were dabbed with handkerchiefs. Even the well-renowned hard men of the dales were struggling to contain emotions at this unexpected tear-jerking reunion.

"Right, on with the wedding, father. Let's not keep the guests, or this lovely couple waiting any longer." Josh took the proffered ring from Pete and the ceremony went ahead without a hitch after all solemnity was restored. Isobel played with a new found gusto which had the old building ringing to the sound of Ruth's favourite hymns.

With the ceremony over, goodbyes said and promises made from old friends to meet again soon, Josh wandered over to Toby. "You're looking well, Toby. Have you managed some of my jobs for me while I've been away?"

"I have Josh," he said earnestly. "I really have. Tell him, Jacob. Tell him I've managed okay, haven't I?"

Jacob put a hand on the boy's shoulder. "Toby has been an absolute rock for us all in your absence, Josh. We could not have managed without his help."

"Well, in that case young fella, I have a surprise for you. Come with me." He put an arm around Toby's shoulders and walked outside. The sun was beginning to fire the tops of the trees as it began its slow descent in the west. Flickering candlelight from the church windows added to the already dramatic family reunion. Toby looked bewildered, puzzled at what Josh could possibly have for him. Only a couple of horses left now, stood quietly outside the stables, highlighted in the stunning afterglow of the sunset. Toby did not immediately recognise the horse with the jet-black coat.

Edging ever closer, the recognition that it was Pal suddenly hit Toby and he was stunned into absolute silence. His mouth was working but he couldn't speak. Then he laughed and cried at the same time as he ran towards Pal.

Pal raised his head and whinnied as if in recognition of the young boy. Hugging the horse's neck, Toby said through the tears, "I never thought I would see you again, Pal. I've missed you terrible. I thought of you laid dead on the battlefield and me not there to help you. Oh my God Josh. I can't believe it. I'm so happy. How did you find him?"

"It's a long story, Toby, but it was all down to your teaching and we got lucky. I'll tell you all about how it happened another day. You just get to know Pal again because he's missed you as well." He tousled the young boy's hair and left him to spend time with his horse.

Josh, near to tears himself, returned to the church where Pete and Barney were busy talking. Embracing them both he asked when they had returned home. Pete explained he was deemed unfit for further action following his injuries, eventually arriving home more than a year ago.

"Barney, what about you? I left you in that old cow byre after we battled through the German line. Did the stretcher bearers find you okay?"

Barney's eyes were alive, sparkling with good humour and life, overjoyed to catch up with his friends. "The very next day, Josh. They got me back to the field hospital. I don't remember much after that, most of it is just a blur, shock maybe. But I do remember you telling me not to moan about me little scratch?"

"Yes, I remember that. I was as good as any mother that day, wasn't I?"

"Well, you did your best, Miss Thrall but have a look at this." Barney shoved his leg out straight, then pulled his trouser leg up to reveal an artificial wooden limb with a makeshift shoe attached. "Some bloody scratch, eh?" A few seconds of silence before Barney eased the seriousness of the moment when his face cracked into a grin. They all visibly relaxed and burst into fits of laughter.

Eventually, Josh said, "Barney, I'm really sorry, but I couldn't think of anything else to say to take your mind off the pain." He paused before adding. "We were so lucky to stumble upon a kind family like we did."

Barney shook his head in disbelief. "I know we were. D'you remember the girl, Josh?"

"I do, vividly. She was a real beauty." Josh frowned in thought, then brightened. "Maria, wasn't it?"

"Yep. I thought so too. Well, she came to visit me in hospital while I was recovering and hopefully, she is coming over here with her grandparents this summer. And guess who she's calling to see?"

Josh's eyes widened in disbelief. "You lucky sod, Barney Stopes. It doesn't take you long to make your mark with the opposite sex."

Many yarns later, when returning to the stables, Toby was still sat with

Pal, Len had Jacob's trap ready and waiting and Ruth and Jim were almost ready to make the journey to Honey Bee and begin their new life together as Mr and Mrs Styles.

One last hug for them all from Ruth before settling on the front seat next to Jim and said, "Thank you all for making this such a special day for us both. We will see you again in a couple of days."

Jim added with a grin, "When we surface."

"Goodnight everyone." Ruth flicked the reins onto Danny's back and they set off across the moor.

Once out onto the open road, Ruth began reliving the day once again. "What an unbelievable day, Jim Styles wasn't it?"

"It certainly was. But it is far from being finished yet, Mrs Styles." He gently prised the reins from her hands, clicking the horse into a faster trot.

"And what might you have in mind, darling husband?"

He put his one free arm around her slight shoulders and kissed her. "All I am saying is, for God's sake, please don't have a headache after all this excitement."

Their laughter rang clear across this wild, desolate moor that they so loved, before being lost in the sighing of the wind.

Acknowledgements

My thanks to Lyndsay Ford of Shutterbox Photography, Stamford. Alice Hannan, Stamford. Judy Fullerton, Bank Farm House, Rosedale. Antony Wootten, Grosmont Writers Group, for book cover design and type setting.

About the Author

John lives at Castleton, a small rural village set in the spectacular heart of the North Yorks moors. Inheritance is his second novel and continues to follow Ruth Brennan's life, and also that of all the characters created in his first book, A Journey of Hope.

Also by John F. Watson

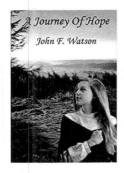

A Journey of Hope

Ruth Brennan, born into abject poverty in the City of York at the end of the 19th century, develops into a character of great courage, passion and determination, possessing a more indomitable spirit on every turn of the page, as she desperately tries to flee the demons of her past. Follow Ruth on her epic journey from birth and early carefree schooldays, through the tragic loss of her parents and cruelty suffered at the Orphanage, before fleeing to make the long, arduous trek toward the coast in search of work. But, by chance, along the way, she stumbles upon a small hamlet set in the very heart of the wild, untamed beauty of the North Yorkshire moors where, at barely sixteen years old, she finds true friendship, religion and love.